I0593397

THE GODS OF WOODMYST

The Gods of Woodmyst

THE WOODMYST CHRONICLES BOOK VIII

Robert E Kreig

WHITEKEEP BOOKS

For Hugh and Claire.

Copyright © 2022 by Robert E Kreig

All rights reserved. No part of this book may be reproduced in any manner whatsoever without written permission except in the case of brief quotations embodied in critical articles and reviews.

First Printing, 2022

The Realm

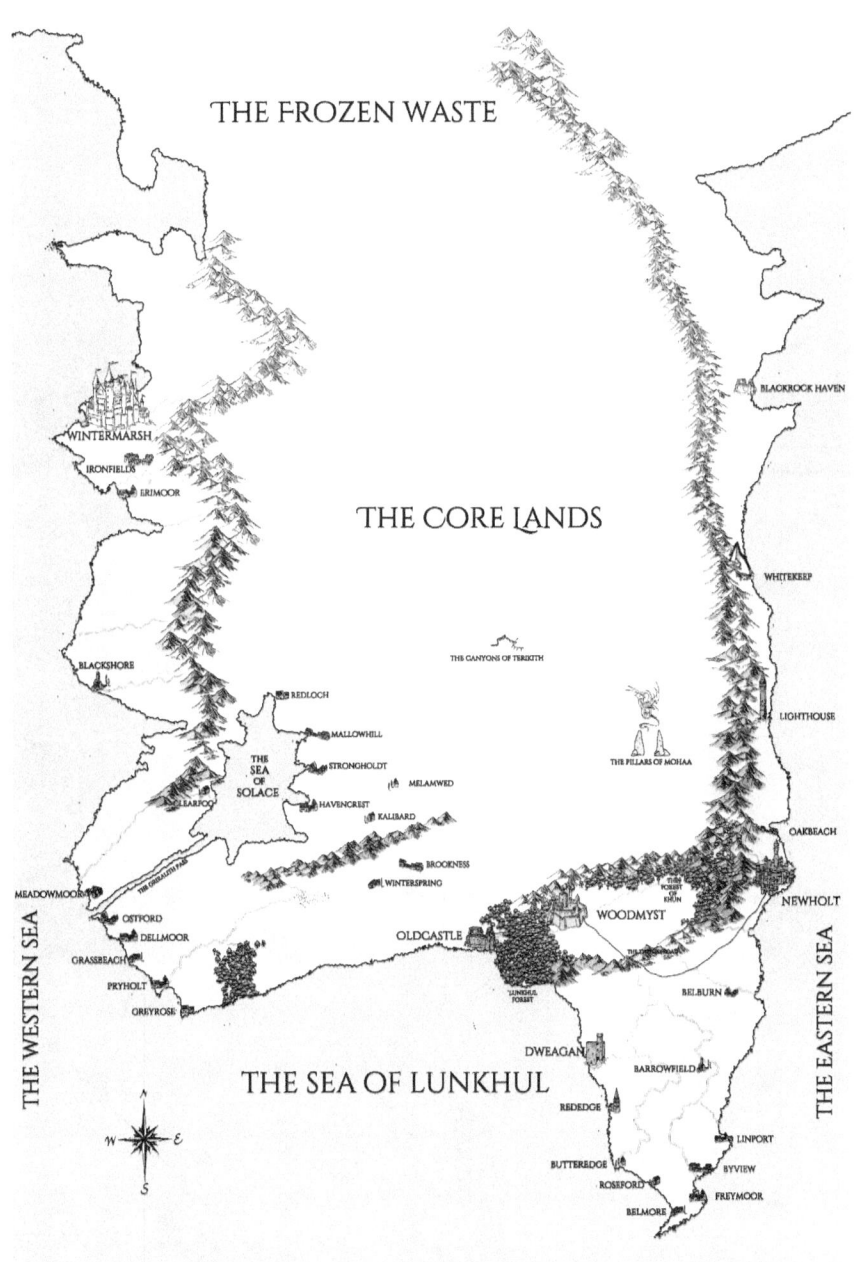

Prologue

She screamed.

A shrill cry echoed over the smooth, green hills surrounding the tiny farmhouse. The sudden outburst spooked sparrows gathered in a crack willow, causing them to flock away like a twisting cloud.

"Hold still, bitch," he growled, pushing the young woman's face against the outer wall of the hut. He was heavyset and smelled of sweat and grog. She knocked over a pail of water by the door as she tried to free herself from his grasp.

Two men, dressed in dark armour and carrying swords, laughed as they clasped her husband by the arms. His threadbare clothing was rent and torn from a scuffle only moments ago.

Four others on horseback chuckled as the man, using his body to hold the woman in place, pulled his trousers down to his knees before attempting to hoist her tattered and patched garments out of the way with his free hand.

"No," she cried, tears welling up.

"Please," her husband begged. One of the two punched him hard in the gut, knocking the wind from him and dropping him to his knees.

She turned her head towards him. Her captor grabbed a fistful of her dark hair at the back of her head and slammed her forehead against the wall. The wooden panel cracked slightly. Dark spots and bright flashes filled her vision momentarily.

Then she saw them.

Two little girls, at least ten years of age and identical in appearance, stood hand in hand with their brown eyes fixed on her. They were just inside the doorway, wide-eyed and clearly frightened.

Their long dark hair fell untidily over their brows and backs. Their pale skin appeared translucent in the hut's shadow. Slowly, together, they moved through the door and outside.

"Look at this," one man on horseback said, pointing with his sword.

"Please," she whispered. "Not in front of them."

The man holding her in place hissed loudly, almost coughing, snickering at her request.

"Not in front of them," he jested. "Bitch, I plan to have both of them when I'm done with you."

"No," the husband cried. A deep pain struck him from inside as the overwhelming feeling of helplessness swept over him.

The man holding the woman turned to meet the husband's frightened stare and smirked.

"I'll take them with me," he teased. "I'll have my way with them over and over again. And then I'll let my friends take turns."

The husband lowered his brows. His eyes filled with rage.

"I'll kill you," he shouted angrily. "I'll tear your throat out, you bastard."

"Shut him up," the man commanded.

One of the two holding the husband pulled a dagger from his belt.

"I'll kill all of you," the husband continued to rant. "I'll break your ne—"

His threats ceased suddenly as the dagger slid neatly over his throat.

"No," the woman howled.

"Shut it," said the man as he positioned himself to take her.

"No," she cried again.

The two men dropped the husband to the ground. Blood spilled over straw and wheat, tossed upon the ground during the earlier scuffle.

One man, holding the bloody dagger in his hand, approached the two little girls. They turned their faces towards him and seemed to study his movement as he drew nearer. In unison, they peered at the body of their father before returning their gaze to the approaching man.

"Do you miss your papa?" he asked. His wide grin exposed yellowing, crooked teeth with blackened spots along the gums. He lowered his head in mock sympathy. "It's all right. I will be your papa now." The other men chuckled as the man with the dagger grabbed his crotch. "Papa has a present for you both."

"Hold still," the first man barked to the woman as he fondled with her undergarments.

"Call me Papa," the other man said, half crouching by the two little girls.

"Leave them alone," the woman screamed.

The girls stared at the man near to them curiously. Their lips remained closed and their eyes wide and full of fear.

"Call me Papa," the man repeated. His voice was stern and a little angry.

"They cannot speak," the woman shouted.

"Shuttit," the man holding her hollered. He pushed her face into the wall again with tremendous force.

A crunch emitted from her head and her body went suddenly limp.

She fell to the ground in a heap.

"You overdid it, Jaku," one horseman said, laughing.

"Bloody heck," the man spat. "She wasn't half bad looking either."

"We still have these two." The other man pointed to the girls with his dagger.

Jaku turned, pulling his trousers back up to his waist. The two girls glared at him.

In any other situation, Jaku wouldn't have cared if two little girls looked at him with such hatred or not. He would have simply grabbed them, torn off their clothes and abused them as he had with many others many times before.

But not this time.

His breathing stopped.

His heart seemed to turn ice cold.

His face became expressionless.

Both girls had locked their gaze upon him. Their brows lowered and their mouths opened agape as if emitting a silent scream.

Jaku felt his body tremble as he saw the girls' eyes glow. White pinpricks of light seemed to pierce his mind and cause an increasingly sharp pain to grow from the centre of his skull. It expanded, expanded, expanded.

His ears rang loudly as the sensation of liquid dripping from his lobes and onto his neck became apparent. The taste of blood and copper filled his mouth as a throbbing ache moved along his spine and down his arms.

He tried to scream, opening his mouth wide to let out a sound.

A misty spray of blood burst from his lips as his face tore open.

"By the gods!" another horseman bellowed as he watched Jaku being torn to shreds by an invisible power.

The girls turned their attention to the others surrounding them.

One by one, in rapid sequence, they ripped apart man and horse, forming them into ribbons of flesh and blood as muscles and organs pulled away from bones.

Within moments, twitching piles of shredded meat and pools of blood lay on the ground around the front of the little farm cottage. Woven amongst the mess were weapons, armour, saddles, and bridles.

The two little girls closed their mouths. Their eyes rapidly returned to a placid brown.

Together, they moved their gaze to the lifeless body of their father. The gaping wound in his neck continued to dribble thick red liquid onto the grass and straw. They looked at their mother, whose nose rested deep in her face, crushed.

One girl shed a tear. The other quickly reached over and wiped it from her sister's cheek.

Together, they looked to the western horizon and saw the sun getting closer to the hills. The sky had changed from soft blue to a strange opaque orange.

Hand in hand, they turned and walked back into the hut, closing the door behind them.

One

Alice kept her composure as another troop of men marched along the aisle, back to the large timber doors of the assembly hall. Their footfalls thundered in unison, echoing throughout the cavernous chamber. Two young Agrodien warriors, dressed in their battle attire, heaved the doors open for the soldiers. The doors emitted a loud creak as the reptilians pulled on the wooden panels with all their strength.

The girl tapped impatiently at the iron claws dangling from her neck as the soldiers passed through the doorway. She noticed that the angle of the sunlight pouring in through the windows high upon the western wall and into the cold, dark auditorium had tilted, shifting so that the yellowish beams stretched farther across the room. They had been here for so long that the shafts of light had crossed from one side of the chamber and almost touched the base of the opposite wall.

Alice took a deep breath and gestured to the always attentive Nola'ee to approach.

The Agrodien passed behind the four high-backed chairs, throne-like in appearance, with cushioned seats and armrests lined up on the platform. Apart from Alice, who sat to the right of centre facing the auditorium, Ursula Wadham seated herself on the far left, Queen Amicia Elynbrigge on the far right and Catherine sat by her sister's side.

"Kayl'sro?" Nola'ee hissed into Alice's ear, stooping low in the space between the girl and the Queen of Newholt.

"How much more of this do I have to bear?" Alice asked in the Agrodien tongue. "If another captain of the guard and his team come through those doors to pledge their fealty, I think I'll slit my throat."

"There are many more," the reptilian answered. "They all wish to assure you of their allegiance."

"They all want my assurance that I won't make Liana burn them in their houses, more like." Alice took a deep breath.

Nola'ee hissed a soft chuckle.

"Relax." Amicia reached over and placed her hand on the girl's arm, sensing her frustration. "You are now the leader of these people. This is what a leader does. A leader listens to the people, no matter how trivial their words may be. To them, their matters are just as important as anything that may vex you. Give them their moment."

Alice took another deep breath as Nola'ee straightened herself and started back to her position at the side of the platform.

"How do I know the words they speak are true?" she asked. "They pledge themselves to us. Yet, they fought for the Maji only five days' past."

"They were under his influence," Ursula put in.

"Not all of them," Alice reminded her. "Perhaps some are loyal to him still."

A draught swept through the chamber, causing the torches positioned around the walls to flicker. Alice pulled her bearskin cloak tightly across her chest before lifting her long braid from behind her to drape it over her shoulder.

"Are you cold?" Catherine asked. Her concern was sincere as she peered at her sister with a hint of anxiety.

"I'm all right," Alice reassured her.

"You're with child now," the older sibling reminded her. "Perhaps we should retire for the day and return home."

Alice shook her head. She instinctively placed her hand on her stomach. There was no visual sign of a belly forming, but the four of them could sense the child inside.

"I don't want to be doing this again tomorrow," she said. "I'd rather be at home with Arthur instead. Let's get it over with."

"Are you certain?" Ursula asked.

Alice inclined her head and signalled to the Agrodien warriors by the door to let the next captian of the guard and his troops in.

***

The sisters strolled arm in arm with Amicia and Ursula on either side. The soft footfalls of the soldiers, both Agrodien and men, followed closely. The queen pulled her cloak about her as she peered up to the moon drifting just above the mountains far to the east.

"I miss my home," she whispered. There was sadness in her voice and the others sensed it.

"We'll reclaim it," Alice assured her. "You will sit upon the throne again."

"No," Amicia replied. Her eyes glistened in the flickering orange light emitting from the lampposts lining the street. "My place is not in Newholt. Not anymore."

Alice felt as if she should ask where Amicia believed she belonged, but she already knew the answer to that question.

It was the same place that they all belonged.

Together.

"Nevertheless," Ursula said, in a comforting tone, "we will reclaim it for the sake of everyone dwelling there."

"Have we any word from Newholt?" Alice asked.

"Only that a small resistance has formed," replied Ursula. She looked over to Alice quizzically. "Word came by a rider this morning."

Alice wore a perplexed expression. She stopped moving and turned to face her personal guard, Nola'ee.

"Were you aware of this?" the girl asked in the Agrodien tongue.

"No, Kayl'sro," the reptilian answered, her face appearing as confused as her leader's.

"How certain are you that this information is accurate?" Alice queried, turning back to face Ursula.

"Very," she replied. "I received a letter addressed to me from Audrey, one of my girls."

The other three understood Ursula referred to one of the three whores from White Keep.

"Anything specific?" Amicia asked as they began walking again. "What of the city? The people?"

"She didn't go into too great of detail," the other replied. "Her writing appeared rushed, but I know it to be hers.

"She wrote that much of the city had been destroyed in an attack from the sea and land. There are black banners everywhere and many have perished. She wrote that my mm–"

Ursula stopped in her tracks suddenly and wept. The three others looked on with concern.

"She wrote they had killed Maud," Ursula blubbered. She turned to face the other three. "She was like a mother to me."

"I'm so sorry," Amicia said, moving to the young woman and wrapping her arms around her shoulders.

"Why didn't you say something before?" Alice asked, moving to the woman's side and placing her hand on Ursula's arm.

"I didn't want to bother you with such a small thing, considering what we needed to do today," the woman replied.

"It is no small thing," said Catherine, pressing her forehead to Ursula's. "We are sisters. We share one another's joy and sorrow. We stand as one. From now on, and forever."

***

It was late when the sisters walked in through the door of their house. All others dwelling inside had retired for the night except for Emily, who waited for her daughters to return home. She sat by the fireplace, nursing a cup of tea as she kept warm.

"There's stew on the stove if you're hungry," she said to them as they hung their cloaks by the door.

"Famished," Catherine said, hurrying through the living room and into the kitchen.

"I think I'll go to bed," Alice replied.

"He's all right," Emily assured her. "I checked on him not too long ago."

"His wounds?" The girl stepped into the room, peering at her mother.

"I changed his dressing at dusk," she answered, "just as the apothecary instructed. His arm…" Emily paused as she turned her head to look at Alice. "Well, you know what I mean. It seems to be healing rapidly. There is still some seeping, however. He is recovering quicker than he should be, according to the apothecary."

"I should wake him to change his bandages again," Alice said.

A sudden loud snort erupted from behind the bedroom door closest to the living room.

"I love you too, David," Emily called back with a giggle.

The sound of loud and steady snoring ensued.

"How do you sleep with that noise?" Catherine asked as she ladled steaming stew from a pot and into a wooden bowl.

"You get used to it," her mother replied as Alice moved through the corridor towards the bedroom she shared with her husband. "Your father was much worse. I rarely got an ounce of sleep with him. And not always because of his snoring."

"Mama!" Catherine gasped.

Alice grinned at the exchange between her sister and mother. She was glad to have Catherine back. They had bonded more closely in the past few days than they ever had in their whole lives.

She opened the bedroom door slowly, delicately, so as not to wake Arthur suddenly. The creak of the hinges seemed louder than usual.

The boy stirred slightly, emitting a soft groan as a sliver of light penetrated through the door and into the room, growing wider as Alice moved inside. Soft candlelight flickered from the dresser as she closed the door behind her.

"Alice?" he whispered.

"Yes," she replied in kind.

"Are you just getting home?"

"Yes," she answered, moving to the side of the bed.

He reached up and wiped his eyes with his hand.

"You've been gone since before dawn," he said as he tried to push himself into a half-seated position. "Have you eaten? There's stew on the stove. I made it myself."

"You made it?" she said, sitting beside him. She ran her fingers through his hair.

"Well," he amended. "Your mother helped. It's hard to use a knife and hold things steady with only one arm."

"You were told to rest," she said sternly, keeping her voice low. "You promised me you wouldn't do anything strenuous."

"I made stew." Arthur looked at her apologetically. "That's all. But..." He wore a pleading expression, like a dog begging for scraps. "I'd like to take a walk in the woods. I need to get out of this house. Having your mother dote on me all day is one thing. My father's affection is another. He smothers me and never leaves me to my own thoughts. I just want to read and be left alone for ten minutes. Five minutes, even."

Alice couldn't help smiling. She bent down and kissed him hard on the lips. He winced slightly, but tried to hide the pain.

"I'm sorry," she blurted.

"It's all right," he told her. "It's not as bad as it was before."

Even in the low light emitting from the candle, she could see the bruises on his face. He was indeed healing faster than natural. Alice knew that was because of her intervention and not so much from the remedial approach from the apothecary. Still, she would change Arthur's bandages, as instructed, and apply the sweet-smelling salve that the practitioner had given.

She would also say her words and place her hands on his wounds as she had been since being reunited with her husband after liberating Woodmyst.

She reached into a drawer by the side of the bed and retrieved fresh dressing and a small clay jar that held the salve. Arthur had already unraveled the bandages that crossed over his chest and back, covering his shoulder and the socket where his left arm had once been.

Alice felt a tear roll from her eye and along her cheek as she remembered him, not all that long ago, with both arms holding her. She quickly wiped it away before he could see.

"It still throbs now and then," he told her. "It's as if my heart jumps from my chest and moves into my shoulder."

"It's just your body trying to heal itself faster," she told him. "Your blood is racing to the wound to repair the damage."

He looked at her quizzically.

"What?" asked the girl.

"Have you been reading my books?" he enquired as he pulled the wrappings away from his body.

"Ones about anatomy, yes," she admitted.

"And you understood them?"

"Some things. There are some words I don't know. And the pictures are strange. Not really like the insides of those I've seen with my own eyes."

"They're close depictions of what it is meant to look like if they were still inside a living person," he explained. "Not spilled out onto the ground during a battle."

She sniggered a little at his words as he lifted the last of the old dressings away. There was a dark stain on the bandages wrapped close to the wound. He dropped them onto the floor by the bed as Alice dipped her finger into the salve.

Carefully, delicately, she applied the ointment to his wound. Arthur held his breath as her finger touched his skin.

"Does it hurt?" she asked.

"Cold," he replied. "A little tender."

She could feel the moist surface beneath her fingers as she smoothed the ointment over the wound. It had all but closed over, new skin forming over the socket, appearing like raw meat. There was still a small section from where a fine trickle of blood oozed.

Alice gently placed her hand over this area and closed her eyes.

"Restore," she breathed.

Arthur felt a wave of warmth flow over his body, just as he had each time Alice had done this to him.

She reached for the fresh dressing and applied it to her husband. He watched her affectionately as her stare grew vaguely distant.

"What's the matter?" he asked.

"We need to talk about something," she replied as she moved the bandage over his chest, under his right arm, and across his back.

"All right."

"It's been on my mind since returning here," she told him.

"You want to move back to the caverns," he speculated. "You've never liked the city. I understand. When do we leave?"

"Leave?" She pursed her lips. "Yes. Back to the caverns, no."

He looked at her for a long time as she continued to wrap his wound. Her lips remained shut tightly, and a deep heaviness had fallen upon her face.

"I knew this day would come," he confessed. "When? After you finish it or before?"

"We need to finish this," she replied. "I'm not about to run."

He placed his hand on her abdomen.

"You have reason to, if you wish," he argued. "We could just go."

She shook her head, placing her hand over his.

"I can't leave yet," she said. She looked to the door, envisioning her mother and sister in the living room just beyond. "I will need to explain it to them. But I'm not ready."

Arthur moved his hand to her waist as she continued to wrap the dressing.

"I don't think any of them will understand," he speculated. "We'll need to prepare. I'll do what I can from here. I won't be able to join you when you go to face him, anyway."

"I know," she said. Her eyes were welling with tears. She tucked the end of the bandage underneath a layer of wrapping and leant in to kiss his forehead. "Let's both go for a walk in the woods tomorrow."

He furrowed his brow. "You don't have any special duties to perform?"

"I have plenty," she answered. "But I don't want to do them."

He clutched a handful of her tunic covering her chest and dragged her close to him, planting a kiss on her lips. She kissed him back, deeply.

He winced a little from the pain.

"I'm sorry," she whispered.

"It's all right." He grinned.

Two

This isn't you.

She pushed the thought away, pressing her thighs against his flesh tighter, trying to think of nothing else except the desire to feel ecstasy and carnal bliss. The bedhead hammered the wall as she let out a deep, guttural groan.

Her fingernails scraped down his back. He let out a soft hiss as his skin opened. A small scratch. Nothing serious.

But his response made her hungry for more of him.

Forcing him onto his back, she moved over his loins. Her palms laid flat against his chest as she continued to rock and thrust back and forward.

This isn't you.

Her head shook, trying to force the tiny voice away.

He reached his hands out to touch her breasts. There was a sudden, pleasurable shiver tingling along her spine and spreading over her entire body.

She almost laughed.

More groaning.

The bedhead continued to thud rapidly against the wall.

Louder and faster.

Louder and faster.

She could feel the movement inside of her.

Louder and faster.

Louder and faster.

Her smile broadened as the movement transformed into elation. Her groans became shouts of euphoria.

Louder and faster.

Louder and...

This isn't you.

She let out a cry of frustration before lifting herself off him and sitting on the side of the bed.

"My lady?" The young man looked confused. "Did I do something wrong?"

"No," she said, reaching for her black robe, which rested on the ground by her feet.

"I could try harder," he said.

"It isn't you," she said, standing up and slipping the robe over her body, feeling uncomfortable after speaking those three words. They were almost identical to those spoken by the voice in her head.

She looked at him and noticed with fresh eyes that he was very young indeed. Not very far into his years of adulthood. "Perhaps you should dress and return to your regiment."

"My lady." He swung his feet over the edge of the bed and reached for his trousers.

As he dressed, she stepped through lace curtains that wafted gently in the breeze, and onto the balcony. She looked out over the ruins of the city and to the Eastern Sea.

The ships from Dweagan had left the coast, moving on to escort the galley transporting the Scarlet Queen northward. Tricia hadn't stopped to visit. The Scarlet Queen had continued on, passing by during the early morning hours.

This did not upset her. After all, it was what the Maji instructed her to do.

That was two days ago.

She wondered if they had reached Blackrock Haven yet.

The chamber door opened and closed, signalling the young soldier's departure. She suddenly felt alone and wished she hadn't sent him away. Her need to feel another near to her was strong. She wanted someone to talk to; be next to; to touch.

To love.

Love.

She frowned as she considered what she had just done. She had ordered a young man to lie with her. To love her.

But she wasn't satisfied.

He doesn't love you.

You don't love him.

She wondered if she needed to find another. Someone who would love her. Someone who would satisfy her.

She thought of her appointed commander, Andris Hill. She would have tried to manipulate him, to beguile him, to lure him into her bed, but he was unbreakable. He was stubborn.

If Andris wouldn't bend to her will, then she would need to search for one that would.

This isn't you.

"Then, who am I?" she asked out loud, a lone tear rolling down her cheek. "Who am I?"

She waited for an answer.

The sea breeze blew through her auburn hair as she remembered a little village high in the mountains. She recalled another auburn girl, older than she. Her sister. They sat together on the floor of their tiny cabin by the fireplace as a man spoke to them both. She couldn't hear his words through the haze of memory, but she knew he spoke of love and charity and things that were good and pure.

A woman sat beside him. She was much younger than the man, but aged with soft, deepening lines and creases in the corners of her mouth. Her eyes filled with wisdom, and her hair like that of her and her sister. She looked affectionately upon the two girls.

There was love here.

So much love.

But the memory was distant, like an echo on a faraway hill, and she couldn't remember the finer details. She had no recollection of her father's voice or where exactly this memory had taken place. Only that, even with snow collecting on the window, it had felt warm and comfortable.

Antony.

It was his name. Her father's name.

Her face softened as she pictured him doting over her and her sister.

Antony Grenefeld.

Antony...

Antony Warde.

The image of a small boy filled her mind. His dark hair and big, brown, innocent eyes staring at her. An innocent face mouthed the word, *Mama.*

Mama.

Mama.

The smile turned to a cry as the look of pain spread over the boy's face.

Mama.

Mama.

The boy's lips silently formed the word over and over as a look of sheer terror swept over his face.

A sharp pain stabbed through her heart.

She shook her head, forcing the image away.

The cabin in the mountains disappeared.

The loving family by the fire transformed into the view of the broken city before her.

The crying boy swept away like a cloud caught in the ocean breeze flowing through her hair.

She was the Black Queen of Newholt again. The ambassador of the Maji.

But she wondered if she should be.

She wondered if she was meant to be something else, someone else.

The pain in her heart deepened as her thoughts continued to spin.

Flashing images of a robust man, smiling as he held her in his arms, laughing as he played with small children, racing away on horseback into battle.

Tears streamed down her cheeks, as confusion spread through her thoughts.

She knew this man.

She had loved this man once.

Perhaps she still did.

But she could not remember him. Not entirely.

Peering down from the balcony, wiping her face to see the black banners posted by the palace gates waving gently in the breeze, she heard the tiny voice speaking to her again.

This isn't you.

She frowned as she rested her hands on the guardrail.

"Who am I, then?" she asked in a whisper.

The tiny voice, caught on the ocean breeze, answered softly.

This isn't you.

Three

Piers Mayne stared at the steaming plate of food placed before him. Bright yellow corn kernels, green beans, spinach, a whole potato cut open slightly to allow a dollop of butter to melt slowly into its white flesh, piled neatly beside the hind quarter of baked fowl. Chicken, the skipper assumed. Smothered in thick gravy.

Very appetising, indeed.

But his stomach, twisting and turning, wasn't about to let him have one bite.

Instead, his thoughts were on the boy and the woman seated near the head of the table.

The distinct clatter of silverware clanking and clinking against the fine, white ceramic kept bringing him back to reality. Other men surrounded him. Some wore neat military dress uniforms. Others, like him, dressed in the finest garb they could muster.

His gaze moved around the room, pausing on the many portraits and few landscapes hanging on the wall, bordered by timber frames adorned with intricate leaves and flora carved by hand. Ladies, mostly, dressed in fabrics of varying colours. One in scarlet, like the lady of the house, only older in appearance. Another in purple and another in yellow.

At the focal point, above the head of the table, two portraits hung side-by-side. One was a woman in green. The shadow of a hood that she wore upon her head obscured her face. Only her lips were visible. Mayne could swear he saw them turn up at the corners ever so slightly as she peered down at those gathered around the table. He took a swig of his wine, something he was doing quite a fair bit as the night drew on, and possibly the reason behind why lady in green grinned.

Beside her was a beautiful blonde woman in white. She was striking in appearance, with blue eyes, soft skin and ruby lips. The skipper felt a compulsion to touch her, as if lured to her loveliness by a spell.

But it was just a portrait.

Someone's interpretation of a person.

Who could say what this woman was like?

Who could vouch for her character?

Surely not the Scarlet Queen seated by the boy.

"You've not touched your meal, Skipper," one of the uniformed men announced.

Mayne snapped back to reality again. He glanced at the owner of the voice, seated across the table from him.

Tricia had noticed his gaze. She studied the portraits above the table of the woman in green and the other in white.

"I'm not very hungry," Mayne replied in a polite tone. "Thank you."

"I'm sorry to hear that," Tricia said. "Perhaps some more wine? You seem to stomach that without trouble."

The skipper shook his head. "Any more of this fine drop, and I don't think I'll be able to walk back to my quarters."

"Don't be silly," she said, and waved to a servant, gesturing for Mayne's cup to be filled. "You'll sleep here tonight. It would be irresponsible for me to allow you to return to your vessel in such a condition. Please, drink and be merry."

The servant, a young woman, moved into a space between Mayne's seat and the occupant to his right. She reached to the centre of the table and took a silver jug standing on a silver tray. Carefully, she poured the thick, red liquid from the jug into the skipper's glass.

He knew he had drunk too much already, but he had never been in a situation where he was fully aware of how drunk he was and how it was affecting his senses.

His mind turned to the servant girl, reaching across him to pour the wine. Her breast rested against his shoulder. Her dark braid brushed against the skin of his cheek lightly. Her soft breath was warm against his cheek as she placed the jug back on the silver tray. He breathed the scent of her perfume as she moved out of sight. He felt allured by her as he had by the portrait of the woman in white only moments before.

"Her name is Agatha," the Scarlet Queen told him, sensing his thoughts.

He shot her a look. *How does she know?*

"My lady?" he managed.

"I could arrange for her to stay in your bed," Tricia said playfully. "Just to keep you warm as you sleep. It gets cold up here, so far to the north. You would like that, wouldn't you Agatha?"

"Yes, my lady," the girl replied. Her grin was more of a reaction to being embarrassed before an audience of men than of playfulness.

Mayne watched as the Scarlet Queen placed a morsel of meat on a fork, only to feed it to Sam. The young boy, ten years old and quite capable, opened his mouth and took it like a babe.

What in damnation is going on?

"Thank you, Mama," the boy replied with a mouthful of fowl.

The skipper glanced around the table to see if others seated nearby were just as puzzled as he. The officers and other well-dressed men continued to clink and clank their silverware against the white ceramic plates, seemingly oblivious to the surreal existence surrounding them.

He took a gulp from his cup, swallowing hard, forcing it down.

"The one in green is Yasmeen Svoboda," Tricia explained. "Or at least the best impression we have of her. She used her men to steal me away from my parents when I was very young, just as she had done with all of my sisters. Just as she had done with these you see around us." The Scarlet Queen gestured to the other portraits with her eyes. "My sisters and I killed her. Right here."

The men seated about the table stopped eating and placed their attention on the Scarlet Queen. Mayne was already there. His gaze locked onto her. He lifted the glass to his lips again as he listened. She continued to feed Sam like a doting mother.

Perhaps that was what she believed she was, Mayne thought. But he perceived her to be something else. Something undesirable. Something from the darkness.

"The woman in white is Sumaiyya Tarkin," Tricia continued, peering up at the portrait. "She is the mother of the Maji. I remember her well. She was much more stunning in person. This painting does not do her any justice.

"She hangs beside the Green Mistress because Takmel believes them to both deserve places of prevalence. This was where it all began."

"Where what began, Mama?" Sam asked quietly.

Mayne's stomach turned again. He drained the last of his glass. Agatha started forward to fill his glass again. He waved her off and reached for the jug himself.

"The Mirikin, my boy," she explained. "Long before the Sovereign took her place as prime; long before they had built her palace; ten witches established the Mirikin near to the seaside not far from here.

"The story, according to some, is that a long, long time ago, during the height of winter, a ship from Dendadia was heading for Newholt and got lost in a treacherous storm. It was carrying people who were looking to begin a new life in a new land, but it crashed against the black rocks by the sea. Some say fifty were on board. Others say over one hundred. It doesn't really matter how many. The story always ends the same.

"The people survived as best as they could, building small huts from the broken timber of the hull, and ate what supplies they had on board. All was well until the food ran out.

"The men did their best," Tricia continued, moving Sam to her lap and stroking his sandy blond hair with her fingertips. "They tried hunting and fishing but came up with very little.

"It was then, out of desperation, that the ten found each other. They were drawn to one another as most beings of a distinct nature are. Just as the wolves come together, or the ravens flock to a fallen creature, the witches gathered in secret and made their plans."

"What did they do?" the boy, wide-eyed and full of wonder, asked her in a half yawn.

"Well…" She smiled down at him. "One day, when the men were fishing and hunting, the ten witches did the only thing they thought was reasonable. Remember, it was the height of winter. The snow was piling up higher each day and night. The storms were growing harsher and harsher. They had run out of food and they needed to melt the snow in pots for water, or at least that's what some say when they tell this tale."

Some, thought the skipper. This was the first he had heard this tale, and he surmised by the looks of deep attentiveness on the other men's faces, that this was the first they had heard of it as well.

"So, when the men were gone, the ten witches slit the throats of every other woman and child." Tricia moved her gaze slowly around the table, locking onto the faces of each of the men gathered around. Mayne thought she stayed fixed upon him for a very long time, as if boring into his brain with her stare, scratching and digging into his thoughts in search of any doubt, disloyalty or defiance. He felt all of it. She continued to tell the tale, peering down to the boy slumped against her chest. "And while their blood was still warm, and while it steamed into the cold air, they drank the corpses dry.

"When the bodies had been drained of blood, the ten witches butchered the women and children and hung strips of meat to dry in the cold air. Afterwards, they sat in a circle by a fire and sang."

"Sang?" Mayne asked. His jaw hung open, gawking at her stupidly, unbelievingly.

Tricia nodded. "Yes," she replied. "They sang. They sang songs to the gods to give thanks for supplying them with a bountiful store."

"They killed innocent people," the skipper put in.

"Innocence is only depicted by the one who believes that they are innocent," she argued.

"What is that supposed to mean?" He got to his feet and pointed to the boy. "This isn't a story for a lad of his age."

"Shhh," she hissed, gently stroking Sam's hair. The boy's eyes were closed, and his breathing relaxed. "I haven't got to the good part yet."

He sat down, feeling as if it was an involuntary reaction to her words. Either that, or an act of the wine.

"The men returned," she continued. "Again, with nothing. But when they could not find their wives and children, they were filled with rage. They came for the ten witches who stayed by the fire and sang.

"As the men approached, the witches sang louder and louder. Their voices rang out and filled the men with a burning sensation that grew and grew until flames burst from their chests and consumed them."

The Scarlet Queen peered around the table. She smiled contently to each of the men as she continued to stroke Sam's hair. He had drifted off to sleep in her arms.

"The ten witches portioned out the remains of the shipwrecked survivors for the duration of the winter and lived. That was the beginning of the Mirikin, and it happened right here before the establishment of Blackrock Haven.

"These women," she said as she looked at the portraits hung about the room, "were part of their legacy. We almost lost them.

"But the Maji has renewed it. The Mirikin has risen again."

Silence filled the dining room. The men could barely breathe.

"Each of you has a role to play in this new empire, gentlemen," she explained. "Play your part well, and we will reward you. Cross me, and you may suddenly feel a burning sensation growing inside of you."

Four

Arthur gripped her hand as he shuffled his feet through the leaf litter. Most of his weight was leaning towards her as he plodded along the western road. He smiled as the sunlight filtered through the branches of the surrounding trees before landing softly, warmly upon his face.

He missed the world outside; almost felt a longing for it.

This, he found strange considering it was usually he that preferred to sit by a fire and read instead of venturing into the woods and what lay beyond. But she had changed that in him.

Being with her gave him a sense of wonder towards the wider world. There was an understanding to be had by being in the physical world that a book just couldn't validate. Out here, he could feel and smell, hear and see the complexities of life. Here, he could experience it all. His books could only tell him about it.

Still, the words of scholars and philosophers had given him knowledge, which helped him to comprehend the hows and whys of the living world around him. Because of this, he could give answers if she ever asked him about something that they encountered.

For now, however, he felt only a strong awareness of how much he was relying upon her to keep him upright. He didn't concern himself with being too much for her to bear. She could take it. She was much stronger than she appeared. Stronger than most men.

His concern was that he may have left his bed too soon. He worried that he possibly needed more time to recover.

"I need to rest a bit," he told her, placing his arm around her neck. She moved her left arm around his waist and guided him to a fallen tree by the roadside.

"Let's sit here," she replied. Her gaze moved to the tall reptilian female following a short distance behind them. They'd asked the Agrodien to keep her distance.

Nola'ee complied. She was about to rush forward to assist until Alice silently instructed her not to.

"How do you feel?" the girl asked, sitting beside her husband on the log.

"A little sore," he admitted. "I find it a little difficult to breathe."

"Should I try again?" she offered, rubbing his back gently with an open hand.

He peered into the trees. A small gathering of sparrows perched high above them watched the young couple curiously.

"No," he answered. "I just need to catch my breath."

"We should probably make our way back home soon," she suggested, looking back along the road, past Nola'ee to where they had come from. The city walls were not that far away. If she was to call for help, the soldiers on the wall would easily hear her. Even now, she could see that a few watched them from the parapet.

They sat in silence, together on the log, listening to the chatter of birds and the soft hiss of the breeze moving through the forest. Arthur listened to the trees groaning and creaking as they swayed.

"I should return to the glade," he blurted.

Alice stared at him, uncertain how to respond.

"This city isn't my home anymore. That little cottage of yours is where I belong. It's where you belong, too."

He looked at her, and his face seemed despondent.

She struggled with her words, searching her mind for the right ones.

"I don't think I belong there either," she replied. "But I know I don't belong here."

He nodded, frowning slightly. His eyes glistened as he looked around to the brushes and colourful wildflowers poking through the coloured leaves resting on the ground.

"What are we to do, Alice?"

She wrapped both of her arms around him and held him as tightly as she could without hurting him.

"I'll leave in the morning," she told him. "I'll come home to you when I'm done. Our real home."

He sighed and leant into her.

The sparrows whisked away, twittering and chattering as they fluttered through the branches of the bare limbs of birch, elm and oak trees, darting into the always green shelter of firs and pines. Arthur watched them vanish into the woods, feeling a deep sorrow that, after returning to the cabin on the glade, he would never return to these woods again.

The sun broke through the canopy and set a warm kiss on his face again.

It was enough to push the sadness aside, just long enough for him to smile one more time.

***

"I don't understand," Sevrina Hill called after her brother, Lor, who was packing his horse near the entrance to the stable house. The steed was being readied for a brief journey as a wagon tethered to two nags waited just outside. Sitting atop the cart were Alan, Lor's son, and Linet, his wife, who held the reins steadily in her hands. "You only just arrived and now you're leaving?"

"Woodmyst isn't safe any longer," Lor replied. "There are still those who are loyal to him hiding amongst us here. Come with us. The glade is a far better place for you."

"I need to stay," she argued, glancing at Linet for help. "Andris might return and if I'm not here..."

"Joanne has taken him," the other woman reminded her. "She won't just simply allow him to leave."

"You can't abandon your nieces," Sevrina argued, trying a new tactic.

"They don't need us," Lor said, tightening the straps of his saddle. "Not here. Not in Newholt either. They'll do what they will without our help. We'll return to the glade and watch over the camp with Arthur and the Agrodiens."

"Come with us," Linet pleaded.

"Please," Alan joined in.

Sevrina frowned and looked through the stable house doors to the city beyond. This was her home and everything she knew was here, within the walls of Woodmyst. However, her brother's words were correct. It wasn't safe.

Sevrina knew that if her husband was with her, he would urge her to go to a place of security, where those who surrounded her were trustworthy. Andris would tell her to go with Lor.

Reluctantly, she nodded, silently agreeing to return to the glade with them.

"Good," Lor said, placing his hand on her shoulder. "Pack only what you need. Clothing and such. None of that fancy linen from Dendadia or remnants from Oldcastle. Just necessities."

She nodded again and started for the doors.

"I'll come along," Linet offered, handing the reins to her son before climbing down from the wagon. She took Sevrina's hand and started along the street.

"Should I take some of Andris' things?" she asked her sister-in-law. "He left in such a rush with nothing more than the uniform on his back."

"We'll take a few things for him," the other replied. "Just in case."

***

David stared into the flames of the fireplace, sitting comfortably in a deep-cushioned chair that had seen better days. His hands pawed at the armrests, rubbing his fingers against the fabric and finding places where the heat from the hearth had baked it slightly over the years.

Alice, Catherine and Emily sat around the dining table in the kitchen drinking tea, while Arthur sat in another seat by his father, balancing a book on his lap and perfecting the skill of being able to turn the pages and keep his place with one hand.

The large man marvelled at his son's swift recovery. It didn't seem that long ago when he had laid eyes upon a bloodied, bruised and beaten meat sack in the prison cells. Now, here he sat, his skin tone returning to its original tone. His bruises had vanished, and his swelling had subsided.

He did still move a little slowly, with a slight limp that was barely noticeable. His arm, torn from him, had not grown back. But with all the wishful hope that it might, David had to recognise that not even with the sorcery and abilities of the Four could such a thing occur.

This brought his thoughts to the Seven. His mind focused upon those who had once dwelt in the very house in which he now sat.

The immense hatred that he harboured for Takmel Hamond, the Maji, was burning in his brain. His desire to reach his fingers around that boy's throat and squeeze as hard as he could grew and grew and continued to grow with each breath he took. With the revelation that Takmel was responsible for the deaths of his wives and daughter, David felt his anger deepen to where he harboured something far superior to revulsion in his heart towards the boy.

But there was another who was just as guilty for what had happened to his family. She sat only a few paces from him. Almost within arm's reach.

She sipped tea and talked with her mother and sister. She looked over at him now and then. *Possibly because of her shame*, David thought. *Possibly because she is remorseful.*

He had to admit that she appeared saddened by her experience. And the fact that she attacked her own husband, the Maji, on the bridge of the market square. She had intended to kill him there and then.

David looked over at her again and locked eyes with her. Catherine was staring straight at him.

Can she hear my thoughts?

Water welled on the edges of her eyelids.

With a soft grunt, he lifted himself out of his seat and ambled to the kitchen. She watched him as he moved behind her chair. He placed his hand on the backrest and leant over to kiss the top of her head.

He had forgiven her.

Emily watched on as Alice continued to talk.

"...and food supplies will need to be packed onto horses," the younger girl said. "No wagons."

"You intend to take the Twisted Road?" Emily asked.

"It's the safer way," she replied. "Snow is falling on the mountain peaks to the north. It's only a matter of time before it reaches the floor of the Forest of Khun. It makes for harder travelling. The horses will tire easily, and the journey will take longer."

"This, we know," David said as he moved to the stove. "Is there any tea left?"

"Enough for a mug," Emily told him.

"We travelled that way once before," the man explained as he poured a cup of brew. "The snow was something that year."

"Then you agree?" Alice appealed to him. "We should take the Twisted Road?"

"Aye," he agreed, returning to the table, sitting down beside Emily. "You should go that way."

"*You?*" Emily furrowed her brow. "You mean *we?*"

David sipped his tea. "I mean *you*," he replied after swallowing. "I'm not going to Newholt. I'll return to the cabin with Arthur."

Emily looked confused. "I don't understand," she said.

"I'm getting old," he explained. "I can feel it in more and more of my bones with each winter. I'll be no good to any of you out there. My reactions are slowing and my muscles ache after the simplest of tasks. The three of you have your magic.

"You two girls," he said, looking to Catherine and Alice, "have tremendous power. I don't think either of you fully understands what you wield. And you, my beauty," he added as he placed his hand on Emily's, "you don't look a day older than the day I first saw you. You can fight like a young warrior and best all the men who dare to face you."

Her countenance dropped as she gripped his hand.

"I wish you would come," she said.

"You would be too worried about me," he told her. "I would only be in the way. And besides, the three of you need your wits about you."

"What do you mean?" Catherine asked.

"He means you are going to face your aunt," Arthur put in. He closed his book and peered over at them. "You will need to forget who she is. She could use your love for her against you."

"We know who she is, Arthur," Alice responded. The corners of her mouth turned down slightly and her eyes were like steel. "She betrayed us. That's who she is."

"You will need to kill her," David explained.

Alice flashed a look at the large man. She knew Joanne would have to be defeated, but the idea of killing her aunt, her mother's sister, hadn't really sunk in until that very moment.

She was about to embark on a mission to execute a member of her own family.

Five

Nathaniel Monteacute pressed his back against the stone wall of the guard post. He gripped the short-bladed falchion tightly. Its straight angled edges stained with blood and dripping onto the ground by his feet.

He looked to the sun, riding high in the cloudless sky behind them. It was casting long shadows on the wall and would give away their position if they were to move any farther.

Carefully, he poked his head around the corner of the building to see what waited before them. Three guards stood by a small fire to keep warm. They chained together twenty prisoners and left to lie uncomfortably on the open ground a short distance away in the centre of the town square.

Monteacute looked over his shoulder to signal the others. He held up three fingers.

Rose Heron pulled her thin rapier from the motionless body of a blackguard. She inclined her head to the sheriff of Whitekeep and crept along the wall to his side.

"Do you see him?" she asked in a whisper as several others followed her into position. "The man with one eye?"

"No," he replied. "But there are numerous prisoners in the square."

"What do we do?" another woman asked.

Rose raised her brow. "We do what we're good at, Audrey," she replied with a small grin. "Unbutton your top. Just a little. You too, Kateryn."

Monteacute peered back around the corner. The three guards were still standing by the fire. He returned his attention to the three women and pursed his lips as they shifted their clothing to expose as much cleavage as they could.

"This won't work," he hissed, looking to their leggings. "You're not dressed like whores. You look like you are ready for battle."

"Here." A young man in the group offered his canteen. "Act as if you're taking water to them."

Two other men handed their water skins to the women.

Monteacute shook his head. "It's the best we can do," he admitted. "Leave your swords. Use your daggers. Make it quick and silent."

"Don't worry, Monty." Kateryn grinned as she placed a gentle hand on his cheek. "You won't lose any of us today."

After handing their swords to others in the troop, the three women rounded the corner confidently, as if they were meant to be there.

"Halt," one guard called.

The three stopped in place, only a few yards from the corner of the guard post. Monty readied himself to jump out of his hiding place and rescue the girls.

"Who are you?" the guard shouted.

"Water maids," Rose replied with a playful look. She held the canteen up for the guards to see.

"We have water," the guard told her.

"Maybe you would like some more," Rose suggested. She popped the cork and tilted the canteen as if to drink, spilling some of the liquid over her chest. "Ooh. How clumsy."

She smeared the water over her breasts a little, as if attempting to disperse it. All the while, she kept an alluring stare on the guard. She ran a finger over her wet skin before placing its tip between her lips to suck it dry.

"Hold on," another guard said as he stepped forward. "I think I'd like to try this water. Ours is a little stale, don't you think?"

"Yes, I do," the third guard agreed, moving towards the three women. "Very old water indeed. It might have even turned bad."

"We only filled the skins this morning," the first guard announced, peering at the other two blankly.

The second turned to the first and placed his hands on the other's shoulders. His eyes locked onto the first guard's. "Nigel, you are an idiot. Listen carefully. The water maids are here to give us water."

"And we already have water," the first guard put in.

"Water, you dimwit, does not mean water," the second guard informed him. "Have a good look at those ladies."

Nigel, the first guard, moved his gaze to the three girls standing by the wall. Suddenly, he understood. He saw the women's over exposed cleavage and read seduction in their manner.

"Oh," he gasped. "Why didn't they just say so?"

"Because we're on duty," the third replied. "And we not supposed to be enjoying ourselves when we're on duty. Are we?"

The second guard removed his hands from Nigel's shoulders and gestured to the ladies. "So we're going to have some water instead. Understand?"

Nigel nodded. He stayed dumb and kept nodding.

"Ladies!" The third guard waved a hand towards the fire. "Come over and keep warm with us."

"We'd be delighted," Audrey replied.

Each of the ladies moved to a guard and wrapped her arms around his waist as they strolled to the campfire. The men were overly eager, almost immediately moving their hands and lips over the exposed flesh of the three women.

With a silent signal, a simple nod, the three lifted their daggers from their belts and slit the guards' throats.

Nigel tried to scream, but Audrey's blade had cut deep. A thick spray erupted from the wound and splashed against her bare chest.

"Bugger," she spat as she looked down at the mess on her skin. Without further hesitation, she plunged the tiny blade into the guard's face again and again. "You dumb bastard."

The three guards fell to the ground, kicking and writhing as they died.

"What was that?" Rose asked, pointing her dagger at the damaged face of the guard.

"Look what he did," Audrey answered, gesturing to the stain on her chest. Her face scrunched with revulsion. "It's dripping down my belly. Disgusting!"

Kateryn shook her head and made her way to the prisoners chained in the open. She scanned the twenty men, searching for a one-eyed man. All dressed in the uniforms of Newholt military. All beaten and bruised.

But not broken.

They looked at her eagerly, holding their clasped wrists up, hoping to be freed. She looked over her shoulder at Monteacute and the other approaching men.

"We need to unchain them," Kateryn called.

"Find the key," the sheriff instructed the others as he raced to her side. He searched the faces of the prisoners. Blood and grit covered their skin. Their faces were swollen, and their eyes blackened and closed over from being beaten.

Then he saw the man who fitted the description.

One looked back at him with one eye staring back. The other was simply not there. A cavernous hole was where his left orb should be.

Monteacute thought he recognised the man as the lieutenant in charge of the docks.

"Are you Sub-Commander Landon Wake?" Monteacute asked.

The other murmured agreement. His whole body trembled.

"Am I alive?" he asked.

Monteacute felt a knot tighten in his stomach.

"Yes," he answered. "You are alive. And soon, you'll be safe. I promise."

Wake wept as Kateryn raced over, holding a small iron object in her fingers.

"I got it," she announced, crouching beside the sub-commander. She unlocked his clasps.

"Who are you people?" Wake asked, obviously not remembering them from the night on the docks when the creatures had attacked. "The resistance?"

"We're a small part of them, yes," Rose replied. "They call us the Whores of Whitekeep."

***

David kicked at the ashes where the great oak tree once stood. The wind had cast most of the grey dust over the expanse of the enclosed grassy area. Only a few piles, formed into tiny hills and dales, remained near the centre of the Great Hall's ruins. The big man peered over at the dragon near the gate. She was fitted for riding, resting on her haunches and watching Alice closely.

"She certainly did a good job with this," David said as he moved to the girl. Do you think it worked?"

"I don't know," Alice replied. She had her cloak wrapped about her and her two swords strapped to her back. "I thought the tree might be a source of power or a place of connection. I may have been wrong. I thought it could have been a special place for them." She paused and swallowed hard. Tears spilled over her cheeks. "It was for me."

Arthur sighed. "It doesn't matter," he told her, touching her on the shoulder. "Even if it possessed any value to them, you still need to go."

"I know," she said, looking at him with sad eyes.

"Don't fret about him," the large man said. "I'll look after him while you're gone."

"I know," Alice repeated with a small sigh, wrapping her arms around the man's waist. David responded by pulling her tightly into his enormous frame.

"You just look out for yourself, princess," he whispered. She sensed his grief and heard a faint tremble in his voice. "And if you get the chance to take her down, do it."

He pulled away from her and held her at arm's length.

"I will," she responded.

"I mean it, Alice," he reiterated. "She may be your aunt by blood, but she is a threat to us all. Your mother may hesitate when they meet face-to-face. You can't afford to do the same."

"I won't hesitate," the girl promised.

She turned to Arthur, who placed his arm around her waist.

"Please be careful," he whispered into her ear.

"I'll be back as soon as I can," she declared.

"I wish you didn't need to go."

She cried.

He kissed her forehead before touching his lips to hers. They stayed that way for a while, not noticing that David had moved to Liana's side. When they looked at the man, he was rubbing the beast on the nose. The dragon emitted a deep purring sound.

Alice climbed onto Liana's back and fastened herself into the saddle. The two men stepped away as the beast spread her wings. With one enormous thrust, she leapt into the sky. A brilliant burst of ash and dust erupted around her, covering father and son with grey silt.

Skyward, the girl and her dragon flew. Higher and higher into the blue.

The two Gyfford men watched for some time as Alice and Liana became a mere speck to the south, eventually disappearing altogether.

Arthur's lip trembled, and his chin quivered.

"Come on, son." David clasped a hand around the boy's shoulders. "Let's get this muck off us and finish packing the wagon."

***

Liana skimmed the mountain tops, tilting steeply and turning sharply as she followed the Twisted Road through the southern range. Alice kept her eyes peeled for any sign of the troop that included the other three of her coven and her mother. The company also comprised of the men from Newholt, a few well-equipped units from Woodmyst's guards, the Agrodien warriors, Schoenbach and the last two of the Erilian women.

The sun had moved far to the west and Alice could only surmise that the travellers would have stopped to set up camp for the night. The darkness brought the cold with it and with little timber to cut down and make fires with along the road, the company would need to make do with their own body heat.

The girl scanned ahead and saw nothing. She hoped she hadn't passed them by. A small tightness gripped her stomach as she feared she had lost them. She considered turning about and starting the journey again, to follow the road from the foothills more closely.

But it was a silly thought.

There was only one Twisted Road through the mountains. If she had missed the multitude of soldiers with her vision, surely Liana had not.

Banking to the right, swooping by a high peak that was lightly dusted with white frost, Alice saw a part where the road wound abruptly to the right to navigate by a large rocky formation before turning back to the left then onward along the edge of the steep embankment. There they were, tucked away to the side of the mountain, neatly positioned and sheltered between two tight, sharp limbs.

The natural formation of the mountain provided a large space to set up camp that was also enclosed by walls of rock, save for a narrow access to the road. The rock formation around which the path diverted provided a little more protection, acting as a windbreaker from the breeze that moved constantly through the southern range.

A woman stood near the centre of the encampment, waving up to the girl. Alice could tell it was her mother, even with the thick coverings and hood pulled firmly over her head and hiding her auburn hair.

"Down, girl," Alice called through the scarf that covered the bulk of her face.

Liana turned and glided for the rock formation. With her wings outstretched and flapping noisily, she tilted her body to slow her approach. Carefully, with her legs stretched out, she clasped the top of the rock and lowered her frame.

Many soldiers stopped pegging their tents, or feeding horses, just to watch the beast. Brondt held a tent pole in place and pretended to not be so in awe. He turned to the men and barked at them angrily.

"Get back to your work."

Thornton gave him a wry look as he continued hammering a tent pole in place.

"Don't say a thing, Captain," the commander instructed.

"I wasn't going to," the other answered. He finished hammering and turned with the commander to retrieve a large rolled-up canvas from the ground nearby. "Only that I think the dragon is amazing as well."

"The men need to see it as if it isn't amazing," Brondt replied, taking one end of the roll in his hands. His eyes moved to the beast as it leapt to the ground with the girl on its back. "If they stop to look at it during battle, as they did just now, we'll suffer losses that we simply don't need to."

"I understand." Thornton took the other end and together they hoisted it over the poles, allowing it to unfurl and drape.

"They need to get used to it," the commander explained, watching the dragon lower its frame to allow Alice to climb off its back.

"I know," the other agreed, peering around at the men. He saw hammering and tightening of ropes as they erected tents. He saw men feeding horses and moving supplies and stores into position. He returned his gaze to Brondt, who was watching the creature intently. "But, it is amazing, isn't it?"

"What?" The commander seemed to snap out of a trance and lock eyes with the captain.

"All the men are working," the captain answered. "Only you appear to be spellbound by the girl's pet."

Brondt glared at the man for a long moment. The captain couldn't tell if his commander was angry or stuck for emotion.

Finally, Jonathon Brondt allowed his face to relax a little.

"Have you always been such an ass, Captain?"

"Yes sir," Thornton growled.

Six

"The resistance is hitting our guard posts more and more frequently," she said, tapping her fingers against the armrest of the throne. Andris had taken a knee before her and bowed his head, staring blankly at the stone floor beneath him. "I just heard that the guard post by the town square was infiltrated and several prisoners are now missing."

The commander of the black forces said nothing. He simply waited, half expecting her to destroy him. The low tone of her voice informed him she was furious. He didn't care. All he wanted was to be at home with his wife. If the Black Queen couldn't grant him that, then he wished to die.

"One of them was the sub-commander of Elynbrigge's military," she continued. "Did you know this?"

"Yes, my lady," he muttered.

"And all of this, I had to find out from my kitchen staff." Joanne leant forward. "Isn't it part of your position to keep me apprised of such matters?"

"Yes, my lady," Andris repeated in the same tone as before.

"Tell me why I shouldn't have you executed for such treachery," she commanded.

This isn't you.

She felt her heart stop cold. Her back went stiff and hit the backrest of the throne hard, emitting a barely audible thud.

"It isn't my place to tell your magnificence what to do," Andris replied. His stare remained fixed to the floor and his head bowed low.

"Magnificence?" Joanne furrowed her brow. It wasn't a customary response. She believed he was taunting her, trying to get an angry response. She looked at him curiously. "Commander?"

"Yes, my lady," he replied.

"Look at me."

Andris lifted his gaze to her. His eyes were empty and cold.

"You are mine to command, no?"

"I am, my lady."

She recognised a broken spirit within the shell of the man before her.

"And you are expected to follow all my commands without question, correct?"

"I am, my lady."

Joanne peered about the room. Several guards stood at their posts near the doors and a few servant girls waited by the side of the throne's platform. She signalled them with a wave of her hand.

"Leave us," she commanded. The guards and the servant girls filed out of the throne room through the doors nearest to them. When she was sure there was no one in earshot, she leant forward again, trying her best to display a friendly face. "Andris." She lowered her voice to a soothing tone.

"Yes, my lady," Andris replied, emotionless.

This isn't you.

The whisper inside of her was a soft thunder, as if a storm in the distance calling to her.

"We have shared a lifetime, you and I," she said.

He looked at her curiously.

"We have experienced things that most could never comprehend. We survived Blackrock Haven together. It only seems fitting that we are both here."

His face tightened as he looked her up and down quickly.

"Together, I mean," she continued. "You protected me, and now I am able to protect you."

"My lady?"

"Well?" She raised her brows a little. "If the guards get word you did not inform their queen of the insurgency, they may get a trifle grumpy. Don't you think?"

He stared at her in silence. His chin quivered slightly.

"Perhaps we could come to some arrangement?"

This isn't you.

The storm drew closer and grew louder.

"No," he replied.

"What?" She glared at him. He could see the anger in her eyes as they turned opaque.

"I said, no." He got to his feet slowly.

Her eyes grew darker and darker. Her lips recoiled, baring her clenched teeth.

"I am your queen." She lifted herself from her seat and pointed to him. "You are mine to command. You are expected to follow my commands without question."

This isn't you.

She pressed her hands to the sides of her head. The voice inside thundered.

A flash, like lightning, filled her thoughts. An image of a small boy looking up at her, cradled in her arms. Antony.

"Yes, my lady." Andris took a deep breath. "But my wife has more hold over me than you ever will."

"I should tear you apart," she hollered, thrusting the thoughts of her infant son away. Her voice bounced off the stone walls, causing her words to resemble a roar.

"As you wish, Your Majesty." He bowed his head, preparing for the worst.

She growled and flung her hands towards a large tapestry hanging upon the wall. It tore violently and toppled to the floor.

"I'm not done with you, Andris," she spat. "I will bed you, even if I have to hold you down to do so."

"You can try, Joanne," he said coolly. "But if you could, I think you would have already done so. If there is nothing more, I would like to return to my duties."

"Your insolence will be your end, Andris," she hollered. "Get out."

Andris bowed politely and left, returning through the doors at the far end of the room.

Joanne lowered herself onto her throne, holding her head in her hands as she wept.

This isn't you.

***

Andris waited until he was out of the sight of the many guards standing along the hallways of the palace before he allowed his composure to relax. Only when he was in his private quarters did he burst into an uncontrollable fit. His breathing became erratic and his legs seemed to give up their strength. He collapsed by his bed and cried.

He must have been there for some time, as when his senses returned to him, the sky through his window had turned dark and stars winked back at him. Lifting himself to the edge of his bed, he tried to get his thoughts together, scrambling internally for rationality.

He found it when he looked at a knapsack he had hanging over the back of a chair by the door. He glanced around the room as he made a mental note of the things he would need and the things he could discard.

The private quarters weren't much to behold; a small room with a bed, a side table, a wardrobe and a chair. It reminded him of his little room in Blackrock Haven so many years ago. Except for the window. It was nothing more than a small square that allowed him to look out upon the courtyard if he stood up.

He grabbed the knapsack and started packing his belongings and discarding any military paraphernalia. After redressing into less conspicuous clothing, a white shirt and grey coat before placing his military uniform in the wardrobe. He strapped his sword to his waist and hoisted the pack over his shoulder.

With a casual step, he strolled from his quarters and moved across the courtyard towards the palace gates. Guards were standing on either side and recognised him as he approached.

"Commander," one of them called.

His heart almost stopped. He kept his calm as he neared the two armed men.

"Evening," Andris replied in a friendly tone.

"No uniform tonight, sir?" the other guard asked.

"On my way to the tavern, lads," he replied. It was true. That would be his best bet to find who he sought.

"Change of clothes?" The guard pointed to the bag on Andris' back.

"Yeah. You never know, boys," he replied as he passed between them. "Might find a whore and stay the night."

"And the sword, sir?" the first guard pressed.

"Besides having enemies out there and the need to be protected?" Andris turned to face them as he continued walking backwards, away from the palace. "Might find someone's wife and stay the night. Who knows? Don't want some jealous husband besting me now. Do I?"

The guards chuckled and waved to him as he turned about and continued down the road into the city.

Andris held his expression for some distance. He felt silly after a while as the men by the gate couldn't see his face.

His breathing changed, trembling as his jaw quivered slightly.

His muscles seemed to vibrate wildly as a deep fear caused him to shiver.

She would hunt for him as soon as she found out he was gone.

She would torture him if she caught him.

Worse, she would rape him. He knew it.

Afterwards, she might kill him.

But he didn't believe so.

He suspected she would keep him alive only to torture and rape him over and over.

There was an unmistakable darkness inside of her; a monster that grew with each passing day.

She was no longer the little girl he had met at Blackrock Haven.

She was different. Her mind wasn't right, and she made him feel afraid.

***

Takmel sat upon the marble seat in the cold marble room alone, save for the four guards, two by the door and one on either side of the throne's platform. His thoughts ventured to the woman in his bed. She had just arrived that morning and he had expected her arrival.

When she had stepped from the carriage, dressed in white, he felt a small amount of excitement. She had then pulled the hood from her head and allowed her long golden hair to fall over her shoulders. Her blue eyes glowed as her lips spoke his name.

He could have melted there and then.

"Isabel," he whispered into her ear. "I missed you."

Their lips touched. Their arms coiled around one another.

And as he held her, caressed her, he couldn't help thinking of how much she reminded him of his mother.

Without hesitation, he had hoisted her into his arms and carried her up the stairs to his chamber. He had commanded that there be no interruptions and closed the door, locking it behind him with a thought.

Delicately, he removed her garments before he undressed. With more kisses, and gentle touching, he made love to her.

How much she reminded him of his mother!

As he sat upon the throne, attempting to steer his thoughts to other things, important things, his mind kept returning to her. He tried to think about the problems to the east. He tried to find a tactical solution to the troubles in Woodmyst. Particularly, the four major and immediate concerns that had proved to be more of a vexation than he had anticipated.

They had hurt him.

They had caused him to almost fall. Even now, he still felt weak. His strength was returning, but very slowly. Catherine, his own wife, his first love, had set something deep inside him. Something that festered still.

Perhaps she has killed me, he thought. *A slow death.*

He rubbed his chin as he gave this concept some attention. He felt her power drawing his essence away from him. He had just escaped her grasp in time to save his life.

But something remained.

Something passed over from her and into him.

Something that made him feel physically uncomfortable.

Like a sickness.

He took a deep breath and sighed. His thoughts returned to the woman in white.

Her blue eyes and ruby lips.

Her smooth, soft skin.

How much she reminded him of his mother.

The sound of approaching boots brought him back to reality. He looked over to the large open doorway at the far end of the room. A guard, dressed in pale armour and a white tunic embroidered with golden leaves along the edges, was approaching briskly. He lowered himself to one knee and bowed his head.

"My lord," he acknowledged the man on the throne.

"What is it?" Takmel replied. "It's late."

"My apologies, Maji," the guard replied. "Some of the infantry in Ironfields have been reported missing."

"Then send a search party," Takmel responded with a slight shake of his head. The news seemed a little trite for his attention.

"We sent a search party, my lord," the guard reported. "They too, have gone missing."

Takmel felt suddenly alert.

"How long has passed since the first troop vanished?"

"We can't be certain," the guard replied. "Their patrol started over two months ago. They were to keep to the border of the Core Lands and report back fourteen days ago. We sent the search party out two days after the overdue schedule. They were to follow the same route as the first and report back six days ago. A scout party was sent and returned with news. We just received word from their commander this very moment."

"What news?"

The guard pulled a parchment from beneath his tunic and held it out to Takmel. From his seat, the Maji signalled to one guard beside the platform to retrieve it. They gave the parchment to Takmel, who read it carefully. It outlined exactly what the guard, kneeling on the floor, had told him.

There was some additional information regarding the scouts' report. Takmel read it.

"Small farmhouse. Two girls," he murmured before looking over at the guard kneeling on the floor. "Am I to believe that two girls slaughtered all of those well-trained men?"

"I didn't write the message, my lord," the guard replied.

"You didn't write..." Takmel looked back to the parchment and read the signature under the report.

The mark at the bottom of the page belonged to Dakoth Risha.

"Risha," Takmel hissed. His thoughts returned to Woodmyst, where he had ordered Risha to take out the inhabitants of the glade. Risha and his men were unsuccessful. The two bitch witches from the east had seen to that. Risha should have taken them out first and made certain of it. Instead, the bastard lost most of his men in the skirmish. The only worthwhile thing he did was to bring the boy to Takmel. But, even after that, Risha displayed his true character. When Alice attacked the city with dragons, Risha and what remained of his men fled. "This worm has the gall to establish himself as Commander of Ironfields. What of General Harak? Wasn't he appointed commander? No?"

"He was, my lord," the guard to his side replied.

Takmel took another deep breath and stared at the guard on the floor.

"Stand up, soldier," he commanded.

The guard complied immediately, bringing his arms to his sides and his legs together.

"My lord," the guard acknowledged.

"Prepare our best company to travel to Ironfields," the Maji instructed. "Perhaps Lieutenant Saruun Versel's squad. When they are ready, come and find me. I will have a parchment for Commander Risha. It will detail instruction for him to present himself before me. Tell the Lieutenant that if he does not comply with these instructions, they are to seize control of Ironfields in my name."

"Yes, Maji." The guard bowed and immediately started for the door.

"Risha." Takmel frowned and shook his head again.

He closed his eyes and tried to envision his beautiful wife sleeping in his bed. He tried to see her golden hair and smooth skin. He strained to picture her ruby lips and blue eyes. He struggled to imagine the woman who reminded him so much of his mother.

Instead, he saw the ugly face of a man whose throat he wanted to wring with his bare hands.

Dakoth Risha.

Seven

Eight sat at the table in the cabin set into the rock. They had finished a simple meal of buttered bread and salted pork that they had brought with them from Woodmyst. Arthur had just set a pot of water on the stovetop and now waited for it to boil.

Lor looked over at his sister across the table. She had both hands on her enormous belly and stared distantly at the tabletop.

"We are safe here, Sevrina," he assured her.

She looked up to him, then around the table to the other faces. It was as if she had just awoken and was remembering where she was.

"I'm not concerned for our safety, dear brother," she told him. Her eyes glistened with tears. "I miss my husband. This one will be with us before long." She rubbed her stomach. "I would like it if he was here to meet his child."

"He'll return home," Linet said.

"How do you know?" the other asked. "You couldn't possibly know."

"I know," Arthur said, giving her a look of assurance. "My Alice will bring him back to you."

David tilted his head silently, agreeing with his son's words.

"She is one little girl," Sevrina contended. "Why don't I share your confidence?"

"Because you haven't seen what she can do," David said simply. "This girl ran the Kyhur Circuit in less than one hour. She leapt over the Rakmha Trench on two separate occasions, on her own legs. She battled with Agrodien warriors and defeated their leader with her bare hands. She fought the Night Demons and faced their dragons and won."

"Haigok," Arthur corrected the man.

"What?" David glanced at his son.

"They're called Haigok," Arthur clarified.

"I know," David said defensively. "Night Demons just sounds more dangerous."

"Sorry." Arthur smiled, returning to the pot. It was steaming.

"And look at her now," David continued, returning his attention to Sevrina. "She is the Kayl'sro of the Agrodien. An ally of the Night Demons. A dragon rider. And gifted with the powers of the gods."

"There are no gods," Arthur interjected. "At least, that's what she would say."

"That's what she would say," the older man repeated with a huff. "It matters not. She will take Newholt. She will free the city and bring your husband home."

"Here! Here!" Lor thumped the table with his fist. The cutlery rattled and rang. Alan, seated beside him, looked up to him, surprised.

Sevrina relaxed a little. "I hope you're right," she said. "I really don't know how I could live without him."

"She'll get him back," Alan told her. "I know she will. She has to."

A sudden, loud, rapid knock at the door caused Sevrina to jump a little. David got up to answer it, opening the door to reveal a few people on the porch.

"Good evening," the large man greeted them. He was face-to-face with a few female folks, Agrodien and human, who dwelt in the glade. "Would you like to come in?"

"I think you should come and see," Becka Dering replied. "Arthur more so."

"What is it?" David asked as his son moved to his side.

"You remember Corandra?" the woman asked.

"Of course," Arthur answered. "Yuri's daughter. Is she hurt?"

"No," another voice replied.

Arthur moved his head to see Courtney Harrow, Ruttger's wife, standing on the ground just off the porch. Ruttger had gone with Alice and the others to take back Newholt. Most of the women had remained in the glade when the assault on Woodmyst had begun.

"Nothing like that," Courtney continued. "Come and see."

Arthur stepped past his father and into the chilly night air.

"You should put something warm on, son," David told him. "You're still not quite yourself yet. We can't risk you getting ill."

"I don't think I'll ever quite be myself," the boy said, gesturing to his left shoulder with his chin.

"Come see." Galonia, Yuri's wife, held her leathery hands out to the boy. He took it gingerly, allowing her to lead him towards the sloping ground towards the stream. They pressed through the long grass. Arthur noticed it was becoming brittle with the approaching cold weather, almost feeling like straw beneath his boots.

"Come see," she said again, her tail stiff and her movement hurried.

Arthur wondered if her behaviour was because she was cold or because she was excited.

He turned to see his father following a few paces behind. The dinner guests had joined the party and the other women followed closely.

"This way," Galonia hissed, pulling the boy gently along.

Arthur hoped they weren't about to cross the stream. He didn't feel like getting his feet and legs wet with freezing water, and he had forgotten where the little bridge was located. The dark often did that to him, causing him to be disorientated. He had only ever tried navigating the glade in the dark with Alice by his side. Truthfully, and he was willing to proclaim it, he wouldn't have found his way from the porch to the large cave without her guidance.

Galonia, being Agrodien, could see quite well at night. Arthur didn't concern himself with his safety as she led him over the grassland. But she was reptilian and didn't feel the elements quite the same as he. She may tolerate freezing water. He, on the other hand, would scream an ear-piercing shriek that would cause blood to curdle.

The Agrodien female turned and headed towards the treeline to the north.

Arthur was silently thankful as he heard the stream bubbling away to his right. They were not going to cross.

"There Corandra." Galonia pointed ahead. Arthur couldn't see her through the dark shadows beneath the trees. But he could hear heavy footfalls. "Corandra," Galonia called. "Come see."

The sound of snapping twigs and heavy crunching grew louder. Something large approached and, to Arthur, it definitely did not sound like an Agrodien girl. His heart thumped and his train of thought raced in a thousand different directions as he contemplated what was happening.

Had she led him to danger?

Of course not. Galonia wouldn't bring me to harm.

Perhaps the Agrodien woman had lost her mind?

Then, all the women of the glade must have as well. Why else would they come and tell me to see this?

The crunching sound became louder and louder.

He feared the worst. A qedia. A bear. A rukyul. Some fell creature he couldn't imagine.

Then he heard a sound that caused his heart to leap with joy.

A soft nicker.

From the darkness, Corandra stepped forward, holding a rope over her shoulder. Behind her, following a few paces behind, was the large chestnut stallion that had belonged to his wife; a gift she had given to him.

"I thought we'd lost you, boy," he whispered, stepping forward and taking his hand from Galonia's to touch the steed on the nose. The stallion emitted a soft rumbling noise.

"I find him in the forest," Corandra told Arthur. "He no like me. I had to trap him and give him food before he come. Many days."

She reached to Arthur with her hand to pass over the rope. Arthur wrapped his arm around the young Agrodien's shoulders instead.

"Thank you," he whispered.

***

Andris kept to the back alleys and narrow access ways as much as he could. He believed the Black Queen would have surely discovered his absence by now and probably had half of her ground troops searching for him. With every sign of approaching guards, or the distinct sound of clanking armour, Andris took cover. He hid behind barrels, crates and under torn and discarded tarps near garbage piles.

Whenever he could risk it, he popped into a tavern, immediately leaving if he spied any blackguards. His search across the city continued. He hoped to find at least one member of the resistance, or at least someone who was sympathetic to their cause.

His biggest obstacle in all of this, however, was himself. He had been the commander of the black forces. For all that the inhabitants of Newholt were concerned, he still was. But he was also a wanted man.

Creeping through the lanes, crouching in the gloom, hiding in the shadows, shivering in the cold, Andris slowly made his way to the west. He looked at the palace tower now and then. It was always there; no matter where he went, he could always see it. Set upon a natural elevation in the centre of the city, built higher than any other structure, for all to see.

And if all could see it, then those within the tower could see all.

He half expected to glimpse her in a doorway, on a balcony, glaring right at him. But it was a silly thought. The tower was too far away. Not even she, with all of her abilities, could find him with only her eyes. The odds were in his favour regarding that.

The guards and foot patrols, on the other hand, were indeed something to worry about.

The farther he moved to the southwest, the more steps falling in cadence resounded around him. The patrols had intensified in this region, mostly because he had recently ordered it.

The Black Queen was an intelligent woman, and Andris knew this well. He had purposely moved a high number of troops to this region because it posed the most likely area of incursion. It was, in fact, where the bulk of the black forces had entered the city. Any army attacking Newholt would come from this direction.

It was also the best and quickest way to get out of the city.

To the east was the sea. Without a ship, it was simply useless.

To the north was no-man's-land all the way to Blackrock Haven. The dark creatures, with their leathery hides and large pointed teeth, had gone that way, leaving the city in the hands of the Black Queen.

Andris was glad to see them leave, as they terrified him. Who was to know where they had gone, except Takmel, who had some level of control over them. Perhaps he had called them to a new location. Perhaps he had set them loose to wreak havoc upon the land until he had need of them again.

North was not the way to go.

West either.

Several of those beasts had come from that way. There was no telling if they had returned to the mountains.

This left south as his only choice.

He would try for Belburn or follow the mountain range and take the Twisted Road home. But he needed to get through the patrols unseen first.

After a close call with two soldiers pissing against a wall as he hid behind a trash barrel within splashing distance, Andris waited for the street to empty and charged down a long street and into another alley.

The sound of laughter and joviality echoed through the passage. He followed the sound to the back door of an inn, the last inn before the edge of the city.

The din of marching soldiers was almost intolerable.

He could risk it and run, possibly get captured in the process. Likely, they would kill him. Or worse, take him back to her.

Instead, he tapped on the door.

It was an involuntary action. Something inside of him simply wanted to get out of the cold. It was almost instinctive.

He didn't even consider that the laughter and cheerfulness could belong to a squad of blackguards. He just tapped over and over until the door opened.

Orange light spilled into the alley, flooding his vision and blinding him momentarily.

"Yes?" a sweet voice asked. Andris felt a hand on his upper arm, pulling him through the door. "Oh, you poor man. Come in." The door closed behind him as he was led to a chair. "Here, take a seat."

He focused slowly, taking in the scenery around him. He was seated in a kitchen. A beautiful, dark-haired woman stood before him. He stared into her hazel eyes and almost found himself transfixed. He shivered slightly, still feeling the cold from outside on his clothes, but there was heat emitting from a stove across the room.

"Thank you," he said. His voice sounded hoarse and raspy.

Suddenly, the sensation of cold steel touched his neck, and his arms pulled tightly behind his back. A sharp pain stabbed through his shoulders, causing him to wince.

It was now that he noticed the two other women in the room. One, with blonde hair, was holding the blade against his throat. The other, with red hair, was standing by the door. They dressed in leggings, reminding him of the attire that the Erilian women, or Alice, might wear. Like hunters.

"Hello, Commander," a gruff voice said from behind him. "Try not to struggle. Else wise, I'll need to break your arms and she'll slit your throat. And none of us wants to clean the mess up afterwards. Got it?"

"Yes," Andris answered. He wanted to swallow, but an irrational fear that the action might cause his skin to press the blade being held against his neck made him rethink the action.

"Not in uniform, eh?" the man holding his arms asked.

"Leaving," he replied.

"Leaving?" the man queried. "What's that supposed to mean?"

"Leaving the city," Andris explained. His throat hurt. He surmised that running and hiding in the cold air had caused the dryness inside it.

"On a mission?" the man pressed. "Something special for your queen?"

"No," the captive responded. "I want to go home. I want to go to my wife."

"A deserter, then?"

Andris wept.

"Yes."

He saw the women exchange looks before peering at the man that held Andris in place.

"There are plenty of soldiers out there tonight, Commander. More than usual," the man stated. "Is that your doing?"

Andris noded.

"Why?"

"They're looking for me."

"So..." The man lowered his voice and moved his lips to the captive's ear. "You're a wanted man, then?"

The sound of laughter and cheerfulness continued inside the inn, past a closed door and out of sight.

"Helps us out a little," said the red-headed woman. "More business."

"Maybe," the blonde woman said, pressing the blade to his throat a little harder, "we hand him over and they might give us some coin."

"Maybe," the man replied.

The dark-haired woman with hazel eyes moved to a bench in the centre of the room. She poured water from a jug there, into a large mug.

"Tell me about your wife," she said as she took the mug in her hand.

"My wife?"

The woman inclined her head.

"She..." Andris started. His eyes welled up and the corners of his mouth drooped slightly. "She has hair like yours, but her eyes are brown. She is the most beautiful creature that I have ever seen, and I would gladly give my life for hers."

"What's her name?" the dark-haired woman asked, stepping forward.

"Sevrina," replied Andris. "She carries my child, and I want to get home to her."

"Why did you leave the Black Queen?" the woman pressed. "And don't say it was to get back home to your wife. There is more. Isn't there?"

"Yes. She tried to make me…" He turned into a blubbering mess.

"Make you what?" the man asked. "Kill someone?"

The captive shook his head.

"You need to understand," Andris said. "I have known her since she was a young woman."

"The Black Queen?" the man queried.

Andris nodded again. His crying ceased. "She was different then," he told them. "She was kind. Her husband was a good man."

"The Maji?" asked the blonde woman.

"No. Tomas," Andris replied. He looked at the dark-haired lady holding the mug. "Tomas Warde."

"The killer of the White Witch," the man said from behind him.

"Yes," Andris assented. "Yes."

"Did she go mad after he died?" the man asked. "Is this why she is here."

"No, that is the Maji's doing," Andris explained. "He has beguiled her, and I believe she is going mad because of it."

The dark-haired woman leant against the bench, cupping the mug in both hands. "What did she do to you, Commander?"

"I followed and gave orders so I could survive," Andris admitted. "I am not proud of what I am."

"And what are you?" the man asked.

"I'm a coward." He wept again. "That's what I am."

"You haven't answered my question, Commander," said the woman. "What did she do to you? Why did you decide to leave her?"

Andris shook, trembling from the cold, but more so from his inner struggle to admit to these strangers what caused him to flee. It seemed silly in retrospect.

"She wants to bed me," he blurted.

There was a moment of stunned silence in the kitchen. The only sound was the din of merriment emitting from the inn.

"Bed you?" the man finally asked.

"I know." Andris felt ashamed. "It sounds silly. She is a beautiful woman and most men would jump at the chance to lie with her. But I am a happily married man. I love my wife and she carries my child. I would rather die than bed another woman."

"It's not silly," the dark-haired woman opined. "Let him go, Monty."

Andris felt his arms drop to his sides. The blonde woman retracted her knife and stepped away.

"My name is Audrey Mountell," the woman announced, holding the mug out for the commander to take. She then looked at the blonde. "The one with the blade is Rose Heron, and the red-head by the door is Kateryn Crane. The beast behind you is Nathaniel Monteacute, sheriff of Whitekeep."

"Sheriff?" Andris managed after swallowing a mouthful of water. He looked over his shoulder at a stocky, much older man.

"Used to be," Monteacute replied. "Those dark things overran Whitekeep."

A vision of the dark creatures filled Andris' mind. He remembered how they had swarmed into Newholt during the invasion. He could only imagine what damage they could do to a small port hamlet.

"We will help you escape the city, Commander," Audrey informed him. "But we could use your help."

"We?" Andris furrowed his brow.

"You've stumbled upon the resistance, Commander," Monteacute replied. "Or, at least, one section of it."

"Resistance?" The commander allowed himself a small smile. "Here?"

"Where the patrols are the more frequent, yes," Rose said. "Right under their noses. We serve them grog, take them to bed and find out all their little secrets."

"Including the times for the changing of the guard, frequency of patrol duties and whereabouts of certain prisoners and personnel," Kateryn explained.

"We've been watching you for a very long time," said Audrey.

Andris peered at each one of them cautiously. He knew he hadn't heard the worst of it yet.

"I want to go home to my wife," he said. "But I don't think you intend on letting me do so."

"We will," Audrey told him. "I promise. But, you're right. We can't let you go, yet. Not until we are certain you're telling us the truth."

"So, I'm your prisoner?"

"Indeed, you are," Monteacute replied, offering a wry arch of his eyebrow.

"We have a bed in the cellar," said Audrey. "It will be your home for a while. The more information you can give us, the more trust you will earn. When, or if, we determine your faithfulness to the liberation of Newholt, we will help you escape."

Andris considered her words. "I don't want to return to her," he pleaded, referring to the Black Queen.

"Don't worry." Kateryn locked the door and stepped towards him. "She won't find you here. You're safe."

Audrey crouched in front of him, locking her hazel eyes with his. "Will you help us, Commander?"

Eight

"No, Kayl'sro."

All heads turned suddenly to the source of the defiant roar. None of them had heard Yuri speak to Alice in such a way. Emily felt a tight knot in her stomach as she watched her comparatively tiny daughter jab her finger at the giant reptilian. She couldn't understand their words as they spoke in the Agrodien tongue to one another. Yuri appeared very distressed by the girl's words and shook his head now and then when she said something he didn't like.

"What's that about?" Schoenbach asked quietly, seated by the fire he shared with Emily, his wife and a few others.

"I've no idea," the auburn woman answered, watching the exchange continue. She looked over to Nola'ee, who was standing a few paces from Alice. The Agrodien female simply looked back to Emily, presuming the mother's thoughts and shook her head as if to say; you don't want to know.

Yuri suddenly dropped to his knees and clasped his hands as if begging the girl. She continued to jab her finger in his direction and tell him her mind in his native tongue. He appeared as if he was about to cry.

"Kayl'sro," Yuri pleaded.

"No more." Alice waved her hand and started towards the fire. "I've said my piece."

Yuri slouched his shoulders and bowed his head. He had lost whatever debate the two were having. Nola'ee gave him a quick, compassionate glance before following Alice away.

"Something we should know?" Ruttger asked as she sat down beside her mother.

"No," she replied sharply. "Any tea?"

"Plenty," Karlena replied, reaching for the pot.

Emily stared at her daughter for what seemed a long time, expecting the girl to say something. Instead, all she heard were two words when Karlena handed over a mug of hot brew.

"Thank you."

"Alice?" Emily chided.

"What, Mama?" There was anger in her voice.

"What?" Emily furrowed her brow. "We have all played witness to something that is so out of character for both you and Yuri. You can't expect us to ignore it."

"It's personal," Alice answered before sipping her tea.

"Personal?"

"I'll make for Dweagan in the morning," the girl announced, attempting to change the subject.

"Dweagan?" Ruttger looked at her curiously. "That wasn't the plan."

"You will all continue for Newholt," she continued. "I intend to destroy the shipping yards and the docks. Perhaps a few ships as well."

"For what reason?" Akasati asked.

"Because of what the Master Bookkeeper said," she explained. "He said Dweagan's ports stock and support all the other strongholds where Takmel's queens are going. If I destroy the docks there, perhaps I can slow the supply runs."

"Makes sense," Schoenbach acknowledged.

"Is that why Yuri is so upset?" Emily queried. "He doesn't want you to make such a perilous journey? If that is so, then I agree with him."

"No, it isn't why he is so upset," she replied irritably. "No, he didn't say he disapproved of my strategy. In fact, he agreed with me. We just don't see eye to eye on a different matter."

"What matter?" the auburn woman pressed.

"A matter that concerns the Kayl'sro and the Agrodien." Alice got up, holding her mug tightly. "I have an early start. I think I'll retire for the night."

With that, she walked away to a tent pitched nearby.

Catherine was already inside, curled up and tucked under a pile of blankets. "So cold," she said to her sister. "Close the tent flap, quick."

Alice complied and lowered herself to the ground. Catherine lifted the coverings to allow the younger girl to slip underneath.

After a moment of getting comfortable, the older sibling nestled herself against the younger.

"They won't understand," she whispered. "No matter how you explain it to them, they just won't understand. Yuri's response proves it."

"I know," Alice replied. "But I needed to tell him all the same."

***

Piers Mayne woke suddenly, forgetting where he was. It took a moment for him to regain his bearings. He rolled onto his side, pressing his flesh against the young woman sleeping soundly next to him. Her dark hair was a mess, draped over her face and all over her pillow.

"No more," she mumbled softly, protesting his action. "I need rest."

"Sorry, Agatha," he whispered as he gently brushed her hair from her face with his fingers.

TOCK! TOCK!

A strange knocking filled his ears. It wasn't coming from the door or window. It almost seemed distant and close at the same moment.

He dismissed it, believing it to be something outside; something beyond his control.

Instead, he tried to recall his dream. The thing that had woken him so suddenly.

All that came to his mind was the boy.

Had he been dreaming about him? He couldn't recollect. Only a sense of something disturbing seemed to plague him, like an itch just out of reach.

He closed his eyes and tried to return to sleep.

TOCK! TOCK!

Slowly, he felt himself drifting away like a cloud sailing in the wind. A dizzying stir lured him towards weakness. Farther and farther away, he fell until…

TOCK!

Blood.

His eyes flickered open, and his heart raced.

What was that?

He reluctantly replayed the image that had appeared in his mind.

Copious amounts of blood had filled the vision. It dripped from silver utensils and spilt over wooden tables and onto a smooth stone floor.

TOCK! TOCK!

Mayne tried his best to find a context for the scene, but came up with nothing.

It made no sense.

TOCK!

He had never seen such a violent sight in his life. The sheer horror of that quick flash of brutality was enough to make him want to stay awake. He feared seeing such a thing again and dared not close his eyes.

TOCK!

And what the hell is that noise?

Agatha writhed a little, moaning softly as she entered a deeper sleep. Soft hisses emitted from her nose, causing Mayne to settle in his spirit a little.

Just a dream.

He grinned a little as he contemplated the stupidity of it all.

It was probably a simple thing caused by exhaustion and a busy mind that thought about nothing else but the Scarlet Queen and her strange relationship with Samuel.

What else could it be?

He relaxed his body and snuggled against the girl before closing his eyes. Her breathing soothed him, and he felt himself drift away again.

A euphoric, dizzying feeling swept over him for a moment.

Further and further.

TOCK! TOCK!

A warm, comfortable sensation grew in his belly. The deeper he drifted into sleep, the warmer he felt.

Further and further.

Warmer and warmer.

So warm it became unbearable. A furnace by his side that he couldn't escape.

He wanted to kick the covers away, but Agatha was beside him. Why should she suffer?

TOCK! TOCK!

Warmer and warmer to the point of almost burning.

He felt sweat forming on his brow, under his arms, around his loins.

He couldn't take much more.

Rolling away from Agatha, he lifted the covers from his body and opened his eyes.

Blood spilt over the kitchen bench and pooled on the smooth stone floor.

TOCK!

His vision focused on a figure standing by the bench. A woman.

She lifted her arm high. A silver cleaver brandished in her fist. With an intense thrust, she brought it down.

TOCK!

And again.

TOCK!

Mayne saw the blood spatter high and wide across the chopping board in front of the figure.

"I thought we had lost you, Skipper," the woman stated. Mayne watched in disbelief as the Scarlet Queen turned to face him. Blood smeared over her chin.

Wake up!

Mayne tried so desperately to open his eyes. But the scene didn't change. He wanted so much to be in his bed beside Agatha, the servant girl.

Wake up!

No matter how hard he tried, he remained in the nightmare. He glanced at the chopping board. Chunks of meat and bone rested on the left side. Fingers belonging to a man were on the right.

He looked down at his arms. They, as well as his legs, were gone.

Cords bound tightly around his arms, just below the shoulders and around his legs, just below his crotch, slowed the blood flow from his body. His frame had sat upon a wooden chair in the kitchen's corner beside the oven.

On the stovetop, a large pot filled with his flesh bubbled and steamed, emitting soft hisses as fat sizzled and spat inside.

"No, no, no," Mayne slurred.

WAKE UP!

His mind screamed at him, not wanting to accept this as his reality.

The burning sensation inside him grew and grew. Sweat dribbled over his brow and stung his eyes. Everything became blurry. He couldn't wipe the sweat away or move away to save himself.

She approached him slowly, an indistinct figure holding a silver blade high above her head.

Closer and closer.

"You won't take him from me, Skipper," she hissed. "But you'll never leave this place either."

WAKE UP!

Despite that, he didn't wake.

How could he?

"You won't feel much," she told him. "I promise."

As the cleaver came rushing towards his face, he understood with a sincere clarity that Agatha was the dream. That he was already awake.

This nightmare was his reality.

TOCK!

Nine

"Wake up," she called, slamming the door behind her as she dashed across the tavern's floor and to the stairs leading to the upper rooms. A distant, deep peal chimed through the air as her feet hit each step with a heavy thud.

"What is wrong with you, Audrey?" Rose called from her bed. "The sun isn't even up yet."

"It's coming up," the other yelled back excitedly. "And it's brought something with it."

"What?" Monteacute opened his door as she reached the top step. He was tucking his shirt into his trousers and trying his best to keep his eyes open.

"Ships!" Audrey cried happily. "Many, many ships."

"Ships?" His face became more alert. He straightened himself a little, pulling his pants higher and lifting his braces over his shoulders. "What type. Merchant or warships?"

"Can't tell," she said before banging her fists against another door. "Wake up."

"Go away," Kateryn called back angrily.

"How do you know?" Monteacute asked.

"Saw them," she returned. "Shadows against a red sky."

"Could be allies to the Black Queen," the sheriff mumbled as he turned back into his room to search for his boots.

"No way." Audrey shook her head. "Listen."

He stopped shuffling about and cocked his ear. Sure enough, he heard the bells ringing. They were signalling from the harbour.

"Do you think they've come to help us, Monty?"

***

Emily woke to find her daughters missing from their bedding. She crawled out of the tent, wrapping her thick cloak about her as she stepped onto the cold ground of their mountain-top camp. Her gaze moved immediately to the fire, where she saw the Four embraced in a tight huddle.

It was a strange sight to behold. Even the troops standing guard couldn't take their eyes off the women. Liana kept her attentive gaze on Alice. She had been fitted with her riding gear and appeared excited.

Their foreheads touched, and they folded their hands over each other's in the centre of their midst. Emily saw their lips moving, but heard no words. Either the four women spoke in silence or the breeze sweeping through the range was a little too loud for her to hear them.

"Sisters talk," a soft hiss said from her side. Emily turned to see Nola'ee watching on. "Sisters talk for long time."

"Do you know what they speak of?"

Nola'ee shook her head slowly.

Eventually, the four women parted. Alice turned to her mother and approached.

"I need to go," the girl said. "Commander Brondt will lead the party through the mountains and make way for Newholt. I'll meet you there, if not on the way."

"I don't want you to go on your own." Emily reached out and took her daughter in her arms.

"I won't be on my own," Alice replied. "I have Liana with me."

Emily kissed the top of the girl's crown. It was then that she noticed dark roots forming near to her daughter's scalp at the base of the white streaks.

"Your hair is changing back," she said.

"I know." Alice frowned.

"What does this mean?"

"It means that we have limited time."

Emily looked at Catherine, who observed the exchange between her mother and sister. She then turned her attention back to Alice to see two big, beautiful blue eyes looking back at her. As a mother, she wanted nothing more than to take both of them away to somewhere safe. She didn't want either of them to face the danger that lay ahead. She also didn't want to cause any grief that could come between them. She needed them and wanted them to need her.

"I'm sorry if I made you angry, last night."

"You didn't," Alice replied. "I just have many things on my mind."

"The troubles of leadership," Emily suggested.

Alice gave her mother a solemn look. "It will all be different after this, Mama," she said sincerely. "Very different."

"How do you mean?"

"Things are about to change." Alice gave Nola'ee a quick glance and spoke to her in Agrodien. "Watch over my mother for me."

The reptilian female bowed her head respectfully. "Yes, Kayl'sro."

Emily noticed the iron claws around her daughter's neck, tucked beneath her cloak. It was easy to forget that the girl was a leader of a nation. It was also just as easy to remember such a thing when she saw the Agrodien warriors minding every word from the little girl.

"I'll see you soon," the girl said, returning her attention to Emily. She moved across the encampment to the waiting dragon. She wrapped her cloak about her tightly and checked her weapons before climbing onto the beast's back. Once she strapped in, the dragon stretched its wings wide and clambered up the rocky formation by the road's side. With one enormous thrust, the beast dived over the ledge and sailed away through the air.

Emily watched for as long as she could until both her daughter and dragon swooped behind another mountain's peak towards the south.

"Be safe," she whispered after her daughter, hoping her words would carry on the wind.

✳✳✳

Twenty riders approached the tiny farmhouse. They could hear a droning buzz as they edged their steeds on. Flies and other insects swarmed ahead of them.

"So," one man said. "Guess we'll have to go looking for Risha later, then, eh?"

"One problem at a time," another replied. "If Dakoth Risha wants to play pretend general and ride all over the countryside to rape and steal from the little folk, let him. We'll catch up with him soon enough. And if not..."

"Some other bastard will," another rider added.

The incessant buzzing of flies grew louder and louder as they approached. Darkened and dried splotches of ground, partially covered with frost, signified places where blood had spilt. And there were many places to behold such a sight.

"That's disgusting," a man announced, copping a nose full of rotting stench.

"Two patrols," another said as he peered about. "So, this is what happened to them."

"What could have done this?" the first questioned.

Piles of drying flash encompassed the ground before the little house's door. Protruding white bones pointed this way and that from blackened meat and clumps of horsehair. Amongst it, dark armour, similar to their own, lay strewn about. Covering it all were copious numbers of flies, maggots, and crawling insects.

The door opened slowly with a long creak.

The soldiers moved their eyes to the void.

Slowly, two little girls stepped from the dimness and into the early morning light. Their clothes were nothing more than stained and torn rags. Their bare legs, arms and feet covered with filth and dried mud. Their dark hair draped over their faces and shoulders like tangled and torn curtains.

The soldiers looked to their leader for instruction.

With a nod from the officer, covered from head to toe in dark armour, one soldier dismounted.

"Permission to speak freely, Lieutenant?" one of the other men asked.

The other assented, steel helmet clinking slightly against the pauldron covering the shoulder.

"Look about you." The man gestured with a tilt of his head. "I don't think this is wise. Perhaps we should try to coax them out to us instead of going to them."

The officer scanned the scene, turning a covered face to the surrounding death. Then, with a flick of the wrist, the lieutenant instructed the soldier on the ground to continue.

The soldier complied, stepping forward with caution. His hands went before him, signalling to the little girls that he meant them no harm.

"Hello," he said nervously. "We are good people. We are here to help you."

The girls kept their gaze fixed upon the approaching soldier as he stepped carefully over a pile of putrid flesh. The flies whizzed by his face. He ignored them and continued forward.

"We can take you to somewhere safe," he told them. "Would you like that?"

A few bugs smacked against his skin. More flies crawled over his chin and cheeks. It tickled, but he felt utter revulsion. He wasn't sure if he could take much more.

They zipped by his ears, buzzing around his head. One crept over his lip and touched his gums.

He spat it out.

"Bugger me," he hissed.

The girls opened their mouths as if to scream.

"No, no," he tried to assure them. "It's all right. I'm not here to hurt you."

An intense breeze swept from the house towards the approaching soldier. It threw him through the air and onto a mound of dark flesh.

"Shit," another soldier called.

Loud creaking and popping sounds erupted from the fallen man as his armour dented and buckled.

A large spray of blood burst from his lips, instantly attracting more flies to his face.

The girls continued to stare at the fallen man, their eyes burning with bright light.

The fallen man writhed in agony as his armour sank upon his chest and back, crushing his body inside.

The lieutenant dropped to the ground.

"Stop."

The voice from beneath the helmet surprised the girls. They ceased their action and looked at the officer. Their eyes changed back to brown.

The lieutenant removed the helmet, revealing long, golden hair and a face that mystified the two girls. A young woman's face with deep blue eyes looked back at them.

"My name is Saruun Versel," the officer said. Her voice was calming and sweet. "I am a lieutenant from Wintermarsh, and my men and I are here to help you. Not hurt you."

The girls stood motionless, as if dumbfounded by the appearance of a woman in armour. Versel stepped forwards slowly with her arms held out towards the girls.

She glanced quickly over to the fallen soldier who was on his back, coughing blood over his own face and slowly dying. The girls followed her stare with their own.

"It's all right," Versel assured them. "You didn't know we were here to help you. You were defending yourselves. We understand."

The girls looked at a body lying near to the house. It had been there for some time, half eaten by worms and bugs. Versel noticed the dress that the figure wore. It was then that she noticed another body, the only other fully intact, not torn to shreds.

"Your mama and papa?" the lieutenant asked.

The girls nodded in unison.

"Did some men dressed like us do something bad to them?"

The girls repeated the action.

Versel looked offered a sad, apologetic expression.

"We'll bury them for you," she said, drawing closer and closer. "But you must promise to come with us. Back to Wintermarsh."

The two little girls looked at each other, as if silently conversing for a moment, before returning their attention to the woman in armour. Again, they nodded. The one on Versel's right cried.

"Hey," the lieutenant whispered. She peeled her gauntlet from her hand before crouching before the children. Softly, she touched her palm to the crying girl's face and wiped the tears away with her thumb. "It's going to be all right. No one will ever try to hurt you again. My master will protect you now."

***

The Black Queen stared from the tower's window towards the sea. An entire fleet sat upon the horizon, their sails furled, and their vessels anchored out of the catapults' range.

Still, she had ordered the weapons into place as a precaution.

She understood the tactical manoeuvre of the ships awaiting off-shore. They were sent as a blockade. Their mission was to thwart any attempt to resupply the city, and to prevent anyone from trying to escape by sea.

Not that she had the power to do so.

Two frigates from Dweagan were moored at the ports. Each was fully manned and ready for battle, stocked with black powder and ammunition for their cannons. They had no chance against the foreign armada that sat in wait.

It was a scare tactic; lining up the ships in such a way to show their numbers. She had counted them several times.

Sixteen. At least sixteen that she could see.

For all she knew, they were conducting patrols along the coast and sinking anything else that sailed along the coast.

"The resistance will strike soon, my lady," an officer standing by a large table in the centre of the room told her. "I believe they will try for our ships, leaving us defenceless."

"We are already defenceless," she replied, turning to face the young man. "At least, concerning the ocean. Are the catapults in place?"

"They are," he replied, looking at a parchment in his hand. "Three along the wharves. Several to the southern end of the waterfront and another five to the north. Should we move the beacon towers to the west over to the shoreline?"

"No," she replied, trying to think like a soldier. She knew she wasn't very good at pretending to be something that she wasn't.

This isn't you.

"What about the catapults to the southern edge of the city?"

"Leave them all in place," she instructed. "These visitors might simply be a diversion for something else. "Move half of the defences on the northern border to the waterfront. We own the north."

"Yes, my queen." The officer bowed slightly and started for the door.

"Has there been any word?" she called after him.

"My lady?" He turned to face her.

"The commander?" she asked. "Any word?"

"No, my lady," the officer answered. "We called off the search for him when the ships appeared. We felt it was better to increase our defences in preparation. Would you like for me to resume the hunt for Commander Hill?"

She felt a stillness in her heart. She longed to have Andris back, to have him to herself. She wanted so much to take him to her chambers, but she couldn't understand why this yearning had consumed her so intensely.

Part of her knew that if they brought him before her, she would torture him. Her mind envisioned how she could break him, both in body and spirit, before she would take him.

She entertained that thought. Savoured it.

This isn't you.

The voice brought her back to reality, to the tower room where she stood face to face with the young officer.

"There's no escape from the city," she said finally. "He's probably dead in an alley, frozen from the night's chill. Or sleeping in a brothel."

She didn't want to believe he could take up with whores. After all, he had refused her advances at every turn. She rather would picture him lifeless.

But she knew better, and deep down, a tiny part of her hoped he was safe.

"Do your duty and strengthen our defences," she commanded.

"Yes, my queen." The officer bowed again and turned away.

***

"How are you this morning?" Monteacute asked, pulling a stool away from the wall to sit beside the cot.

"Not sure," Landon Wake replied, rubbing his brow. "I think I heard bells earlier."

"You did," the other replied. "Ships have appeared on the horizon. I'm not sure who they are, but I can gather a guess and say they are probably from Dendadia."

"Is that good or bad for us?" Wake asked.

"I hope it's good," Monteacute answered. His countenance changed, offering the sub-commander a sombre expression. "Do you remember much? You were vague when we found you and you were in and out over the last couple of days."

"They made a mess of me, didn't they?"

"Aye, they did."

Wake took a deep breath.

"I remember you," he said confidently. "Sheriff of Whitekeep, right?"

"That's right," Monteacute said.

The sub-commander moved his eye back and forth as he tried to gather his thoughts. The sheriff couldn't help staring at the empty socket instead, noticing some twitching and flexing from beneath the skin inside.

"You were with four, five women and a bunch of soldiers," Wake said.

"Five women," the other confirmed. "One went with your queen almost a month ago. We haven't heard from them since."

"I remember," blurted Wake, as if suddenly recollecting. "That was when Commander Brondt made me his subordinate. That girl. She made the lightning dance."

"Correct," Monteacute said. His expression changed again, to sadness and despair. "Another, an older lady, died during the assault. One of those devils took her."

"I'm sorry to hear that." Wake frowned. "Was she your wife?"

"What?" The sheriff raised his brows. "No. Nothing like that. She was like a mother to the others, and she kept me in check whenever she could."

"And the other three are here?" the sub-commander asked. "I think I've seen them. I think one of them told me about the resistance. She called herself something. Something to do with Whitekeep."

"The Whores of Whitekeep," Monteacute informed him. "The men gave them that name."

Wake gave him a disapproving look. "Not very nice."

"It's what they are," the sheriff replied. "Or were. They have a special set of skills that they have used to gather information for us. The Whores of Whitekeep." He contemplated the name. "It's an apt title."

"So, what next?" Wake tried to sit up. He winced as a sharp pain moved through his ribs.

"You rest," Monteacute ordered, pushing gently on the man's shoulder to make him lie down. "They beat you pretty badly. You need time to heal. Here." He reached into his pocket and pulled out a bandage.

"I'm not bleeding," Wake told him.

"For your eye," the other replied. "I couldn't find a decent leather patch, like the one you had before. I hope it will suffice."

"Thank you." The sub-commander took the cloth and held it in his hands.

"One of the girls will bring you breakfast soon. Is there anything else I can get you in the meantime?"

"This is a tavern, is it not?" Wake asked.

"Yes, it is."

"Then, how about a tall mug of rum, if you can spare it?"

"A man after my own heart!" The sheriff grinned. "On its way. Might even join you."

Ten

As Brondt led the march along the winding path towards the southern foothills of the ranges, Alice rode high in the sky towards the coast. Liana spread her wings wide and glided on a stream of air that washed towards the ocean. Without needing to exert herself, she simply tilted her frame every once in a while, to correct her trajectory, always pointing her snout to the southwest.

Alice relaxed, resting her body against the dragon's shoulders and drifting off to sleep. Her night had been a restless one, with images of fire and blood. She imagined they were things that were yet to come. Perhaps things she could change.

With her scarf wrapped over her nose and mouth, her hood tightly pulled over her head and her hands folded against her chest, she napped. During the short snooze, she saw her aunt Joanne.

She had dressed in black, as she had done for some time now. At first, the woman was standing on a balcony overlooking a burnt city. Smoke rose from places over the landscape and soldiers skirmished in the open.

Looking to the sky with fear, Joanne reached her hands out as if about to cast a spell. Instead, she fled from the balcony and into a room beyond the doors, passing by lace curtains that flapped loudly in the offshore breeze.

Joanne was then upon a cliff that peaked high above the ocean. Tumultuous waves crashed against black rocks far below. The Black Queen, her aunt Joanne, seemed to look directly at her. Alice felt something tighten in her gut as she saw her aunt's lips move, only there wasn't any sound. The woman's eyes were sad and pleading.

Then, without warning, she flung herself from the cliff.

Alice sat upright and breathing rapidly.

Liana chirped, as if sensing something troubling the girl.

With a stroke of her hand against the dragon's leathery skin, the beast's concerns eased.

Alice calmed her breathing and pushed the dream away.

She scanned the horizon where she could see the unbroken line of where the ocean met the sky. There was still much land to cross before they reached the coast, but it wasn't very far away.

She followed the shoreline with her eyes from the north to the south and found the city in the distance. The white palace was visible from so far away, standing over everything else around it.

"Keep low," Alice called to the dragon. The beast obeyed, diving shallowly until it skimmed the surface, just above the highest trees.

The ground rolled, presenting itself as smooth green hills with coppices of green wood that trailed through tiny vales and long dells. These, she followed in order to keep lower than the surrounding hilltops.

But soon the hills flattened out into lengthening plains. The sight of a great dragon bursting from behind a knoll set cattle running and herders screaming.

It wasn't long before she reached the edge of the city.

"Up," Alice commanded the beast. Liana flapped her giant wings and started for the sky. The girl leant her frame towards the tower above the palace. "There."

Liana understood. She directed her body towards the target, gliding higher and higher over the houses beneath her, passing over small market places.

Closer and closer she flew.

"You know what to do, girl," Alice said.

The dragon pulled up sharply, hovering a few yards from the looming tower. Below, on the streets of Dweagan, Alice could hear the terrified screams of women and children as they fled.

As Liana hurled a thick jet of flame over the tower, Alice wondered if the people of this city deserved to share the fate of their queen.

Jade banners hanging from the tower's balconies burned and stone crumbled from the heat. Liana was relentless, continuing to breathe her fire until the entire structure was blazing with great flames and sending a dark pillar of smoke into the sky.

As Liana sucked in air, Alice looked down to the people running about, fleeing for their lives. The girl decided their fate. They were loyal to the Maji. Not one of them had offered to help or warn them of the arrangement that Takmel had made with them. They had supplied him with ships and transport.

"There." Alice pointed to the waterfront. Several docked vessels were resupplying.

Liana banked away from the tower and glided over the city to the wharves.

"Burn it all," the girl commanded.

Swooping along the docks, the dragon spat a line of fire, consuming the wooden walkways and storage buildings. She circled and came back several times to complete the task before turning her attention to the ships.

Men jumped from their vessels and from the docks to take refuge in the water. In most cases, it proved futile as Liana's flames swept over them, scalding their flesh and causing them to perish.

An enormous explosion erupted from one warehouse as black powder ignited. The force from the blast caused Liana to rock a little off course. She quickly corrected herself and made way for a large vessel armed with cannons along its sides and a catapult upon its foredeck.

It was only now that some of the city's archers found their way to the waterfront. They flung shafts into the air but came short of their target. Alice guided Liana away from the coast and higher over the water. From there, she safely executed her plan to destroy all the vessels anchored away from the port.

The move didn't stop the archers from trying. They continued to shoot fire their bows and call after the girl, naming her a coward amongst other words that she found offensive.

Black ships, merchant vessels and tiny fishing boats burned before sinking beneath the waves. Plumes of smoke filled the air on the docklands. The archers continued to fling their arrows relentlessly.

Alice watched the last ship disappear into the water before turning her attention back to the waterfront. There were still two ships moored near the burning warehouses.

But the archers had them covered.

Part of her struggled with the idea of attacking. They were mere men.

But they are loyal to him, and they always will be.

The troubles of leadership, her mother had said to her.

Alice turned Liana to face the archers, hovering high above the water.

"Where is your queen?" Alice called to them.

"Come closer," one man yelled back, taunting her. "We can't hear you."

The others joined in, waving to her, beckoning her over.

"Where is your queen?" she yelled louder. "Where is Gilda Smythe?"

"Fuck you," another cried out, firing his bow. The arrow arced high before falling short of its intended target.

Liana trumpeted a loud grunt in defiance.

Alice sighed and shook her head.

"Burn them," she said.

Like lightning, the beast dived towards them, spreading her jaws wide. A great flare of bright, furious fire swept over the men as she passed over their heads. Within an instant, they were on the ground and writhing in agony.

The dragon swept back to the sky before turning towards the moored vessels. In one huff, she engulfed in flames and the remaining docks set alight.

Liana took to the sky again. Alice glanced to the city where she saw men in armour swarming down the streets towards them. Infantry and cavalry made their way along a primary artery from the city's centre towards the waterfront.

Liana gave another guttural call as she levelled out and turned towards the sea. Alice expected the beast intended to turn back and swoop upon the soldiers.

"One last pass and we leave," the girl said out loud.

The dragon tilted its frame to the right, turning in a tight circle. Flame and smoke veiled the tower. A dark cloud covered the port, and the ships had all but disappeared into the sea. Dweagan was a sight to behold.

Directly before her, right in her line of sight, riders and foot soldiers rushed along a wide road towards her.

Liana flapped her wings and pointed her snout towards them. She emitted a deep growl as she gained pace, smoke already billowing from between her teeth.

Alice turned her face to flint. She gripped the saddle tightly with her fingers as the men grew larger and larger in her view.

The smoke thickened around the dragon's head.

The eyes of the men grew wide with horror.

Bright flames spewed from the beast.

Screams of terror filled the air.

In a flash, girl and dragon were high in the air again.

Alice looked over her shoulder to see a long, wide stream of flame consuming the road where the men had once been.

They had no chance.

Alice rubbed her hand against the beast's leathery shoulder.

"Good girl," she said. "On to Newholt."

***

The stench of burning flesh was putrid and made her stomach turn. She could still hear people screaming as rubble crumbled or another cache of black powder erupted in the distance.

She cowered against the wall of the guardhouse, peering at the smoke billowing from the tower above her. She watched as the top third of the tower toppled backwards and away from her, into the bulk of the palace. An eruption of dust, smoke and flame followed. It was as spectacular as it was tragic.

There was no saving the building. She wept as she rested on her haunches to watch it burn.

"My lady?" A guard crouched beside her. "I don't think it's safe here. The dragon may return."

"She won't," the Jade Queen replied. "Not today."

"My lady?" the guard furrowed his brow.

"She came to do one thing, and one thing only."

The soldier looked at the smoke rising from the waterfront, understanding what the queen was referring to.

"She didn't get to you, my lady," the guard reminded.

"She would still be here if she intended to get to me," said the Jade Queen.

"Begging pardon, my lady. But how could you know this?"

"Because that was Alice Warde," she explained with tears in her eyes. "And nothing escapes Alice Warde. When she hunts, she kills. And she has killed today."

"My lady." The soldier rose to his feet. "We should get you to safety." She shook her head.

"There is nowhere safe in Dweagan," the Jade Queen said.

"Then we should try to get you to somewhere safe outside of Dweagan," he replied.

"No ships." She half-smiled. "So where can we go? We have failed the Maji. The supply ships burn and drown. The storehouses are aflame."

"We could go south," he proposed. "Perhaps Linport or Bellmore have vessels."

"And then where to?" She looked defeated. "To where?"

"West," he suggested. "One of the other queens would take you in. Surely they would be able to…"

He stretched his arm up and away, gesturing to the sea, exposing his dagger attached to his belt.

She didn't think she could be so fast.

Before he could finish his words, she snatched the blade from his belt and dug it deep into his throat, twisting it and pulling it a little to the left. A wide wound opened and spilled blood over his chest and sprayed against her face.

It was warm and pleasant; she thought. She jabbed the knife into his chest three more times before he fell.

With a blank stare, she watched him bleed out. She peered around to see if any had witnessed the event.

None had.

Any nearby fixed their eyes upon the destruction in the city.

She looked back to the toppled tower and palace, now engulfed in flame.

The unbearable aroma of burning flesh was thick in her nostrils.

Her breathing shook as her flesh trembled.

"I failed you, Takmel," she whimpered. "I failed you, my love."

She lifted the point of the blade to the side of her neck and pressed it deep. The skin seemed to pop as the knife penetrated her flesh. With one tremendous pull, she cut a long gash through her throat from one side to the other.

A warm flow spread over her breasts and down her torso.

The stench of burning flesh drifted away and the heat from the flames engulfing the palace grew colder and colder.

Darkness swept over her.

She found this a little confusing, considering the sun was still high in the sky.

But now, even that was gone.

Gone.

Eleven

Takmel felt the sudden disconnection. It was as if someone had plunged him into darkness for a fleeting moment, suddenly bringing him back into bright light and causing him disorientation.

There was emptiness; a void that had made him less than whole.

"No," he gasped under his breath. He looked over to his right, where Isabel sat. Her finely fashioned chair was not as regal as his marble seat, but nevertheless, it spoke of imperial magnificence and a place of importance.

She stared blankly at the floor, appearing dazed and confused. He could tell that she had felt it as well.

One of the queens was lost to them. A life extinguished.

Isabel cried, shedding tears over her cheeks. Takmel wondered if he should mourn as she did. He contemplated this long enough for her to turn to him in hope of comfort.

Instead, he felt anger and frustration.

He now needed to fill the void.

He needed another wife to take the place of the one taken from them.

"You feel it?" she asked him. "Gilda."

"Yes," he slurred. "And her actions have brought a lot of trouble for us."

She stared at him blankly. He couldn't tell if she felt concerned for him or taken aback because of his lack of sympathy. He summoned a guard by beckoning with his hand.

"They'll remember," she whispered as the guard approached. "They'll remember their husbands and children. They'll remember what you made them do."

"Do you?" He glared at her.

"My lord?" The guard dropped to his knee at the base of the platform.

"Any word from Lieutenant Versel?"

"Only the scout's report, my lord," the other replied. "They bring twin girls that were discovered near Ironfields."

"No idea of how far they are from arriving?"

"None, my lord."

Takmel waved the guard away and returned his gaze to the woman in white. How she reminded him of his mother.

"I remember," she told him. There was scorn on her face as she leant towards him. Tears continued to stream over her cheeks. "I remember everything. I remember murdering my husband. I remember carving and boiling his flesh. I remember devouring it all. I remember choosing you over him. I choose you still."

"Then why are you angry with me?"

"Because you feel nothing for Gilda," she explained. "Only the need to fill the hole she left behind. And I know you well enough, Takmel. You are already considering these twin girls we have received word about. You regard them as replacements."

"And?" He shot her a puzzled look.

"And they're too young," she answered. Her voice was a fraction too loud for his liking. It reverberated off the walls a little. "They would not even be of the age to flower yet, and you're considering taking them as your wives."

"Yes," he acknowledged sharply. "I need nine. I am down to seven. What would you have me do?"

"Search for others who are more suitable," she advised him. "Others who are ready to receive you."

"Older women?" he questioned. "What if there are none? These two have power. I can use that."

"You took Lucy," she argued.

"Out of necessity," he explained. "Besides, she is dead. What good was she in the end? She had no power. She wasn't one of us."

Isabel stared at him with a blank expression. She knew him to be cruel, but not heartless. Not after all the things she had heard him say that had made her love him so much.

But now she understood. Lucy was a means to an end. And with the death of Gilda, the Jade Queen, she had a revelation that the Seven were nothing more than a convenience. They completed the circle at the time of need.

If any of them were to fall, he would simply replace them, keeping the ten active. This was the new coven. Each of them was expendable so that the pitiless Maji could reign on and on.

Still, she loved him.

As he sat with his fingers gripping the ends of the throne's armrests, squeezing and releasing as he breathed deeply, she felt deep affection for him. She could sense that he was still regaining his strength after the skirmish in Woodmyst, and his escape across the breadth of the land.

He needed the nine to complete the circle. He had been rebuilding himself slowly, but it had been difficult without Lucy to complete the collection. Now, it would be even harder with Gilda taken from them. And Catherine had torn herself away.

As much as she didn't want him to take the two little girls, she knew he needed to close the gaps.

She knew it to be wrong. But she had been privy to murder and infanticide. Surely there was no other act more wicked.

To want to take two children as wives, however, seemed appalling.

But she loved him and didn't want to see him suffer longer than he needed to.

"You will need three," she told him, wiping her eyes. "Not two."

"Three?"

"Catherine is not a part of us," Isabel explained, placing her hand upon his. "Not anymore."

He frowned, considering her words.

"You're right," he said, looking over to her. How much she reminded him of his mother. "We must begin a search. Perhaps we will find more suitable replacements instead. More mature."

"Perhaps," she said, with a glimmer of hopefulness.

***

Lieutenant Saruun Versel continued to scan the path ahead. She moved her troops at a slower pace than usual. The horses plodded along steadily, occasionally snorting as they progressed. She surmised the beasts were protesting about the leisurely dawdle, being used to travelling much faster.

But they had two passengers, and they were precious cargo.

One of the little girls sat on the saddle against Versel's stomach. The lieutenant kept an arm over the little one's torso, holding onto her as they strolled towards Wintermarsh. She was breathing rapidly and not enjoying the experience at all.

"You're all right," the lieutenant kept telling her.

The girl kept looking at another horse travelling to the side and slightly behind them. Sitting atop the steed was another soldier carrying her sister in his lap. She was wide-eyed and smiling.

Tethered to that steed was another carrying the body of the soldier that the twins had crushed inside his armour. A tarp lay over the man after they strung him across the horse's back.

The girl riding with Versel gave the canvas-covered corpse a sorrowful glance before returning her eyes to the road ahead. The lieutenant had noticed and petted the girl's stomach slightly in an attempt to comfort her.

"It's all right, little one," she said. "You did nothing wrong."

***

Porf and Hygo had appeared on the western edge of the glade carrying wood axes. Sweat covered them and they looked exhausted.

"Water," David said to Alan as he noticed the two men approaching. Alan got to his feet and moved away from the hearth in the middle of the encampment to retrieve a water skin resting on the ground nearby.

"Hard day?" Lor asked as the men drew nearer.

"Aye," answered Porf, reaching out to the boy for the waterskin. "We could use some help if you can spare it. We felled five trees, but we haven't yet cut them for storage."

"We can do that," David said, looking at Lor and Alan.

"Would love to assist." Arthur gestured to his missing arm. "But I don't think I'm quite up to it."

"You could drive that horse of yours," Alan put in. Arthur was a little annoyed but tried not to show it. He would have rather stayed by the fire and read his book.

"We can hitch a cart or something to it to bring a load of timber back," Alan went on.

Arthur saw his opportunity and seized it. "Well, we can't get a cart into the woods over there," he said apologetically. "It's too thick and bumpy."

"It's a good idea, Alan. We can put ropes on the harnesses instead," David interjected, sensing his son's disinclination to get involved. "We'll drag the logs back into the open and portion them here."

"We could use any horse for that," Arthur replied.

"But yours is so much bigger and stronger than the others." David grinned. "In fact, why not get a few of the horses to help us."

"Let's go," Lor said to Alan, slapping the boy's back as he got to his feet.

The two moved away towards the open field where the steeds ran free with the livestock.

Arthur shook his head slightly, closed his book, and placed it on the ground beside his chair.

"You can't sit here all of your life, son," David said softly. "I don't care if you want to pine away waiting for Alice to return or whether you want to feel sorry for yourself because your arm was taken from you. Do that. But do it when all the tasks are done. We need firewood. We need food. We need a lot of things that we won't get by just reading books and worrying."

"I can't do much," Arthur said. "How can I help? I'm a cripple. Look at me."

"Rubbish," the big man spat. "You'll learn to use that one arm of yours as if it is two. You can lead the horses easily enough. You just have to hold the rope in that hand. There's your start. Later, you can learn to fish again and maybe hunt."

"I can't shoot a bow," the boy argued.

"I know." David frowned. "You never could. You were always hopeless at it. But you can trap."

Arthur shook his head. Not because he disagreed with his father, but because of the other man's optimism.

"All right." He managed a smile, forcing himself to his feet.

"Small steps, son." David placed his hand on his son's back.

***

A fine spray of blood splashed against the stone wall of the warehouse. Rose pushed the soldier away, allowing his open throat to drain over the boardwalk. She watched him stumble and tumble over the edge and into the water.

The clang of swordplay surrounded her as she strode confidently along the pier. A small skirmish had begun after one catapult on the waterfront had been set alight. The flames reached high into the air and had already spread along the wooden structure of the walkways.

Unfortunately, the flare was also a signal to the soldiers in a nearby guard post who came rushing to the scene in a frenzy.

There was no point in using her womanly charms. The soldiers had come for blood. Instead, she ordered the others with her to kill everything.

She had time during the assault to see two more plumes of smoke rising from other locations by the seaside; a sign that the groups accompanying Audrey and Kateryn were successful in their efforts to sabotage the large weapons of the foreshore.

"We flee," she called to the others, still fighting around her.

The men disposed of their opposition as hastily as they could before running along the boardwalk behind her.

A great clanging cymbal rang out from some distance away. It either heralded the fires or notified the city of an attack. In either case, more soldiers would be on their way.

She directed her team along back streets and alleyways, hoping to avoid anyone in uniform. Leaping over barrels, scrap piles, and almost tripping over a cat or two, the group sprinted as fast as they could.

When they were a safe distance from the waterfront, she turned and counted her men.

A few were missing.

Fallen during the skirmish, she believed.

Dead, she hoped.

One of the last things she wanted was for any of them to be tortured for information.

The very last thing she wanted was for any of them to inform.

"We're missing five," she said, panting after the run. "Did anyone see what happened to them?"

"One fell by my side," a man replied.

"Another two by me," answered another. He was holding his left hip where blood seeped through his fingers.

"Can you manage to keep going?" Rose asked him, gesturing to the wound with her chin.

"Aye," he said.

"I saw one get cut down near the catapult," another man offered.

"That leaves one unaccounted for," she said. "Did no one else see any fall?"

She waited, but there was no reply.

"Bloody heck," she spat. The sound of footfalls grew louder and louder. She couldn't tell if the noise was someone approaching or an echo bouncing off the surrounding buildings. "We need to move."

With that, the group fled through the lanes, criss-crossing streets and zig-zagging through the city, always heading to the southwest.

Before long, they gathered by the back door of the Petty Beggar. Rose knocked three times, waited and knocked twice more. They heard the unmistakable clicking of the lock before the door opened wide. Nathaniel Monteacute was waiting for them with water.

"Get in," he muttered.

The group moved into the kitchen and relaxed as the sheriff closed the door behind them. He latched it and turned to face the young woman.

"Have you seen Audrey?" he asked.

"No," she replied, taking a mug from the table. "We've been a little busy."

"Kateryn made it back a little before you." He pointed to the door leading into the tavern. "All are well except for a few scratches. What about you?"

"Four dead for certain. One wounded." She pointed to the man with the injury on his hip. "One missing."

"Shit," Monteacute spat. He peered around at the faces of the other men in the room. "You did well, lads. We hit three of their catapults and it looks to be a success. Let's hope the other divisions accomplished their tasks today as well." He gestured to the door leading into the tavern. "You should all take refuge inside. I'll wait here for Audrey. There's a barrel of rum waiting on the bar."

"Bless ya', Monty," one man said as he moved through the doorway.

"And get someone to clean that gash before you go drinking yourself to death," the sheriff instructed the wounded man.

"It's just a scratch, really." The man followed the others into the tavern.

Three taps on the door made everyone freeze in place. The last of the men in the room pulled their swords free.

Another two taps set them at ease, just a little. They stood ready for the worst as Monteacute opened the door.

Hazel eyes and a flushed face stared back at him. Audrey huffed as she moved past the sheriff and into the kitchen. Twelve men followed and piled into the room.

Monteacute closed the door quickly and locked it.

"They're everywhere," she said, moving to Rose's side. "Did all of yours get back?"

The blonde woman shook her head as the last of her men sheathed their swords and moved out of the kitchen.

"Bugger," she said as she looked at Monteacute.

"What about you?" he asked. "How many did you lose?"

"None," she answered. "We left with thirteen. Came back with thirteen. We didn't have as much opposition as your lot." She looked at Rose again. "We saw you on the pier and tried to get over your way as quick as we could. But it meant running back into the streets and around the warehouses to get to where you were. By the time we reached the back of the warehouses, the alarm rang out. We headed directly for here."

"We can't account for one," Rose informed her. "We know four fell, but that one... We just don't know."

"We may have to relocate," Monteacute put in, looking at Rose. "If they have captured your man, he may talk."

"I'd like to think that if they captured any of us, we'd be able to hold our tongues," said one of the men in Audrey's party.

"No offence, son," said Monteacute as he stepped towards him, "but have you had any military training?"

"No," the man replied awkwardly, glancing around to the others.

"Have you ever been captured by the military and tortured?"

"No," he replied, appearing more and more uncomfortable as the other drew closer.

"What is it you do for a living, may I ask?"

"Before this?"

"Aye, before this," Monteacute said. "You don't get paid for this."

"I'm a merchant mariner."

"A seadog?" the sheriff clarified.

"Aye."

"Most of you lowly bastards are seadogs, right?"

The others grunted a chorus in the affirmative.

"My bet is that once I hammer two nails through your balls and into a cold, wooden chair, you'll be singing whatever tune I want you to, son," Monteacute said to the man. "That's the sort of thing those animals will do to our man out there, if he's still alive. Got it?"

The man assented and lowered his head apologetically.

"What about you lot?" the sheriff asked, turning to the other men in the room.

With a silent nod of their heads, they accepted the sheriff's words.

"Good." Monteacute frowned as he pointed towards the tavern. "Now, get out there and drink my rum. You've earned it today."

Twelve

The Black Queen leant against the banister of the tower balcony. Her face felt flushed with rage as she absorbed the scene unfolding before her.

All catapults on the waterfront burned. A thick black cloud rose from the east, almost obscuring her view of the foreign ships offshore. She could see the vessels' sails unfurling in preparation to reposition themselves.

"We have no defences," she murmured.

"My lady." The officer standing behind her stepped forward. "We have dispatched more men to the eastern sect—"

"We have no defences," she repeated, turning to face him.

He stopped in his tracks and felt a chilling sensation pierce his heart as his stomach gripped into a tight knot.

Her eyes had turned pitch black and dark, twisted lines stretched from them under her skin and over her face.

"Your name," she demanded.

"Uh..." The vision of horror stepping closer to him took aback.

"Your name," she yelled. Her voice resounded like a thunderclap.

"Captain Leonard Funteyn, my lady," he replied. He felt his knees shake and his chin tremble.

"Well, Captain Funteyn," she said, pointing to the rising smoke behind her. "They have the gall to attack in broad daylight. Where were your men?"

"Uh..." he stammered, fear gripping him so tightly that he struggled to speak. "The commander had ordered most of the men to night patrols, my lady. We weren't expecting such a well-organised attack from the resistance during the day."

"The commander has fled," she reminded him. She stretched out her hand and took him by the throat.

A look of shock and awe swept over the officer's face as she lifted him off the floor. He couldn't comprehend how a woman of such stature could possess such strength.

Then, looking into those black eyes, he remembered with whom he was dealing.

His feet dangled and swayed. His hands gripped her wrist in desperation to be free of her grasp.

"My lady," he said as she squeezed her fingers tighter and tighter. His face drained of colour.

This isn't you.

She saw the boy in her mind. He looked at her with an overwhelming love as his lips moved.

This isn't you, Mama.

Her orbs melted from black pools to their usual hazel pigmentation. She threw the officer through the doorway and into the room. He toppled across the floor, rolling over and over until he smacked hard against the wall on the far side. Several books on a nearby shelf fell to the floor and a small wall side table toppled onto its side after the impact.

"The ships will attack from the sea. The resistance will seize the opportunity and attack from the land. Ready all of your men for battle," she growled as she stepped through the door and into the room after him. "You are commander now, Funteyn."

***

As the ships moved into position, drawing closer to the waterfront and turning their hulks to point their cannons towards the shore, Monteacute readied himself for battle. He strapped his leather breastplate on and belted his sword and sheath in place before moving back downstairs to the tavern.

"Sober up," he called to the fifty men gathered in the room. "I think they might need out there us."

"We're not even drunk yet, Monty," one man called back.

"Good!" The sheriff looked over at him. "Because, when we hear the guns firing, we attack."

"What's our target?" Audrey asked, placing her mug of rum on the bar top beside her.

"Every damn soldier we find," he answered. "I'm wagering that most of the infantry will move for an assault nearer to the palace. With the ships attacking from the coast, and the other factions of the rebellion attacking from wherever they are, the city will be thrown into confusion. They will need to gather around their queen."

"Makes sense," said a voice behind him, from higher on the stairs.

Monteacute turned to see Sub-Commander Landon Wake descending slowly, his hand gripping the rail as he carefully navigated each step.

"What are you doing up?" Kateryn called. "You should be resting."

"This is my city," he replied. "I intend to fight for her."

"You'll be dead before you cross the street," the red-haired woman scolded, moving to the base of the stairs. She placed herself under his free arm to help him down. "Monty, tell him to get back in bed."

"No," the sheriff said to the woman. He then turned to the soldier. "But you won't be joining us either. You're in no condition to fight."

"I can't just lie on my back," Wake replied as Audrey helped him to a table. He sat down, wincing slightly as he lowered his arm from Audrey's neck.

"You'll stay here," Monteacute ordered. "Talk to the man we have in the cellar. He knows the Black Queen and was commander of her forces. Perhaps he can tell us something we don't know."

"Why isn't he dead?" asked Wake.

"He says he wants to go home," Rose explained.

"A deserter?" the sub-commander raised his brows. "They'll kill him if they find him."

"Perhaps," replied Monteacute. "All the more reason to get what we can from him before they do."

"All right," Wake said. "I'll talk to him."

"No torture." Kateryn pointed to the sub-commander.

"I'll talk to him," Wake repeated.

"Because, if he is who he told us he is," she continued, "then he is as much a victim of circumstance as we are. And lately, I have lost my trust in soldiers to keep their word."

"You could say that for every bastard out there wearing a black tunic," one of the other men said.

"I'll talk to him," the sub-commander said again. "I won't poke him or prod him. I'll just talk. All right?"

She glared at him for a moment, seeming to measure him with her eyes before she nodded.

***

Hundreds of archers wearing black tunics positioned themselves on rooftops and in the spaces between buildings, using the smoke rising from the burning piers as cover. They aimed their shafts for the approaching ships that were turning in order to point their cannons towards the shore.

"Volley," one officer hollered from the rooftop of an inn.

The archers let loose a torrent of arrows that shot through the clouds of smoke, over the water, and towards the closest vessel.

Onboard the frigate, the captain stood atop the fo'c'sle, peering over the bow of the ship to monitor potential obstacles beneath the water. He was an elderly man with leathery skin, aged by sun and sea.

Several bolts struck low into the port bow as he watched on. Others splashed harmlessly in the water by the vessel.

"Fuck me," he hollered, half jumping out of his skin. "Master Gunner."

"Aye, Captain," a young man called from mid-deck.

"Get those cannons loaded and blast the shit out of that area there." The old man pointed to the shore.

"Aye, sir," the master gunner replied before turning his attention to a doorway leading to the companionway. He poked his head through the door and looked at the gun deck. "Did you hear that? Captain wants us to blow a hole in Newholt."

"Aye," the men cheered as they finished loading the port side cannons.

"Cannons ready," another man bellowed.

"Gun Mate reports cannons ready, Captain," the master gunner reported.

"Down sails," the old man called to all the deckhands. "Drop anchor." He pointed to the adolescent operating the wheel. "Get this bitch in position. I want to fire my guns."

"Aye, sir." The youth spun the wheel to the right.

The ship continued to turn as the rigging lowered and the anchor caught the sea bed with one of her flukes. The chain connected to the anchor pulled tight, causing the ship to stop with a gentle sway.

"Fire when ready," the captain shouted.

"Fire when ready," the master gunner repeated.

"Fire!" the mate commanded.

Twelve guns burst to life, smothering the port side of the ship in a blanket of white smoke.

A noise like many claps of thunder choked the sound of screaming archers as shards of iron and orbs of steel tore them to shreds.

"Again," the captain commanded.

"Fire when ready," the master gunner called.

"Fire!" the mate shouted.

The men were well trained and had practised often. The teams were already preparing the powder and stock for the third load before they had even shot the second.

The cannon operators ignited the flints.

"And again," the captain called.

***

Other vessels found their places along the waterfront and followed the frigate's actions. Cannon fire boomed and echoed across the cityscape, alerting the resistance to take action while the black forces were in a state of flux.

"Here we go," Monteacute roared as he opened the tavern doors and ran onto the street. Three women and fifty men piled out after him with swords in their hands.

There was hardly a soul in sight but for a few street-peddlers gawking at the rising smoke on the waterfront and commenting on the cannon blasts and some people milling about looking lost, possibly wondering whether they should go home or run away.

"There," one man in the group yelled. He was pointing along the street.

Monteacute followed the man's finger. He thought the man was gesturing towards the palace at first, but then he saw them; two soldiers standing by a merchant's cart. They were taking trinkets and hand-carved wooden statuettes that resembled the four gods and placing them into canvas bags strung over their shoulder.

The merchant, an old man dressed in raggedy clothes, obviously protested, trying to cover the goods with his own body to stop the two uniformed men from stealing his supplies. One soldier, toying with a figurine of Grolle, turned to the merchant and pushed him onto his rump. The merchant hit the ground hard and rolled, smacking his head against the stone wall of the building next to which he was peddling.

"Right then," Audrey huffed before running towards the soldiers as fast as she could. Her knuckles turned white as she gripped the hilt of her sword tighter and tighter with each stride.

The other two women and the fifty men looked at each other stupidly for a fleeting moment before taking off after the dark-haired woman. They erupted in a loud cry as they swarmed down the street.

The two soldiers looked at the oncoming horde, awestruck. They were so taken aback by the sight that they didn't see the woman closing in.

Audrey plunged her sword towards one soldier with such force that it penetrated his chest plate, slipped through his body and out the other side.

The other soldier looked at his comrade, who was spewing blood over his chin and neck. He then glanced at the fifty men bolting towards him. With a quick weighing of the situation, the soldier turned and fled along the street towards the palace.

Audrey was almost pulled off her feet as the man attached to her blade fell onto his back. She tried to pull the sword free, but it had stuck hard. She placed a foot on the dead soldier's chest plate and gripped the hilt in both hands, tugging as hard as she could.

Two women and fifty men charged right by her in pursuit of the fleeing soldier. They continued their battle cry that boomed through the narrow passageway and echoed from the stone walls of the tightly packed buildings.

The street fell suddenly silent, save for a groaning old man who had propped himself against the wall, holding a hand to his head where he had hit the ground, and the sharp little grinding noises of Audrey's sword slowly coming free as she continued to pull it out of the dead soldier.

"Bastard thing," she spat.

"Thank you," the old man offered.

"What?" She peered over at him. She was so focused on retrieving her weapon that she had almost forgotten he was there. She looked around to see other merchants and people watching on. "You could bloody well help, you know?"

A few observers snapped out of their trances and moved forward to help the old man. Others continued to stand in place, either watching the others helping the injured peddler, gawking at her as she struggled with her sword, or observing the rising smoke in the distance as cannon fire resounded.

She continued to tug and tug. The sword slipped a little more each time, but nothing substantial. It was going to take a very long time.

She pictured Monteacute, Rose and Kateryn getting farther and farther away without her. She needed to be with them, not here with her blade stuck in a dead man that didn't want to give it back to her.

"Bastard," she spat as she tried one big heave. It scraped a little against the armour and nothing more. She stood back with her hands on her hips.

"Why don't you just take that man's sword?" the old man asked.

"What?" She turned to face him.

One helper was pressing a white cloth against the elderly merchant's head. Audrey could see a little blood on the fabric. He must have hit the wall hard, she thought.

"That sword there." The old man pointed to the dead soldier's sheathed blade. "He isn't going to use it anytime soon. Is he?"

She stared with her mouth open wide.

"I'm so stupid," she finally muttered. She reached down and took the sword from the dead soldier's casing. It was slightly heavier than her own, but it would do.

She looked at her own blade, still stuck in the soldier's chest and had some second thoughts about leaving it behind.

"Don't worry about it, love," the old man said. "I'll make sure it gets back to the Petty Beggar for you."

"Thank you." Audrey smiled at him before charging off after the others.

Thirteen

Andris stared at the cellar doors as they opened. Some sunlight flooded in, spilling down the stairs to the cobblestone floor. The only other light was from the thin candlestick on the bedside table, its tiny frame flickering as a small draught moved through the opening and into the dank room. He moved from his back to the edge of the cot and placed his feet on the ground. The stones were cold to the touch, but he didn't want to show weakness to whoever was coming to see him. So, he took a deep breath and tried his best to bear the sting that the chill brought to his skin.

Heavy boots made their way through the doorway. The boards of the stairs creaked slightly with each step as a shadow cast into the room.

"My name is Sub-Commander Landon Wake," said the visitor as he reached the lowest step. He wore a bandage over one eye and moved awkwardly, as if hurt.

"Andris Hill," the other responded.

"I know full well who you are," Wake replied as he reached for a short step-ladder, placed against the wall by the bottom of the stairs. "Commander of the Black Forces."

The sub-commander opened the step-ladder's hinges wide. Two coarse ropes held the legs in place, keeping the joints from opening wider. He placed the ladder on the floor a short distance from the cot and sat upon it, using it as a stool.

"You hear that?" Wake asked, pointing his finger to the ceiling. The drone of constant thunder made its way into the room. "That's cannon fire, boy. Your forces are about to be beaten."

"I know." Andris felt the corners of his mouth droop.

"Are you a little worried about your men?"

"No," he answered, shaking his head slowly.

"Then why are you so upset?" Wake asked.

"All I want to do is get home to my wife." Tears welled in his eyes. "I have the feeling I won't see her again."

Wake bit his upper lip as he contemplated the man before him. He tilted his head to direct his eye towards the captive.

"You should put something on your feet," the sub-commander told him. "You won't be any use to your wife if you die from a cold."

Andris gave the man a perplexed look as he reached for his boots.

"You're the strangest interrogator I've ever encountered," he said.

"Interrogator?" Wake shrugged. "Tell me about your queen."

"She's not my queen," Andris replied.

"But you are the commander of her forces, are you not?"

"Was," the younger man answered. "Not anymore."

"Why not?"

"I ran," Andris said as he started lacing his boots.

"And why would you want to run?"

"Because I love my wife," he replied. "More than I love my own life."

Sub-Commander Wake took a deep breath. He pictured a young woman with a dark braid over her shoulder. She was wearing a wide-brimmed cavalier hat on her head, slightly tilted. A long, dark coat covered her thin frame, and a rapier was slung upon her hip.

Davine.

How he missed her.

He felt some connection to the man before him. He too, loved a woman more than his own life. He just hoped that he lived long enough to see her again.

"Explain what you mean," Wake instructed.

Andris lowered his gaze to think of the words he needed to say.

"The Black Queen wasn't always like this," he began. "She wasn't cruel. But something has changed in her."

"Changed how?"

"I knew her when she was a child," Andris continued. "I was a slave of the Sovereign. A prisoner in Blackrock Haven."

"The Green Mistress of the Mirikin?"

"Yes," the other confirmed. "Her men captured women and young girls under her instruction and shipped them back to her. Most were used by the men for..." he looked to the sub-commander. "Well, you probably can guess what for."

Wake nodded.

"Some were taken by the Sovereign herself to be trained," Andris explained.

"To become witches?"

"They were already witches. She wanted to train them to harness their power to the will of the Mirikin. Eventually, they would become replacements for the Mirikin. The Black Queen was one of these girls, among the last to undergo such training. She always fought it. She seemed to oppose the guidance of the Sovereign. Eventually, she and the other six held captive with her destroyed the Sovereign."

"You know this, how?" Wake asked.

"I was there," Andris replied. "I saw it with my own eyes."

"What happened next?"

"Blackrock Haven was burnt. The Black Queen, Joanne... Her sister was there with others from Woodmyst."

"I know this story," Wake interjected. "Some men of Woodmyst went north and defeated the Green Mistress. The White Mistress escaped and gave birth to a son in the west. And so on, and so on, until he becomes the Maji and here we sit. What has that got to do with her being here?"

"He beguiled her, I think," Andris answered. "He beguiled all seven of them. He made them his wives, and now they control strongholds in the coastal regions of the land. Newholt is a key location. It only made sense that he placed the strongest of all of them here."

"I don't understand." Wake furrowed his brow. "Why here? Why does that make sense to you and not me?"

"This was the seat for Amicia Elynbrigge," Andris explained. "The Fuchsia Mistress. The only survivor and traitor of the Mirikin. Newholt isn't only a city worth controlling for her trade ports and location. It is a stronghold for power beyond our comprehension. Something changed here when the Fuchsia Mistress rebelled. It caused the first break in the chain that was the Mirikin. The Maji wants the chain mended."

"Those cannons would say his chances of succeeding with that are pretty limited," Wake said, pointing to the ceiling again.

"Don't underestimate him," Andris replied. "And don't underestimate Joanne. She hasn't used her powers yet."

The sub-commander looked at the young man and grimaced, understanding the heaviness of his words.

"You still haven't answered my question," said Wake. "Why did you run?"

"Joanne is losing her mind," Andris answered. "At least, I think she is. She was once a sweet girl. Now she is cruel. But there is a struggle between the two. Sometimes she is callous. At other times, she seems reluctant to be so.

"By all my recollections," he continued, "I should have met her wrath over a hundred times by now. But she always lets me live on."

"Why would she want to kill you?" Wake questioned.

"Because I won't bed her, or let her bed me. She could do it easily enough. She is strong and could physically overpower me. She could use her tricks and make me believe I wanted to do it myself; or make me see my wife instead of her. But she hasn't. She just yells at me when I tell her I love my wife and will do nothing to hurt my Sevrina."

"Sevrina is your wife's name?"

"That's right."

Wake looked to the floor and rubbed his hands together. It was cold in the cellar. A fire burned in the hearth upstairs and he could feel it calling to him.

"I think she'll kill you if she catches you, Commander," Wake said.

"Andris," the other corrected. "I don't want that title anymore."

"Andris," Wake repeated. "I think you would be better off here. Hidden and out of the way until we can get you out of the city."

The young man lowered his head, agreeing with the sub-commander's words.

"Could I get an extra blanket or two?" he asked.

Wake smiled. "Grab your gear. I'm moving you upstairs."

***

Joanne sat upon the throne.

There wasn't much else she could do for the time being. The relentless rumbling of the cannon fire had caused her head to ache and the glare of the sun caused her to retreat from the balcony once again.

She had moved from the upper rooms of the tower where the table, the maps and the tiny set pieces representing the forces in the streets were all laid out, to the throne room on the first level. There were no windows here. The sound of the outside world seemed far away and the sun, the cold air sweeping from the mountains and the outside elements couldn't reach her here.

A throbbing had started in her temples and spread to her brow. She sipped at the large goblet in her hand. Water.

It didn't help.

"Something stronger, my queen?" a young woman dressed in white linen asked.

Joanne shook her head.

"Just quiet," she replied in a whisper. Her fingers pinched the bridge of her nose as she closed her eyes.

The low reverberations from the docks softly echoed off the walls. She could feel their vibrations through her boots.

She pictured a large dark cloud above the city and saw people fighting on the ground below the tower. Some she recognised.

Reptilians fought alongside men and women she had once called friends. The faces belonged to Erilian warriors and men of the glade.

Ruttger Harrow, Jeremy Schoenbach, even her sister was amongst them, slicing her blade through men wearing the black cloth.

In their midst, three with white streaks in their hair and piercing blue eyes stared directly at her. Amicia, Ursula and Catherine. She felt their gaze bore into her heart.

She heard the words.

A murmur on the wind as distant thunder erupted in the dark cloud. *This isn't you, Mama.*

She looked up at the source of the thunder. To the source of the voice.

Bursting through the clouds, spreading her majestic membraned wings, came the dragon. A great plume of flame spread from its mouth, engulfing her men below.

She heard their shrill screams as fire and heat melted flesh and bone.

Riding on top, she saw the one she feared the most.

Snowy streaks flowed through her long, dark hair and blue eyes bit into the soul.

The girl opened her mouth and emitted a long hiss that drained out all other sounds.

Mistress.

Joanne sat upright and both her hands gripping the armrests. The goblet had toppled to the floor and smashed into pieces.

"My queen!" The young lady in white rushed forward. "Are you all right?"

Joanne could feel her heart throbbing in her chest, could hear it in her ears.

"I must have dozed off," she said in response.

Two guards appeared at the door.

"My lady?" one of them called.

"I'm fine." She held her hand up to them. "Return to your posts. I'm fine."

The men vanished back into the corridor beyond as the young woman dressed in white carefully picked up the shards of glass.

"Don't cut yourself," Joanne told her. Her voice sounded sincere.

"I'll fetch a broom for the rest," the girl replied. "Shall I get you another goblet, my queen?"

Joanne thought about it for a moment before nodding.

"Something stronger, this time."

***

Alice found them crossing a stream on the plateau some distance east of the Twisted Road. Some had stopped a little farther on and started setting up camp. This perplexed her until she noted just how far the sun had travelled into the western sky. She had spent most of her day gliding across the air with Liana.

She looked to the open land to the south and saw cattle roaming freely. With a gentle lean, she guided the dragon over. The magnificent beast dived for the ground and, before long, lifted a heifer in her claws. The cow objected to being so rudely interrupted from its grazing and cried loudly as the dragon climbed high into the sky again.

Moments later, Alice guided Liana back to the ground near to where the camp was being set up. Emily was waiting for her with Catherine by her side.

"You brought dinner," the older sister said with a gesture to the cow.

The heifer mooed as it clumsily found its feet and stood near the dragon.

"That's hers." Alice pointed to the beast as she leapt to the ground.

Liana responded by sinking her teeth into the cow's neck and shoulders. Loud, wet crunching and cracking sounds emitted from the cow as Liana bit down hard, killing the animal instantly.

"She deserves it after today," the girl said as she moved to her mother. The two embraced.

"Gilda is dead," Catherine said as Alice wrapped her arms around her.

"I know," the girl answered.

"Not by fire," the older sister added.

Emily looked at the two with curiosity.

"No," Alice answered. "It was after I left."

"Strange that we should know this," Catherine put in.

"You are still linked to them through him, I think," the younger suggested. "And you are linked to us. Not that strange really."

Emily continued to watch her daughters carefully. She then moved her gaze to the east.

"Can you..." she looked back at the girls. "Are you linked to your aunt Joanne? Is she all right?"

Alice looked to her mother sadly and moved to her side where she took her hand.

"I don't know," the girl replied. "I know she's there. But you need to remember, Mama. She's not the same person anymore."

Emily wept. "I know," she admitted, gripping her daughter's hand tightly. "I am just hoping that if your sister can return to us, perhaps mine can too."

"There's nothing wrong with hope, Mama." Catherine pressed herself to Emily and wrapped her arms around the woman.

The moment would have been sweet, with the three of them holding onto each other, except for the sound of wet crunching bones and slurping cow flesh in the dragon's mouth behind them.

Catherine was the first to giggle. The other two weren't far behind her.

Alice looked towards the camp. She saw a large figure standing before her with his head low.

"Kayl'sro," he growled. "I sorry."

Alice stared at the reptilian for what seemed a long time. Her eyes welled with tears as he ashamedly kept his gaze to the ground. She suddenly rushed to the Agrodien and leapt off the ground. Her arms wrapped around his neck tightly as she hung onto him. He instinctively put his giant hands around her and squeezed her to his chest. His head lowered to rest upon her shoulders.

"You my Kayl'sro," Yuri told her. "I obey."

"You're my friend," she replied. "I should never have spoken to you like that. I'm sorry, Yuri."

Emily felt a tear roll over her cheek and a lump form in her throat. She saw her little daughter's feet dangling high off the ground, touching the giant reptilian's thighs as she clung to him.

It was moments like these that reminded her of just how small, just how young Alice was. She had been handed such great responsibility, commanded an entire nation and now led an army to battle.

Emily believed her daughters both had been robbed of their childhood. But none more than Alice. Her heart sank as she watched the girl embracing the Agrodien. Alice had two swords strapped to her, and she had used them. She was married to a boy and with child.

This life that her younger daughter lived was not what she had intended to give her.

But it was what had been dealt.

The gods, fate, whatever shaped the world, had placed this path before Alice. Alice had simply followed it to this very moment.

It began with Tomas being taken from her, Emily believed. Everything that shaped their lives to this moment happened after that. Takmel sneaking about and subtly sowing seeds of discord. David's wives and daughter being taken too soon. Secret alliances in Woodmyst and the betrayal by the Seven. What hurt her the most in all of that was that her own sister had turned.

All of that had made Alice what she had become.

But it wasn't fair, Emily thought.

If none of these things had happened, we wouldn't be here.

She wept quietly as she watched on. She was proud of her little one.

Alice had negotiated peace between three very different species, strengthened an alliance with the Queen of Newholt and done things that Emily could only imagine were possible.

We need to be here.

The little girl and the giant Agrodien had no intention of letting each other go anytime soon. Emily felt her other daughter's hand grip her own tightly. She looked over to Catherine and saw tears streaming over her cheeks.

The auburn woman pulled her elder child in tightly against her and wrapped her arms around the girl.

Fourteen

Tricia dipped her spoon into the bowl of steaming soup. Large oily bubbles floated on the surface, and swirled a little, as she scooped a small portion of the mixture. Diced potato, carrot, peas and meat. She allowed herself to slurp a little, rather un-lady like, un-queenly, when the spoon met her lips.

The soup was a little salty to the taste, but she couldn't be held responsible for that.

At least it was warm, and very much appreciated on such a frosty night. Snow had built upon the windowsills, setting a white frame against the dark night beyond, and the fireplace blazed brightly, filling the room with a warm orange glow as she sat at one end of the long dining table.

There were no men seated about the room tonight. No chatting about ships and voyages. No conversations regarding the portraits hanging on the walls.

There were others in the room with her; two female serves, dressed in white. Young women barely out of adolescence, they stood by the doorway leading into the kitchen, waiting for a signal from their queen, to which they would eagerly respond.

Another presence in the room shared the table with her and sat to her left. He scoffed down his bowl eagerly, as if it was the last meal he would ever eat. Before she was halfway through, his silver spoon was scraping the bottom of the ceramic bowl.

"Would you like more, Samuel?" she asked.

"Yes, Mama," he said with a grin. "It's so good."

She summoned a serve over with a click of her fingers.

"My queen?" One girl bowed as she moved to the scarlet woman's side.

"More for my boy," Tricia ordered.

The girl lifted the bowl from in front of Sam and retreated to the kitchen.

"What is it?" he asked.

"Just soup," replied Tricia.

"I know that." He giggled. The sound of his snicker made her smile. "I meant, what's in it?"

"It's a secret," she answered with a grin and a tiny wink as the serve returned with a topped-up bowl of steaming soup. "Now, eat up. Eat it all."

***

"It's late, Lieutenant," said the soldier with the other twin on his lap. She was fast asleep. Versel had noticed that her passenger had also been snoozing for some time. The day had been long for both of them.

"You're going to suggest that we keep the girls for the night," the lieutenant replied as she looked at the enormous castle on the hill.

"I was thinking it," he replied. "Yes."

"He would probably have our heads if we did," she told him. "My orders were to find out why our men went missing and report back to the Maji."

"Orders were to take care of Dakoth Risha, too," the soldier replied. "But that didn't happen."

"Can't do something like that if the target has taken absence," she said. "I'll inform the Maji of the situation and accept what consequences he feels fit to deliver."

"Let's hope he takes it out on you and not the rest of us," the soldier told her.

She shot him an annoyed glare, to which he responded with a smile and a shrug of his shoulders.

A short time later, the horses had pulled up in the castle's court-yard. Both twin girls were woken from their sleep and led by Versel into the foyer.

"This way," a guard told her as he started leading the lieutenant and the two girls through a large door and into an enormous marble room.

The twins gripped each of Versel's hands tightly. The woman could feel their fingers trembling as they walked along the length of the room, their feet brushing against the icy marble floor.

"They have no shoes!" Isabel gasped as she looked on from her chair beside her husband. "The poor things."

"Get them something," Takmel commanded, looking at the guards standing around the room. "A rug or some socks. Hosiery or stockings. Anything."

Several men left the room in a hurry.

"My lord." Versel bowed to her knee. "My queen."

The two girls looked at her strangely before peering to one another. Then, with a look at the man upon the throne, they followed suit and dropped to their knees as well.

"Lieutenant Versel," Takmel replied. "How did you fare?"

"I bring good and bad news, my lord," she replied. "We can attribute the missing men to these two ladies. They do not speak, or at least I don't believe they can. I believe they were acting in self-preservation. From what I could gather from the scene, Risha's men killed the girls' parents."

"All dead?" he asked.

"Yes, my lord," the lieutenant answered. "They killed one of my men when we first encountered these two. They appeared very frightened and again, I believe they were acting out of self-preservation."

He nodded, looking at the two girls covered in dust and filth.

"The poor dears," remarked the White Queen.

A guard hurried back into the room carrying woollen socks that were clearly too big for the little girls' tiny feet.

"They look as though they are meant for men," Takmel said, looking at what the guard carried.

"My apologies, my lord." He bowed. "It's the best I could do at short notice. They're from my supply."

"I hope they're clean," Isabel chided.

"Yes, my lady," he answered. "These have never been worn."

The guard offered them to the girls, who looked on curiously.

"What other news, lieutenant?" Takmel asked.

"They've probably never seen such things before," Isabel said as she rose from her seat and stepped from the platform to crouch beside the girls. She reached over and took the socks from the guard. Holding one out in her hand, she pointed to the girl' feet. "They slip over your toes and up your legs."

"We rode to Ironfields," Versel reported to the Maji. "Dakoth Risha was nowhere to be found, my lord."

Isabel handed a sock to the girl closest to her. The girl looked at it for a long time before moving her attention back to the lady in white. She then pointed to her feet.

Isabel nodded, "Yes, that's right."

"So, he's vanished?" Takmel questioned the lieutenant.

The girl took the socks from the White Queen and handed two to her sister. The other little girl watched with interest as the first slipped a sock over her foot, using her hand on the still kneeling Versel's shoulder to keep balance.

"No, my lord," the woman in armour replied. "We questioned some people who told us he's begun raiding the local farms and villages for stores. Others have told us he has claimed these raids as *patrols* that were sanctioned in your name."

Within moments, both girls had oversized socks on their feet.

"Much better!" Isabel giggled delightedly.

"In my name?" Takmel queried.

"Yes, my lord," replied Versel. "From what I can gather, these girls' parents were victims of such a patrol."

The Maji looked the girls over again. They appeared a little comical in the large footwear.

"And Risha is on one of these raids now, I suspect," he said.

"That's what we were told, my lord," the lieutenant answered.

"They're in desperate need of a bath," Takmel noted, returning his attention to the twins. "And new clothes."

"I'll take care of them," Isabel offered a little too quickly. Takmel shot her a glance.

"Fine," he told her. "When they've been cleaned and fed, put them in a bed chamber with a fire and set two guards on the door. You can stay with them for the night, if you wish."

"My lord." Isabel bowed.

***

A cold, gentle breeze swept down the mountain slopes and over the foothills. Catherine pulled her cloak around her tightly. She struggled to keep it in place as she used both hands to hold a rib as she attempted to strip meat away with her teeth.

Above the campfire, skewered onto a spit, hung the roasting carcass of a stag. A few of the soldiers found a herd of deer near the base of the mountains where the Twisted Road began. They killed quite a few for the night's supper. Several fires had been lit across the open ground and the tents erected before dark. Now, the troop sat around the many hearths, enjoying the feast.

"Good venison," Ruttger mumbled as he threw a polished bone into the fire.

"Mmm," Catherine murmured as she pulled on her cloak again.

Alice stifled a chuckle as she watched her sister struggle with the rib and her cloak.

"It is good," Amicia replied, rising to her feet. She dropped the bone she held in her hands into the flames. She then reached her hand out to Brondt seated beside her. He handed her his dagger, which she used to slice a portion off the stag's rump. She handed the blade back to her husband and sank her teeth into the meat before she lowered herself next to him. "Very good."

"You could have sliced a little off for me while you were there," Brondt said playfully as he got to his feet.

"I am the queen," she stated, almost laughing. "I will not do such lowly chores for my subordinates."

"You are a cheeky woman who needs to be taught a lesson or two in how to appreciate her husband," he riposted, pointing the tip of his dagger towards her. She giggled as he slipped the blade into the stag's flesh.

"Anyone else, while I'm here?"

They all declined.

"So," Schoenbach said as he reclined against a fallen log and peered into the flames. "We ride onto Newholt tomorrow." He looked at Brondt first before moving his attention to Alice. "Do we have an actual plan?"

"No," Alice replied.

"No?" The other raised his brow. "So, we're going in blind? We'll make it up when we get there?"

"Most of us know the layout of the city," the girl replied. "We strike from the south-west and move through the streets until we reach the palace. When we take the palace, we take Newholt."

"They have a ground force much larger than ours," Karlena put in.

"We have a dragon," Brondt refuted. "And four witches to their one."

The Erilian nodded.

"We also have the resistance," Amicia said with a mouthful of stag. She swallowed the morsel. "With any luck, they will provide additional support."

"But no actual plan?" Schoenbach persisted as he peered into the flames.

"We've got through many bad times before without a plan, Jeremy," Akasati told him. "How many times have we fared well, sometimes by the skin of our teeth, when we were the crew of the *Adelandria?*"

He sighed. "Many times."

"Many times," she repeated. "I don't understand why you have such questions about plans. Not unless you are afraid."

He shot her an irritable glare.

"Not afraid," he said. "Just wary. That's all."

"Wary?" Captain Thornton asked from Ursula's side. "What's that supposed to mean?"

Schoenbach lowered his eyes to the flames and took a deep breath. "I look at you all and see very brave people," he stated. "I don't regard myself as a coward at all, but I don't see all the faces I once battled alongside. Some are here. Others are gone. A few are back in their homes."

Emily immediately thought of David, back in the glade with his son.

"I'm getting old," Schoenbach admitted.

"Old, my arse," Ruttger snapped. "I'm older than you, and I'm here."

"I know." The other held up his hand apologetically. "I didn't mean any offence. It's just that I've noticed that I'm slowing down. I don't move how I used to. When we were retaking Woodmyst, I was very lucky. There were a few times when I thought I was done for."

"I'll be by your side, my love." Karlena rubbed his arm.

"I know," he acknowledged. "But you shouldn't need to be. I shouldn't be such a prevalent thought in your head while you're trying to fight." Schoenbach looked at Emily. "Isn't this why David stayed back?"

"He stayed to care for Arthur," Alice rebuked.

"He also has a wound in his leg from an arrow," Emily reminded her. "From the night when Shadow was taken from you."

Alice remembered the rukyul that had called the glade its home for a short time. She recalled its enormous frame and dark fur. A deep solemnity swept over her as she recollected not being there when the attack occurred. Instead, she had been dealing with the Haigok, far away to the north in the Core Lands.

"It is healing, but slowly," Emily continued. She looked to Schoenbach. "He too, shares your concerns. He told me he can feel age preventing him from doing what he wills."

"I'm not afraid to go into battle," Schoenbach said to the gathering around the hearth. "I'm not afraid to die. I'm afraid I will hinder our success. Especially if you concern yourselves for my wellbeing instead of focusing on the task before you." He looked at Karlena. "Don't concern yourself with me. Make this your plan. Take the palace, and if any of us fall along the way, take the palace in any case."

She pressed her forehead against his.

"I will," she said. "But if either of us falls, we come back for the other afterwards. Yes?"

"Yes," he replied. "I'll never leave you."

"And I'll never leave you," she whispered.

***

Fiery arrows streaked through the air like swarms of arcing birds made of flame. Some flew to the east, some to the west, others north and south as pockets of skirmishes broke out across the city. Buildings blazed and innocent bystanders appeared befuddled, as they couldn't determine where to run or where to hide.

Swords clashed and sent a ringing din echoing through the alleys and thin streets. It was difficult for anyone to judge the exact whereabouts of the scuffles. The Whores of Whitekeep had kept together for the best part of the night, but they had lost track of Monteacute and at least twenty of their men that had followed him north, towards the palace.

"Watch it," one man called, pointing his sword at the sky.

They all peered at the stars above. Kateryn found the sight of bright white lights twinkling from so far away an enthralling spectacle. She even smiled a little.

That was until she noticed the flaming bolts streaking through the air from the northwest and directly towards them.

"Over there," Audrey called, gesturing to a building on the northern side of the street. "Against the wall."

The men with her complied, pressing their backs against the stonework. Rose and Audrey quickly dashed across the street to the other woman's side.

Arrows hit the roof of the building, some bounced off the cobblestones of the street, and the rest stuck into the rooftops of the structures on the southern side of the road.

"How can they see us down here?" Rose questioned. "We're surrounded by houses."

"They're firing in every direction," Audrey told her. "They don't know where we are. They're just hoping to cause damage."

"They could hit their own people," one man put in.

"I don't think they care," Kateryn replied.

Audrey followed the road with her eyes. "The way is clear," she called to the others. "We should try to find Monty. He may need us."

With that, she sprinted along the cobblestones, leaping over a body of a fallen soldier in black. The others followed closely.

Audrey stopped at the edge of a building, positioned on the intersection of a crossroads. The upper level of the structure was ablaze, flames bellowing out of the windows high above her. She poked her head around the corner and saw soldiers; at least twelve by her count.

The men in black were herding children, young girls as far as Audrey could tell, and as many as fifteen. They had tied the younglings' hands, stringing each of them together in a line.

As she watched, Audrey saw one man put a child, who appeared not much older than six or seven, in place on the line and start tethering her wrists with a length of cord. Another soldier was keeping a woman away from the child, pushing her back against the wall of a house each time she tried to reach out to the little one.

"Give her back to me," the woman cried. "She's frightened."

"Shut it," the soldier snapped, slapping the woman across the face with his gauntlet.

She fell to the ground in a heap, sobbing uncontrollably. The other men in the troop laughed.

A hot flush ran through Audrey's face, neck, and down her spine.

"Give me back my daughter," the woman slurred, reaching her hand towards the little girl.

"Mama," the child shrieked.

The soldier plunged his sword into the woman where she lay. Her body went limp and still.

"By the gods!" Audrey gasped. She turned to face the others behind her. "They're taking little girls."

"What for?" Rose asked.

Kateryn shot her a glare. "What do you think?"

Rose's face instantly changed from inquisitive to wrathful. She moved away from the wall of the structure, strode past the other two women and into the street where the soldiers and captive girls were.

"Shit," Audrey spat, wanting to pull the other back into their hiding place. It was too late.

"What's this, then?" a soldier called.

The others in the troop looked over at the young woman approaching.

"Who gets this one?" another shouted.

"Watch it boys," another yelled. "She's armed."

The soldiers erupted in laughter as they noticed the sword in Rose's hand.

"You've been busy, boys," she called to them, gesturing to the captive girls with her blade.

"What's it to you?" called the soldier who had just killed the woman.

"I'm afraid I'm going to have to relieve you of these little ones," Rose replied.

"You could try," the other said, moving towards her. "And when I'm done beating the shit out of you, I'll use you to show these little girls what they're in for."

"You could try," she sneered, repeating his words.

"Just kill her, Gordon," another barked. "We want to get this lot back to the guard post."

Rose ran at the soldier while the other distracted him. She swung her blade wide and brought it towards his neck hard and fast. He blocked it with his own sword. A loud ringing sound resounded along the street.

Gordon recoiled and swung his weapon in a downward arc, intending to hit Rose in the loins. She jumped back just in time, feeling the breeze from his blade as it flashed past her face.

She responded by swinging her sword from her left, chopping into him just below his right arm. The blade sliced through his armour and sank deep into his ribs.

Rose pulled her blade free, sending a splash of blood over the wall of a nearby house. Some children made a frightened noise. Others watched on in awe.

"Bugger me," one man huffed as he pulled his sword from its sheath.

Gordon fell to the cobblestones and leaked blood over the street.

"You bitch," another man hollered as he lifted his weapon to the ready.

The others in the troop did the same, preparing themselves to cut the blonde woman down where she stood. They moved into position, placing the captured girls behind them and forming a line across the street.

"Can't get all of us," another said. "We're too many."

"You're not enough," Rose yelled back.

Two more women and almost thirty men bolted from around the corner, swords held high and eyes filled with fire.

The eleven remaining soldiers' faces dropped as an intense fear for their lives gripped them. Five dropped their swords to the ground, lowered themselves to their knees, and placed their hands above their heads in surrender.

It was a pointless gesture.

Within moments, all eleven soldiers lay in the street with either limbs missing, intestines strewn about or heads rolling away.

"We can't go after Monty," Kateryn said as she and Rose used their daggers to free the captive girls. "Not now."

"Right." Audrey turned to face the men. "You can go on if you wish," she told them. "But I would greatly appreciate it if some of you could accompany us back to the Petty Beggar. These girls need our protection and we can't leave them out here."

The men talked a little amongst themselves. The sound of distant sword clashes continued as more fiery arrows drifted through the sky above. After a time, ten of them stepped forward.

"We'll go back with you," one said.

Audrey offered a polite smile. "Thank you."

Fifteen

Arthur woke well before dawn. He lay awake in bed for what seemed like endless hours, tossing and turning in a desperate attempt to find comfort. It was strange, he supposed, that he felt so tired yet could not close his eyes for even a moment without them flickering back open again.

He missed her, and he didn't need to struggle with admitting it to himself. He knew it. The bed was just not the same without her in it. Having her beside him was simply enough to bring the right amount of solace that would allow him to slumber.

Loud snoring from the neighbouring room informed him that his father wasn't suffering the same dilemma. It appeared that David could sleep in any location under any situation.

But Arthur wasn't his father.

Unable to bear it any longer, he got out of bed, dressed, and made his way to the kitchen. He set a pot of water on the stove, buttered some bread and prepared a pot of tea; a task that was not so easy to do with one arm.

After eating a slice of bread, he poured a mug of the brew and let it sit on the bench while he put his coat on. He grabbed the steaming mug and made his way out the door, placing his cup on the floor to perform each task before and onto the porch. All the while, the sound of his father's snoring resonated through the walls.

Standing just off the porch, munching on some grass by the edge of the house, the chestnut stallion turned his ears back and forth. He captured sounds emanating from all around the camp and the forest surrounding the glade. Arthur made a mental note of how the ears kept twisting back to the cabin each time David snorted loudly.

Arthur put his mug on the porch and reached his hand out to the steed to scratch its muzzle. It responded with a soft nicker and moved forward to give Arthur a friendly nudge in the chest.

"I guess you can't sleep either," the boy said in a low voice. He looked up to the stars in the clear sky above the glade and saw patches of deep tones that he had never noticed before. "Too nice a night to sleep, anyway."

He rubbed the stallion behind an ear, almost hugging the horse's head in his arm. The steed nickered again and seemingly relished the moment.

"Guess I'll have to learn how to ride you again, boy," Arthur said to the horse after a while. "Guess you'll have to learn how to take me on your back. I think it will be difficult for both of us. You'll have to be gentle with me. No rushing off like you used to for her. No more battles or adventures, I'm afraid. Just easy riding from now on."

The stallion nuzzled him again, urging the boy to keep scratching behind his ear. Arthur smiled and obeyed. He glanced down at his steaming mug of tea. He guessed it would turn cold quickly in the chill morning air.

He didn't really care.

He could make another pot of tea any time.

***

Tents and bedrolls had been packed before the first hint of red could be seen on the horizon. Breakfasts had been eaten and fires doused as the sky showed the first signs of the morning sun. Horses were saddled and mounted as the sun breached the horizon. The infantry from Woodmyst were well on their way to Newholt as the day began.

Alice was the last to leave, after cleaning up what little mess remained and making sure the fires were out. She would catch up easily enough and planned to try for the peaks to the west of the city to spy out what was happening there. With luck, she would go undetected and be able to report back to the travellers before they arrived.

"You ready, girl?" she asked the beast as she tightened a strap across the dragon's chest. Liana replied in a friendly chirp before lowering her head to Alice. The girl responded by rubbing her hands over the dragon's snout. "It won't be as hard going as yesterday. I promise. But you will need to fight, I think. I hope you've built up your strength enough." Alice looked at a discarded horn, partly adorned with blood and a small amount of tissue, from the heifer that the beast had devoured.

Alice took time to make sure she was ready to go. She slipped her scabbards' loops over her waist belt, placing her swords on her hips. She put on her hooded cloak, followed by the dark bearskin tunic worn by the Kayl'sro.

The girl clambered on top of the dragon and strapped herself into the saddle. She pulled her cloak tight, lifted her scarf into place, tugged her hood over her head and slid leather gloves over her hands.

"All right," she called.

Liana spread her wings and bounded a little across the ground on her legs before she flapped her mighty wings and lifted into the air.

It wasn't long before they reached the rest of the troop. Ursula waved her hand, rewarded with a reply in like from the girl on the flying beast.

Alice continued, banking slightly to the left and climbing higher as Liana made her way into the mountains. Grassland gave way to exposed rock and steep, sheer cliffs where pine trees seemed to cling precariously, defying the gods by refusing to fall.

There are no gods, Alice thought, hearing the words in her father's voice.

The trees thinned, leaving room for exposed areas of rock and frost. Snow had recently fallen on the highest peaks. Alice rarely felt the elements, but she could feel them now. A biting chill made its way through her layers of clothing to her skin. She pulled her scarf higher upon her nose and tucked her gloved hands under her bearskin. A slight shiver erupted over her body, causing her to haunch over and form herself almost into a ball.

She could direct Liana to turn more to the southeast, taking her down a little lower in altitude and closer to the foothills. In fact, it tempted her to.

But she aimed to avoid being seen, so, over the mountains, she flew in the most direct path to Newholt.

Liana kept herself above the peaks, gliding upon updrafts and cross-winds to save her energy. It was a spectacular sight as the morning light seemed to give the mountains new life with shades of orange, red and yellow striking the snow and rock. Alice would have loved to stay up there forever to watch the scenery pass by, except that the cold was becoming unbearable, and she could see the seaside city in the distance.

Liana found a suitable perch on the side of a towering rock face, high upon a mountain that sat a short distance to Newholt's western border. Alice scanned the sight as she rubbed her hands against her body in an attempt to warm up a little. The dragon snorted, blowing a thick vaporous mist from her nostrils as she settled onto her haunches.

Alice saw several vessels anchored at the foreshore. Smoke rose from many places throughout the city. Much of it was burning. In some cases, entire sections had been flattened and had turned black like charcoal. The wharves were aflame, and the clock tower had toppled.

It was horrific.

The only salvageable object that she could see was the large white palace in the city's centre. Surrounding the palace, she saw pockets of movement here and there. She watched intently as she tried to figure out what it was.

Then she realized.

There was fighting in the streets.

Alice faced a sudden decision.

Should she leave and report what she could see to the others who were still a good half day's journey away, or should she go down and offer her help?

It wasn't a hard decision. She already knew the answer before the question popped into her head.

"Let's go, girl," she said to the dragon.

Spreading her wings and leaping from the rock face, Liana dived through the air, picking up tremendous speed before arcing skyward. She flapped her wings and pointed her frame towards the city.

***

Joanne gripped the guard rail surrounding the balcony. She stared down at the streets below, where the sound of swords and shouts of battle continued to make their way into her pounding head.

The scent of burning timber, black powder and flesh made its way into the palace and clung to the walls inside. It was worse in the open air, Joanne thought. She considered returning to the throne room far below and was just about to do so when she heard an unmistakable guttural roar.

The sound made her blood run cold and hear heart seemed to stop.

She turned to face the south.

There was no great cloud of smoke in the way, just thick plumes rising from buildings below.

There were no witches in the courtyard, only her guards waiting for the inevitable at the gates as the resistance, along with the ships' crewmen, made their way along the road to the palace.

It was nothing like what she imagined.

But there she was.

Alice approached upon the great dragon's back.

The Black Queen instinctively reached out her hand, not knowing exactly what she would do. She needed to do something; something that would stop the girl and her monster from bringing any harm to her.

This isn't you, Mama.

Alice looked directly at Joanne as she shot by the tower and out over the eastern sector of the city. The dragon gave another horrendous roar that shook the balcony with a tremor.

This isn't you.

Joanne lowered her hand and turned from the balcony. She rushed inside, through the room and into the corridor beyond. Before she even realised what she was doing, she dashed down the stairs of the tower, hastily making her way to the lower floors of the palace.

"My queen?" A guard waiting at the base of the stairs bowed.

The dragon roared again.

"I need to leave," Joanne blurted. Her eyes were wide with fear. "I need to get north."

"My lady?"

"Now," she yelled.

"Yes, my queen," the soldier replied. "This way."

He led Joanne through the corridors and passageways out to the courtyard. Commander Funteyn was there, barking orders to his men and peering to the sky now and then to see where the giant beast had gone.

"Commander," the soldier called.

Funteyn turned to see the Black Queen gawking into the sky.

"My queen," he called to her. "You should be inside where it is safe."

"Safe?" She kept her gaze on the sky above. "Tell me where you would feel safe with that thing circling the city. I want to leave, now."

The commander shook his head. "We're cut off," he replied. "The road is being overrun by the enemy as we speak."

"I want to get north, now," she snapped. "Use every man to clear a way for me."

"My lady..." he contended.

"Now, Commander."

He saw the fear and anger in her eyes. It was a dangerous combination in any person, but this was the Black Queen, and he had witnessed just a fragment of what she was capable of.

"All men on the gate," he barked. "Prepare to attack."

***

Monteacute dropped another in a black tunic to the ground after sticking his sword through the man's neck. Before he had time to congratulate himself for his efforts, he blocked another soldier's attack. He parried each blow, feeling the vibrations jarring along his weapon and into his arm.

His elbows and wrists ached. His knees and ankles felt as if they were going to break at any moment. He was thirsty, exhausted and ready to collapse. Only the will to live kept him going.

He kicked out with his boot, knocking his opponent backwards and into striking distance of other resistance fighters. Monteacute saw the soldier get hacked apart. But again, before he had time to savour the moment, another adversary appeared.

The monster swooping above them had drawn the attention of a few enemy soldiers away momentarily, giving the upper hand to the resistance. But suddenly, the black forces attacked with a more intent ferocity.

Something was happening.

Monteacute kept looking at the palace gates. He and his men had teamed up with several factions of fighters from across the city and somehow, miraculously, had made their way to the base of the climbing road that led to the palace. The end goal was in their sight.

A horde of men dressed in armour and black tunics had run through the gates and down the road towards them. They held their weapons high and a great battle cry went out.

The swarm of men pushed the resistance back and away from the palace road, into the surrounding streets. From his position, Monteacute could still see the gates.

Several horses fled from the courtyard and down the road. The sheriff followed them with his stare as they spun to the north and galloped away. One steed, he could swear, carried the Black Queen. She was cloaked from head to toe, but he could see her auburn hair sticking slightly out from under the hood.

It must be her.

He blocked another barrage of blows from his opponent, quickly found his footing and hacked his blade again and again at the enemy soldier. The man in black slipped a little in the guts of a fallen comrade, opening himself to a kiss from Monteacute's sword. The blade's edge dug deep into the face of the soldier, splitting his lip and right eye socket open.

As the soldier fell, the sheriff peered along the street to where he saw the Black Queen riding. She was gone.

"The dragon has lit the catapults to the south," a voice called. It was an enemy soldier, pointing to a plume of rising fireballs along the length of the city.

"Good," called a resistance fighter, and stuck the other man through with his blade. "That means they're our friend and not yours."

Maybe that's why the Black Queen flees.

Monteacute hacked into another soldier, who was distracted by the sight of the dragon shooting into the sky again.

"Keep fighting, boys," he shouted. "Focus your attention on the here and now."

***

The girls sat on a rug by the fireplace, huddled together and shivering from fear. They looked to the ceiling as if they might see through somehow to the sky above and the monster that called out now and then.

"You don't need to be afraid," Andris tried to tell them. It would have been more believable if he didn't jump in his chair every time the guttural roar bellowed through the air. He heard a loud tearing sound whoosh by overhead. The noise of great leathery wings ripped through the sky. It was close. Very close.

"Has it come to eat us?" a little girl asked, tears streaming down her cheeks.

"No," he answered gently.

"How do you know?" Rose queried, crouching by the girls.

"Rose," Audrey chided as she brought a mug of ale to Sub-Commander Wake, who sat beside the other man.

"What?" The blonde woman shrugged. "I'd like to know how he could be so sure."

"That's Alice up there," Andris explained.

"The dragon's name is Alice?" A girl looked at him strangely.

"No," he said. "The dragon's name, if I remember right, is Liana. She was a gift from the Night Demons. Alice is her rider. She is a friend to Newholt."

"Alice must be a powerful warrior," said another girl, a little older than the others.

"Oh, she is," Andris confirmed. "She can fire a bow at many targets much faster than any man I know. She carries two swords and can defeat all the men in the Woodmyst guard. She has fought both Night Demon and Agrodien. She is so strong and powerful that the Agrodien made her their leader."

The girls listened to his words in awe. The dragon roared again, and while they still felt afraid, their faces seemed comforted by Andris' story.

"She must be a beautiful woman," said another girl. "A warrior princess."

"That she is," Andris agreed. "But she isn't a woman. Not yet anyway. She's not much older than you. And she is a powerful sorceress."

"You lie," one girl said. "No one can be all of that."

"I assure you she is," he told her. The dragon roared again. "I'd like to hope she is finding a way for all of us to be free. If anyone can do that, it's Alice."

***

She banked to the south, leaving the western defences in ruin. The catapults and beacons burned behind her as Liana flew high into the sky again.

Alice peered over her shoulder as they flew away from Newholt. There wasn't much else she could do for now. If she attacked the soldiers on the ground with Liana, she would also wipe out friendly forces. She considered finding her aunt, but didn't want to risk her dragon being hurt closer to the ground. Landing on the surface would place the beast in a vulnerable position and she imagined the ground forces belonging to the Black Queen wouldn't hesitate to attack with spear, arrow, and sword. So, she kept to the sky.

Joanne would have to be dealt with later.

Sixteen

He sat at the head of the table, delicately eating a hearty breakfast of pork strips, eggs and toast. A young servant girl poured tea from a finely fashioned silver pot into a white ceramic cup. He had grown a habit of drinking a steaming brew with his meals; something he had picked up during his time living in Woodmyst.

He thanked the girl when she was done, watching her as she moved away to the side of the room to await further instructions. He entertained a thought as he took in her appearance. She was comely with raven hair tied up on the back of her head, strong features and a well-developed form.

Perhaps she would make a good wife.

He smiled as he bit into his toast. His gaze moved to the empty place beside him. There sat an empty plate with an empty cup. Isabel had not made her way to breakfast yet. He wasn't overly concerned, except that he spent the night alone.

After a sip of his tea, he dug into the contents of his plate. He used the rest of the toast to mop up the runny egg yolks at the end. He polished off his cup of tea and sat back.

"Very good, thank you," he said to the girl. "Could you pour me some more tea before taking my plate?"

"Yes, my lord." She bowed slightly as she moved to the edge of the table.

Perhaps a good mistress.

The sound of footfalls approaching drew his attention from the servant girl towards the door at the far end of the room. Isabel walked in with two little girls that Takmel barely recognised from the night before, holding the White Queen's hands. The girls clothed in clean floral dresses in various tones of blue and green. Leather boots covered their feet and their dark hair tied back in a neat braid. They were clearly uncomfortable in the new attire, walking awkwardly as they moved around the table.

"Two more places," Isabel commanded the servant girl.

"Yes, my queen," she replied, lifting Takmel's plate and hurrying away to the kitchen.

The White Queen paused behind her chair and smiled at her husband. "So?" she asked. "What do you think?"

He peered at them for a while. The dresses suited their form much better; he thought. But he wasn't certain of the colour. What impressed him was how they appeared with their freshly clean skin and neat hair. He could see their faces, and for two little girls, they were certainly very pretty.

He entertained another thought; one he had earlier, before he had even seen them with his eyes. Now, it seemed to make sense.

"Very nice, girls," he approved before gesturing to two seats beside the place set for Isabel. "Please join me."

He rose to his feet and moved along the table, pulling the chairs out for each of them, starting with his wife. After he had been a gentleman, he returned to his place.

"I spent the night with them," the White Queen informed him. "They were a little upset for a while, but they drifted off soon enough."

"Were your beds comfortable?" Takmel asked. The girls nodded. "Good," Takmel said as he lifted his cup to his lips and sipped. He placed it back on the table, keeping his eyes on them. They watched him cautiously. "If there is anything you need, don't hesitate to ask for it. If you need more blankets, pillows...or..." he leant forward and lowered his brow, "...men's sized socks. You just let us know."

They giggled silently, recalling the incident from the night before.

"I thought I might take them to the market today," Isabel announced as a few servant girls entered from a side room with more plates and cutlery for the twins. "I'd like to get them fitted for more clothing. There is a seamstress with a quaint store that the serves talk about. The finest on the Western Sea. Isn't that right?" She looked to one of the servant girls.

"Yes, my queen," the other answered as she placed a cup before one girl. She looked over to the Maji. "The finest linen and cloth I have ever seen, my lord."

Takmel imagined the serve had seen little of the finest of anything except what was available inside the walls of his home. His gaze quickly flashed around and took in the expensive white ceramic plates and cups, the silver cutlery, the finely crafted timber chairs, and dining table. He noted the tapestries draped over the walls and the various adornments, like the silver candelabra resting upon the oak benches around the sides of the room and the iron sconces holding the flickering torches in place. The rug her feet touched, or the stone floor beneath it, or the dust that had settled between the joins was probably worth more than anything she owned. If she owned anything.

Still, he humoured his wife, who was peering at him eagerly for a response.

"We could have the seamstress visit us here," he said. "It is a mite cold out there."

"Please, Takmel." She scrunched her forehead slightly and tilted her head a little. "I really wanted to make a day of it."

He looked at her for a moment. He didn't like her using his name in front of the servants. But her blue eyes begged him, and he felt his heart melting as he continued to gaze at her.

"All right," he agreed as he looked to the twin girls. "Get them everything they need, and then everything they desire."

"Thank you." Isabel reached over and touched his arm.

He lifted her hand to his lips and placed a gentle kiss there.

"Anything for you, my love."

***

The y heard soft clicking sounds emitting from outside, blending with the howling wind that had just hit Blackrock Haven. Creaking timbers and the rustling of sleet sweeping from the north against the outer walls caused the men sitting inside the warm tavern to feel a chill to their bones.

Each of them nursed a room-warm mug of rum and had downed a few others during their time inside the inn. Most did so because there was not much else to drink; others because it was the only thing that made them feel warm or numbed the cold.

The door flung open and smacked against the outer wall, caught by the strong gale. Every eye turned to the newcomer moving through the open passage. He looked as if he was half frozen. His arms hugged his torso tightly and his hooded, long coat smeared in white powder.

"Close the door," the barkeep hollered.

"There are more coming," the other shouted back.

The men inside the room glared at him irritably.

"Close the door," they shouted in unison.

"Ya, dumb shit," one finished.

This got most of the others chuckling as the newcomer wrestled with the wind as he pulled the door closed behind him.

He brushed the snow off his arms and onto the floor before taking his gloves off and placing them into his coat pockets. He then lowered his hood and unbuttoned his covering. He peered about as if lost, turning his scraggly face this way and that as he looked for a place to hang it.

"Just drop it on the floor, ya princess," the barkeep shouted.

The men laughed again.

The newcomer did just that and approached the bar.

"Rum?" the barkeep asked.

"Yeah." The man smiled through his unkempt beard.

The barkeep poured a mug and slid it across the bar to the newcomer. The man lifted it to his lips and drank it down in one go. He placed the mug on the bar and let out a large breath.

"More," he said, looking at the barkeep.

"Money?"

The newcomer reached into his pocket and produced three copper coins.

"How's that?"

"That'll get ya three," the barkeep informed him. "A silver will get ya ten."

"All I got is coppers," the newcomer replied.

"One copper, one mug of rum," said the barkeep, taking two coppers out of the other's hand before pouring him another mug.

"Good thing I have a lot of coppers, then." The newcomer moved closer to the fireplace.

"Why you out in this shit for, anyway?" one seated by the hearth asked.

"A mooring rope came loose on our ship," he replied, leaning his shoulder against the wall by the fireplace. "We were staying on board and felt the whole ship swinging a little too much in the aft, even in this weather."

"What do you mean you're staying on the ship?" another piped up. "There's plenty of places to put yer gear on dry land around here."

"You call this dry land?" another chortled.

"My skipper didn't want us to leave the ship," the newcomer replied to the first man. "He wanted to be gone as soon as possible, but we haven't seen him for a couple of nights now."

"Funny that." Another raised his brow. "Our captain has made himself absent as well. We just figured he was up there in that nice big house on the hill, shagging the Red Queen and all of her handmaidens."

"Scarlet," the newcomer said as he lifted his mug to his lips.

"What's that?" the other asked.

"Scarlet Queen," he corrected. "We brought her here from Dweagan."

"You're from that big galley, then?"

The newcomer nodded.

At that moment, the door flung open again.

A strong gale swept through the room and caused the flames in the fireplace to bow and flicker violently.

"Close the door," all the men in the room chorused.

"Ya, dumb shits," a few chanted afterwards.

The room erupted into laughter as one man pulled the door shut.

"Three rums," one of the new arrivals called to the barkeep as he peeled his gloves from his hands.

"You got coppers or silvers?" the barkeep asked.

"Coppers," the other called back.

"One copper, one rum," replied the barkeep, lifting three mugs onto the bar.

A man, younger than the others, was faster at peeling his outer layer off than the others. He made his way to the bar, paid for the drinks, and approached his crewman by the fire.

"That rope's no good, Will," he said. "We just fitted a new one. The other one looks as if something chewed it right through."

"Chewed?" asked Will, the first of them to arrive. "What do you mean, *chewed?*"

"He means worn," another said. He looked at the young man sternly. "I told you, ain't nothing that can chew through a mooring line."

"Just saying what it looked like, that's all," the young man said, and shrugged.

Sleet scratched its way across the roof. The men in the room peered up and followed the sound with their eyes from one side of the room to the other.

"Bugger me, it's coming down hard out there," a man by the fire said. "You got any others on that galley of yours?"

"Yeah," the last of the newcomers replied. "They'll stay beneath deck. The old boat has seen worse than this."

One of the older men by the fire looked up.

"Can't have been much worse than this," he mumbled.

A deep clicking noise resounded through the chimney and into the inn.

The men peered quizzically at the hearth.

"What was that?" one questioned.

A sudden thud against the wall behind the bar made the barkeep shout in fright.

"Did you lot see anything out there on yer way over?" he asked.

"Nobody," the young one replied. "That storm is pretty bad. I could barely see two yards in front of me."

Another thump from an adjacent wall caused all faces in the room to turn.

"Who's out there?" the barkeep hollered.

"There's no one out there," one of the older men said, laughing. "It's just the bloody wind. You lot are very jumpy. It's not midday yet and you're all behaving like little children telling ghost stories. You want to hear something really scary? I remember a time when I was about your age, lad." He pointed to the youngest of the newcomers. "We anchored in the Bay of Nay'ia, far to the east of Dendadia. We were on our way to deliver goods to Alarelith and pick up a load of tea and... Well, that isn't the point.

"The point is that we were told not to anchor in the Bay of Nay'ia under any circumstances," he continued. "Some say there is a hidden fortress there, abandoned for centuries but filled with the spirits of those who were slain there. Others say there are witches living in the woods above the cliffs along the shore who devour men who shelter in the bay."

One of the men noticed smoke clinging to the ceiling and pointed upwards to inform the others. But they were too engaged in the old man's tale.

"All I know is," the older man continued, "that there was a very intense tempest and our captain, at the time, drove the ship into the bay without hesitation. We anchored and sheltered from the storm. We joked about the stories we had heard and even laughed a little.

"That was, until we heard the screaming coming from high above us, from the top of the cliffs. We didn't see any fortress or any witches. What we saw was our captain yelling at us to raise the anchor, so we could get the fuck out of there."

The youngest of the newcomers stared at the older man, who locked eyes with him and stared back.

A long silence ensued.

The wind continued to howl.

The sleet scratched across the walls and roof.

An incessant clicking grew louder in the hearth, echoing down the chimney.

"BOO!" the old man yelled.

The younger man jumped and thrust his hand to his heart.

"Oh shit," he gasped, before snickering.

The rest of the room fell into a loud roar of laughter.

The door flung open again and smacked loudly against the outer wall. A blast of freezing wind swept through the room, causing the flames in the hearth to flap and shrink.

"Close the door!" the men shouted in unison. "Ya, dumb shit."

They laughed again, but there was no one there.

"Close the door," the barkeep hollered, wrapping his arms about himself and stepping to the open entrance. He peered out and looked into the storm that seemed to flow over the town like an endless white wave.

The others watched on, keeping close to the fire, or huddled in the places about the room as far from the cold as they could get.

Without warning, the barkeep disappeared, as if picked up and taken by something unseen.

The men heard him scream, pleading for help.

But fear had struck the men. After all, what could they do? Most of them were merchant sailors armed with nothing more than knives.

"Close the door," the older man said.

The younger man dashed across the room and reached around to grab the door. He peered into the storm and saw a large mess of blood and flesh a few yards from the inn.

He pulled the door as hard as he could, fighting the wind with all his might.

Then he saw it.

A dark, lanky creature with long white teeth and leathery skin. It moved as if oblivious to the freezing weather.

It started emitting a strange clicking noise as it stalked along the ground towards him.

The young man kept tugging on the door, straining to pull it shut. With each success came a powerful gust of wind that pushed the door back against the wall.

"Come on," he called out loud, as if it would make the door move for him.

The creature screeched a long, high-pitched squeal.

The young man saw countless more of the beasts appear from behind buildings, crawling through the snow towards the inn.

There was a sudden clatter behind him. The men started moving and shouting as chaos erupted in the room. He turned to see another creature crawling from the hearth, having just exited the chimney.

One man bolted right by him and out into the cold.

"Wait," the young man called after him. But it was to no avail.

Three of the awaiting creatures lunged and tore the man to shreds in moments.

The other men started for the door, not knowing what had just occurred beyond their view.

"There's more out there," the young man shouted. "They're every-where."

As he yelled, the one that had crawled from the fireplace attacked the older man seated by the fire. Another appeared from the chimney and lunged at one of the other men in the room.

The younger man turned to face the storm again and was confronted by large white teeth bearing down on him.

The lunging creature dug its claws into the young man's head as it bit into his face.

The others inside the inn screamed in horror as the young man writhed and kicked in agony on the floor by the door.

They could neither run outside nor live if they remained in.

In desperation, they gathered behind the bar and threw mugs, flasks, and as many objects as they could get their hands on. The creatures whimpered and swiped at the tossed articles before continuing into the room.

The screaming was swept away into the howling wind as the storm continued to devour Blackrock Haven.

***

The Scarlet Queen watched from a window from high above the town.

"What is it, Mama?" Sam asked from his seat by the fire. He sipped warm milk laced with honey and wore a creamy white moustache on his upper lip.

"Wipe your mouth, Sam," she instructed. He used his sleeve. "Use a napkin next time, my little one." She returned her gaze to the window.

She could feel the presence of the dark ones and smiled a little as they feasted upon the seafarers occupying her huts and ships moored on her docks.

They would need their strength, she thought. Takmel had told her so.

"With winter coming," he had said, "they will need to sleep. Before they sleep, they will need food."

So, she watched through the window as the dark creatures scurried through the township; as they crawled over the snow-covered huts and clambered over the vessels secured to the pier.

It was all a part of his plan.

Seventeen

The Black Queen rode her steed hard, surrounded by five others, including Commander Leonard Funteyn. They charged over hills and through dales, keeping the ocean to their right.

The sound of waves crashing against the black rocks lining the coast thundered in their ears. Joanne peered over her shoulder in fear that the dragon had found them. Something deep inside told her she was right to flee. She didn't believe for one moment that Alice would spare her.

Not after what she had done.

This isn't you, Mama.

The words kept crying out in her head over and over and over. The irritating sound of the boy's crying made her want to pull her own brain out of her head if it meant that he would stop. Another part of her wished she could hold him again in her arms. The voice was the only part of him she had left.

She looked again at the sky.

There was no dragon.

Even the smoke rising from the city seemed far in the distance now.

"We should make Oakbeach by day's end at this pace," Funteyn called to her.

Oakbeach, she thought. There was a place that she never wanted to see again. It was where the marauders, who had burned her village and killed her mother, had taken her to the black ship. The black ship had carried her to the Sovereign. The black ship was where her virtue had been ripped from her as the grotesque, foul-smelling captain raped her again and again.

She didn't need to see that place.

Not ever.

But where else was there to go?

So, she rode on.

*∗∗

"It's all but destroyed," Alice informed them. She sat upon Liana's back and faced the head of the troop a few yards away.

"What do you mean, destroyed?" Amicia asked. Her voice was shaking, and her hands trembled as she gripped the reins of her steed.

"It's horrible," Alice replied. "Most of the city has been burned. Many buildings have fallen."

"The people?" Brondt asked. "Could you see many alive?"

"There was intense fighting near the palace," she reported. "Some more skirmishes in pockets throughout the city. Some ships are moored and anchored near the shore. They aren't yours. And they're not from Dweagan either."

"Dendadia perhaps," Schoenbach put in.

"Perhaps," Brondt replied.

"What of our men?" Captain Thornton queried. "Did you see any of our soldiers in the fight?"

"None were carrying the queen's banner that I could see," Alice replied.

The men under Thornton's command lowered their heads, and a few said curse words under their breath.

"That doesn't mean they aren't there," he snapped at them. He turned to Brondt. "I think we should keep hope close, sir. If young Alice saw fighting in the streets, we should be encouraged that our people are keeping strong. The sooner we can get there, the sooner we can assist them. Perhaps if they see the queen alive and well, they will be encouraged too."

"You're right."

"What of my sister?" Emily asked eagerly. "Did you see her? Is she well?"

"She's the bloody Black Queen," William Vawdrey said from behind Thornton. "Who gives a fu—"

"Shut your mouth right now," Thornton growled. "This isn't the time for your horseshit."

Alice shot the soldier a glare before looking back at her mother.

"I saw her," she replied. "We saw each other fairly well, I suspect. She was in her tower as I passed by. I didn't see her on my second pass. She looked well enough."

Commander Brondt looked to Amicia, who was turning in her saddle to face the auburn woman.

"I know this isn't easy for you, Emily," she said in a soft voice. "I know this is a struggle. Joanne is both your sister and our enemy. Are you capable of doing what must be done? Do you wish to sit this one out? We are going to face her, and I fear there will only be one outcome."

"She's my sister," Emily replied, tears in her eyes and her chin quivering. "I should be there for her. Even if she hates me to her last breath, I should be there."

"Are we ready to go?" Brondt asked.

Emily assented.

"We're ready," Amicia answered.

"We still have a good hour's ride ahead," the commander called to the men in formation behind him. "We should pick up the pace a little." He waved his hand in a gesture to follow. "Forward."

Alice stayed on the ground, watching her mother ride away. She knew this would be a trying time for the woman that had raised her. She couldn't imagine what she would do if she faced a similar situation.

It had come close, though.

She had spoken harsh words to her sister when the older sibling was by the Maji's side. Catherine had said words to the same measure back.

Alice had imagined slicing Catherine's throat open more than once. Luckily, their paths had led them back together and now they were side by side again, just as sisters should be.

She hoped her aunt Joanne would find a path back to them. She hoped the Black Queen would cease to be and Aunt Joanne would return.

But she put little faith in that hope.

***

It was a little after midday when they reached sight of Newholt. Amicia wept when she saw the state of the city.

Smoke continued to rise from countless places. Toppled buildings lay scattered about and the docks simply did not exist any longer.

Only the palace and its tower stood intact, high above the surrounding metropolis. Black banners still flapped from the masts and high windows of the stronghold. And they could hear the sound of battle resounding from the streets.

"Look!" Lieutenant Hugh Brook pointed towards the palace. "In the streets below the road leading to the gates. The fighting seems to be concentrated there."

Brondt tried to focus on what the other was gesturing towards. He saw buildings and movement, but he couldn't be sure if this was caused by the haze of smoke or his aging vision.

"I see," Thornton acknowledged.

A great roar thundered from above them as Alice swooped by overhead. She was flying directly towards the fray.

"Well, that's that." Brondt frowned. "If she's heading over there, then that's where we should be too, don't you think?"

"Most certainly, sir," Brook agreed.

Brondt turned to Amicia. "I'd feel better if you were to stay back here," he said.

"My prime has gone in on her own," the queen replied. "I should be there with her. This is my city and they are my people down there, and I should be amongst them. I won't be staying behind, dear husband."

"I didn't think you would," he said with a wry smile. "I just said that I'd feel better if you did."

He lifted his sword from its sheath and gave a shout as he urged his steed on. The troop charged towards Newholt at great speed, their horses' hooves thundering along the open ground, passing farmhouses and other small clusters of huts. They ran by the charcoaled catapults and beacons on the southern edge of the city before racing along the narrow cobblestoned streets.

"Make way for Queen Amicia," Brondt called as he led the charge towards the palace.

People rushed to their windows, and out from their hiding places to glimpse their queen's return.

Gradually, the troop made their way to the base of the road leading up to the palace gates. The way was packed with soldiers wearing the black tunics over their armour. The resistance fighters were struggling to make ground.

Brondt could see they were exhausted, covered in muck and blood, and nearly at their wits' end. He leapt from his horse and charged into the clash without hesitation. Thornton was right behind him, followed by Brook and the rest of his men.

Ursula, Catherine, and Amicia stayed a suitable distance away from the skirmish, watching from horseback in the safety of a thin alley.

The Agrodien warriors were next to get into the action, scaring the life out of many black soldiers and resistance fighters alike. Once Yuri had cut down a few of the soldiers standing on the road leading up to the gates, the resistance fighters felt revitalised and moved to his side where they gave him and his kind help.

More of Brondt's men and the guards from Woodmyst rushed in with their swords held high, some even remaining on horseback. The steeds charged into small bands of black soldiers, knocking them off their feet where they were made easy targets for resistance fighters nearby.

Slowly, they advanced along the road.

Fighters gave chase into the streets as more than several black soldiers turned coward and ran away. Others continued to hack and chop into their enemies, covering the way up to the palace with blood.

Bodies fell, both allies and enemies. They were trampled so badly under foot and hoof that it was difficult to determine who was friend or foe.

The black forces had thinned out severely by the time Brondt and Thornton had reached the top of the road. The remaining soldiers in black tunics retreated into the courtyard and locked the enormous gates.

"Fucking cowards," Thornton growled through the bars. "Come back and fight."

"We climb." Yuri pointed over the tall walls.

"No," Brondt said. "They'll have bows aimed at you before you could get over."

Emily moved through the crowd of allied soldiers and free fighters. Blood covered her extremities, but appeared unhurt. She looked at the commander and the captain strangely.

"Why are you standing here?" she asked.

They peered back at her, perplexed.

"What do you mean?" Brondt questioned. "They've locked us out."

Emily pointed to the sky over the eastern sector of the city. The men followed her gesture and saw the dragon moving from north to south, far out and away from them.

"She's waiting for you to get out of the way," the auburn lady told them.

Thornton was the first to grasp what they were being told.

"Shit," he barked. "We need to get off this road."

Brondt suddenly understood and yelled to the others gathered behind them.

"Back down the road," he hollered. "Back down the road, now."

The throng moved into the side streets, and away from the wide path leading to the palace gates. No sooner had they all cleared the road than Liana swooped in.

A great stream of fire flung from her mouth as she engulfed the ground outside the palace in flame. The mass watched as the barracks near the gate was set on fire. They listened as the shrieks and screams of men burning reached their ears.

Liana swung high into the air to the west of the city and turned about. She dived back to the east, making another pass by the palace, spewing more flames over the barracks and courtyard.

There were more screams.

Amicia watched on with a heavy heart. It was not a good way to die, and she hoped none of her people were up there, trapped in the dragon's fire.

Liana dropped from the sky and hovered above the gates, grasping them in her talons. She flapped her mighty wings and tore the large iron gates from their hinges before letting them fall harmlessly into the courtyard.

"Stay here," Brondt called to his wife. "I won't take no for an answer this time."

"All right."

The commander charged up the road again, noticing the carnage of body parts and blood beneath his boots. Thornton and his men were on his heels. Together, they raced into the courtyard and observed the scene before them.

Flames poured out from the windows and door of the barracks building. Its roof had been burnt away and parts of its stone walls had fallen in. Charred bodies of men were littered about and the gardens had turned to charcoal.

The palace, however, had remained untouched.

Brondt turned as he felt a heavy gust of wind strike him from behind. The dragon was landing as the girl pulled her hood from her head.

"Sorry for the state I left this in," Alice called to him.

"Quite all right," Brondt told her. "Did you get all of them?"

"I think so," she replied. She gestured to the palace. "I didn't see any go inside. But I can't be certain."

"We'll take care of that." Brondt waved a hand at the surrounding men. "And Alice?"

"Yes?"

"Thank you for not damaging her." The commander pointed to the palace with his blade. "I'm truly grateful."

"It's Liana who has the good aim," she expressed with a shrug. "I just go along for the ride."

Brondt chuckled as he started for the palace door.

"Cobham, Cheyne and Sparrow," Thornton called. The men ran to their captain. "You lot stay here in case anything comes out of those doors while we're inside. Got it?"

"Yes sir," they chorused.

They watched the commander, the captain, and the other men move into the building.

Eighteen

Joanne first saw the decaying seaside village from the top of a hill as they galloped towards the north. Surprisingly, many of the buildings were still standing in place, but given in to overgrown vegetation and weathering. Several structures had collapsed over time and the thatched roofs that once sheltered houses and stores had vanished, leaving empty stone shells behind.

There were a few buildings that had clay slates resting on their rooftops. Most of the tiles were still very much in place. Funteyn steered his horse towards one of these structures.

"It's getting late," he called out, looking towards the sun. It had dipped below the mountains, which cast a long shadow over the village and into the sea. "We should stay here. It is the only reasonable shelter between here and Whitekeep."

Joanne followed him without question.

Whitekeep was at least two days' journey away, if not more. The only other place that might provide some shelter was the ruins of a lighthouse that acted as a sort of halfway post between Oakbeach, where they were, and Whitekeep.

Without tents and bedding, having left Newholt in such haste, and with snowdrifts littering the ground, their chances were looking slim. They would need to shelter here for the night.

Joanne looked to the sky to the south as they pulled up by a small stone hut. There was no dragon chasing them. The smoke rising from Newholt had passed out of view. No one could see them. No one was following.

But she still felt on edge and afraid.

Alice was coming.

She knew it.

***

"Let me pass," Monteacute said to the guards by the entrance into the palace courtyard. Four men stood sentry where the gates had once endured. "I need to speak to Ursula."

"What business have you with Lady Ursula?" Lieutenant Hugh Brook asked, crossing the courtyard from the palace doors. He stopped short of the sentry guards and peered at the man wishing to enter. "I know you."

"Sheriff Nathaniel Monteacute," the other announced.

"From Whitekeep." Brook jabbed a finger in his direction. "Let him pass."

The guards moved aside to allow Monteacute through.

"Come on," the sheriff said to two people behind him. They moved past the guards together, but they let only Monteacute into the courtyard. "Wait," he said to the men. "They're with me."

Brook waved his hand. "Let them in as well."

The guards moved aside. Brook watched on as a woman wearing a wide-brimmed cavalier hat strutted by the guards. She wore a long coat, unbuttoned so that her rapier's hilt, sheathed to her waist, was clearly visible and blood streaks smeared her blouse. Behind her strolled an impressively tall man, dark of complexion and carrying a large curved sword on his hip.

Brook recognised the woman immediately.

"Captain Staiger." He bowed slightly.

"Lieutenant." She bowed back. She gestured to the other man. "This is my first officer, Stalekk Rank'sku."

"Sir," the tall man said, and bowed slightly.

"A pleasure," the officer replied. He started towards the palace door and looked to Monteacute. "Lady Ursula is inside. Everyone has gathered in the drawing-room."

The sheriff and his two companions followed the lieutenant, but their attention drew away to the enormous beast at the far end of the courtyard.

"Impressive, isn't she?" Brook said.

The dragon was tilting its head to allow a girl, with two swords strapped at her sides, to scratch at the skin beneath its jaw. Standing about the girl, as if guarding her, were reptilian warriors. The sight was beyond impressive, but the captain's focus fell upon the girl.

"They both are," Staiger replied. "Who is she?"

"The dragon's name is Liana," Brook answered, knowing full well that he was being asked about the girl. Captain Staiger shot him a reproving glare and a cheeky grin. "Her name is Alice. She is the dragon's keeper, amongst many other things. Those standing about her are her subjects. She is their chosen queen; I think that best describes it."

"They elected a child to lead them?" Rank'sku enquired.

"I'm uncertain how she came to lead them," the lieutenant replied as he ascended the steps to the palace door. "But if I were to wager a guess, I would say it had something to do with those swords of hers."

"She's a fighter, then?" the tall man pressed.

"Fearless," Brook replied as he stepped inside the doors.

He led the three into the foyer and through a door to the right. There, some seated, and some standing, was a large group of individuals. Some Monteacute recognised. Others were strangers to him. All, except for three ladies, were as filthy from battle as he.

"Monty," he heard one of them call excitedly.

Ursula bounded from her seat by a fireplace against the far wall and navigated through the room at a quick pace.

"Ursula!" He put his arms out, then suddenly remembered how he looked. "No hugs, me pet. Not until I get time to clean up."

She stopped in her tracks just inches from him and smiled.

"Are you well?" she asked. "Were you hurt?"

"I'm fine," he replied. Before he asked her anything, she was speaking again.

"The girls? Maud? Where are they?" She looked past him expectantly.

"The girls were out there with us today," he answered. "I lost them somewhere during battle. I intend to go back out and search for them."

"We can get some men to do that." She turned to Brondt. "Can't we?"

"Of course," the commander replied, moving slowly to the sheriff and extending his hand. Monteacute took it. "Commander Jonathon Brondt at your service."

"Sheriff Nathaniel Monteacute of Whitekeep at yours," he responded. "But I must decline your offer for help, Commander." Both Ursula and Brondt gave the sheriff a perplexed stare. "You have so much on your hands at the moment. I'm sure I will find them on my own. They are probably back at the Petty Beggar waiting for me." Monteacute gestured to the two behind him. "Captain Staiger, her first officer, and I were about to go there. Your subordinate, Sub-Commander Wake, is my guest. I'm certain he'd like to hear from you or a representative, if you could spare the time."

"Guest?" Brondt questioned.

"He was tortured and injured during the takeover," Monteacute informed the commander. "We've been tending to him."

"I see," the commander responded.

"We also captured the commander of the black army," the sheriff continued. "He says he escaped and was on his way home when we found him."

"Andris?" Emily enquired. She had been in conversation with Amicia a little further in the room and now was drawn to the conversation by the door. She turned back to the other woman. "Sorry, Your Majesty."

"Quite all right." Amicia smiled politely, touching Emily on the arm. "Go on."

"Are you talking about Andris?" Emily asked, moving to the Brondt's side.

Monteacute nodded.

"How is he?" she asked. "Is he well?"

"If you're asking whether we tortured him," Monteacute replied sternly, "the answer is no. We don't behave in such a manner. He was fed and kept under our roof. Admittedly, he is being kept in our cellar, but he is a prisoner."

"He should be allowed to return home," Emily said to the commander.

"We may need to question him," Brondt replied.

"About what?" Emily furrowed her brow. "The black forces are defeated."

"He might know something about the Maji that we are unaware of," Brondt clarified. "Some tactical information that could serve us towards a victory."

Emily looked at the commander critically.

"He needs to go home to his wife," she said.

"And he will," Brondt assured her. "After we have asked him some questions. He won't be hurt. He won't be tortured. If he has truly escaped, as he has told Mister Monteacute, then he would want to help us. Wouldn't he?"

"No harm will come to him." She pointed her finger at Brondt's chest. "I have your word?"

"You have my word," he replied in all earnestness.

Ursula returned her attention to Monteacute.

"You haven't mentioned Maud."

The sheriff frowned and looked at the floor.

"It's not good news, my dear," he said. "I don't know how else to say it, but she's gone."

The young woman standing before him stared blankly at him.

"How?"

"You don't need to know that," he replied.

"How, Monty?"

His chin trembled. "We were hiding inside the cellar at the Upright Banker," he faltered. "One of those dark animals found us and…"

Monteacute looked at the other apologetically. "I tried. I really tried. But it got to her." Ursula had tears streaming over her cheeks. "I'm so sorry," Monteacute sobbed.

She nodded, not knowing what else to do.

"We should get moving," called a voice approaching from the foyer.

All eyes suddenly turned to the door where Alice entered, oblivious to the conversation that had transpired in the room. She froze in her tracks as she surveyed the scene.

"What happened?"

***

"Did you enjoy your day out?" Takmel asked from an upholstered chair that had been placed by the fire in the sitting room. He had his back to the door as he peered into the flames. Isabel noticed his arm moving but couldn't tell what it was that he was fondling with.

"We had a splendid day," she replied with a smile, looking down at the twin girls standing beside her. They were still dressed in their floral dresses. "Didn't we, ladies?"

They nodded silently, grinning back at the White Queen.

"I suppose you will parade your new finery for me," Takmel said, moving his hand over something out of the girls' view.

"Not yet," Isabel replied.

"My lady?" One of the servant girls stepped through the door. She and three others held packages of differing sizes, wrapped in brown paper and tied with coarse string.

"Upstairs," said the queen, and pointed to the stairwell leading to the levels above. "In the girls' bed chamber."

The servant girl bowed and led the others away.

"Are they just too good to show me?" Takmel asked, turning his head a little in their direction. A small, soft whimper emitted from his direction. "Shhh," he hissed, turning his attention to something in his lap.

Isabel furrowed her brow.

"The seamstress needs to make the dresses," she replied. "Should take no longer than a few days."

"So…" Takmel raised his brows and continued moving his arm slowly. "What will these two lovely ladies wear in the meantime?"

She stepped into the room cautiously, the girls on her heels and hiding behind her dress. They stared to Takmel warily, keeping the white woman between them and the man in the chair.

"We found some suitable garments in the market," Isabel answered. "Nothing extravagant. But practical."

"Practical?" he questioned. "Are they suitable for playing in?"

"Some are," the woman replied, tilting her head to see what was on his lap. "It all depends upon what you mean by *playing*.

"On the ground," he replied. "With animals, let's say."

"Animals?"

"Yes," he said, and chuckled. "Like dogs, for instance."

He got to his feet and revealed two little puppies, streaked with a variety of grey tones. One of them whined as he moved, disturbed from a comfortable slumber.

"Oh, my!" Isabel smiled joyfully.

"Not for you, my love," he said. "One each for the most beautiful twins I've ever seen."

He held his arms out, extending the pups to the younglings.

They bolted from behind the White Queen and snatched the dogs from Takmel's hands. Their faces lit up as they squeezed the pups tightly to their chests. The pups responded with a ferocious attack of licking.

"Where did you…?" Isabel asked as she watched on fondly.

"The kennel master offered them," he replied. "One of the bitches produced a litter a few weeks ago. They've been weaned, but this will be the first night away from their mother and the others in their litter." He crouched before the twins. "You must promise to take good care of them." They nodded and smiled jubilantly. "Feed them and clean up after them," he continued. They looked to him and persisted with nodding. "They are both boys and will need lots of training. They will grow to be huge. If you don't control them, they will control you. And you don't want that. Understand?"

Both girls tightened their lips and tried to appear serious, nodding incessantly as he spoke.

"Good!" He stood to his full height. "The kennel master has offered his assistance and will teach you how to care for them."

Isabel kissed him on the cheek and wrapped her arms around him.

Takmel grinned, quite pleased with himself, as the girls dropped to the floor to nurse their new wriggling and writhing, face-licking puppies.

Nineteen

It was a small party that travelled north during the night. Alice had chosen only a few to be her companions. Amongst them was her mother. Alice selected her before the others. She had told her it was because she needed her by her side. The truth was that she wouldn't have been able to stop Emily even if she tried.

Her sister, Catherine, had insisted on going. Again, Alice couldn't argue with her and believed it would be pointless to do so. She simply told the other to dress appropriately and keep warm.

Schoenbach, Karlena and Akasati joined the small band of riders, along with Ruttger Harrow and three Agrodien; Yuri, Nakrah and Nola'ee. Alice instructed the others to stay behind and keep watch over Liana.

The dragon appeared upset when she noticed Alice on horseback instead of her own. She chirped to call her rider back. She crawled after the troop, making her way across the courtyard.

"Stay here," Alice commanded the beast, holding a hand up to her.

She whined and growled, lowering her neck and bobbing her head up and down.

Alice turned back to the road and continued as the dragon called after her again with chirps. When that failed, she roared. The sound boomed over the city like thunder.

"Why not just take her?" Catherine asked as they reached the bottom of the sloping road that led to the palace.

"I need her rested," the younger sibling replied. "She will be needed for when I go to Blackrock Haven."

Emily moved her gaze to her daughter.

"You plan to take Tricia on your own?"

"I do," Alice replied.

"We should come with you," Catherine argued. "The Four should be together."

"I need you to go to Dweagan," Alice instructed. "All of you. There may be loyalists to the Maji there and we need to bring a swift end to anything that supports him. Right now, they are in a state of confusion, just like Newholt. Their shipyards are destroyed, and a great number of their soldiers have fallen. Their queen is dead, and they have no established leaders to run the city. It's the best time to intervene. Perhaps their people will submit to our cause."

"You truly believe that?" Schoenbach asked.

She shook her head. No.

***

"My one-eyed idiot," Staiger whispered as she gently ran her fingers over Wake's cheeks. He held her tightly around the waist and pressed his forehead to hers. "Do you have yer own room here?"

He quickly moved his eye around the tavern. Most people ignored their display of affection, but the girls rescued from the street were all watching intently.

"Not really," he replied. "We could go back to my home."

"Fire ripped through it, remember?" she said. She had told him earlier that she noticed his home was a smouldering pile of rubble as she made her way to the Petty Beggar. He had simply been too excited when he saw her walk in through the door to take notice of anything spoken by anyone.

"Right," he said, scrunching up his face.

"We could go back to the *Gypsy*," she whispered into his ear.

"It's a long way to the waterfront for someone in my condition," he said earnestly.

"Oh, for the love of the gods," Rose snapped. "Take my room and get it over with. Second door to the right at the top of the stairs." They looked to her with astonished faces. "What are you waiting for? Off with you."

"I won't say no," Wake replied as he took Staiger by the hand and led her away and up the stairs. The others watched in amazement as a new vigour and agility took hold of him, and he climbed the stairs faster than his injuries should allow.

Ursula chuckled. "I had almost forgotten what it was like being in a brothel," she said.

"This isn't a brothel, young lady," Monteacute scolded. "This is a fine establishment, thank you very much."

"And just how did you procure this fine establishment, Monty?" she enquired.

"I found it empty just after the takeover," he replied. "So, I moved in and changed the locks."

"What's a brothel?" one of the younger girls asked.

Audrey turned to her and smiled. "A fine establishment."

"And what are they doing upstairs?" the little girl questioned.

"Shagging," Thornton growled from his seat by the fire. He nursed a large mug of rum in one hand and used a poker to rouse the flames with the other.

"George!" Ursula snapped. She wore a wide smile on her face.

He shot her a playful grin.

Monteacute sniggered as the younglings turned their head to face the soldier in the chair. The older girls smirked and shot embarrassed glances at one another. The younger ones stared at him blankly.

"What's shagging?" the curious little girl probed.

"Try explaining that soldier-boy." Monteacute chuckled.

***

"Anything you could share would be of great help," Brondt said. He sat by the fire in the palace drawing-room. Amicia sat beside him and leant forward, listening intently to Andris, who sat in a cushioned chair across from them.

"I really don't know what else to say," he admitted. "She is struggling with her loyalties, I think. Part of her wants to be true to Takmel. The other wants to be true to her real self. It's driving her insane."

"You base this upon the way she behaved with you?" Amicia asked.

"I do."

"Why would she want to lie with you so keenly?" Brondt asked. "No offence intended. You're a good-looking lad and all. But, why has she got this fixation?"

"I'm not sure," he replied. "The last time I experienced anything like this was when we were both captives at Blackrock Haven. The Sovereign wanted Joanne to lie with me. She wanted all the girls to lie with their man-servants. It was a manner of taking power."

"It wasn't a way of taking power," Amicia corrected him. "It was a way of inflicting authority. The potentials would command their man-servants to bed them, even if it was against the will of the man."

"Rape?" Brondt asked. His face betrayed his stoic demeanour, showing disgust and abhorrence towards the idea. "You're talking about rape?"

"Yes," she replied. "To force one into submission is to gain power. Or, at least, power over that individual. It was also a way of allowing a vulnerability to the one committing the act. Or so that was how the Sovereign saw things. She perceived that if she could get her potentials to force their will onto others, she could strip away those pieces of them that didn't want to cause harm to others. The parts that allow us to be kind and forgiving. Then, she would have a foothold and be able to instil the things that would shape them into what she wanted them to be."

"And you know this, how?" Brondt asked.

She looked at him critically. "You know how I know."

He seemed stunned. "Oh." He looked away from her and to the rug on the floor. "I see."

"What were her plans if she was to lose the city?" Amicia asked the other man.

"There were none," Andris replied. "I don't think there was any contingency. They were all so sure they would succeed. The prophecy said that the Maji would be ruler of all. How could they lose?"

"The prophecy," the queen mumbled as she peered into the flames. "The prophecy is a sham. Something that the Mirikin created to give them purpose."

Andris looked at the flames.

"You intend to go after him?" he questioned. "You and Alice?"

"We do," she replied.

"If he isn't in Woodmyst, he would have returned home," the young man offered.

"Wintermarsh," she said. "We know."

Andris frowned and looked at her in shame.

"I cannot go with you," he told her. He looked at Brondt, then back to her. "I need to go home to my wife. She is with child. Or she was when I last saw her. I need to be there."

The commander shifted in his seat and leant towards him.

"I'll have a horse and some supplies ready for you in the morning," Brondt said, rising to his feet, signalling the other that they had finished for the night. "I'll be sending men to scout the land between here and the Twisted Road tomorrow. You can travel with them if you wish. But, you will be on your own after that."

Andris assented as he lifted himself from the chair and reached for the other man's hand, "Thank you, Commander." He then turned to Amicia, who looked over at him from her chair. "Thank you, Your Highness."

"Quite all right, she replied as she stood up. She took his hands in hers. "Take care."

Andris bowed and turned to leave the room. They watched him go before resuming their seats.

Brondt took a deep breath and looked at the flickering flames in the fireplace. She could feel his unease as if it was an invisible entity, a deeply uncomfortable feeling pushing against her skin.

"We can talk about it," she said eventually.

"I don't know if I want to," he replied. "Do you want to?"

She frowned and felt a tear roll over her cheek.

"I am not proud of my past, Jonathon," she said in a low voice. "I was never a good woman until I found you."

She turned to face him. His heart sank as he saw the tear streaks over her skin. He used his thumb to wipe them away and kissed her forehead.

"You don't need to tell me anything," he said.

"She made us do it," Amicia blurted. "We were just little girls, and she made us do it with them. And afterwards, we killed them. I killed him with my bare hands."

She erupted into a crying fit. Loud, uncontrollable moans erupted from her. Brondt waved the guards away with one hand as he embraced her with the other. He didn't know what to say, so he just held her.

"That boy almost suffered the same fate," she blubbered. "He has no idea how close he came."

"It's over now," he whispered. "You're safe here with me in our home. There is no more Yasmeen Svoboda. She is gone. She won't be making any more little girls do anything like that ever again."

She pushed her face against his chest and wept profusely. He wrapped his arms tightly around her and said no more.

***

The winds had picked up and a fine dusting of snow drifted to the ground around them. Yuri tugged his thick cloak, lifting the hood over his brow so that the only recognisable part of him was his snout protruding out from beneath the lid.

Nola'ee almost laughed, emitting a soft hissing that reminded Alice of snickering. The girl turned to smile at her personal guard.

"Quiet," she whispered in the Agrodien tongue. "He might hear you."

"Not under all of that fur, Kayl'sro," the other replied. "I don't think he could hear your dragon roar if she were right here."

Alice chuckled, moving her eyes to the way ahead. She could hear the waves crashing against the rocks to their right and see the dark forms of the mountains reaching high into the sky to the left.

Now and then, she caught the noise of creaking branches from the pine forest that covered the foothills. She could smell their sweet aroma wafting through the breeze, much subtler than the scent of horse, man and reptilian. Much more appealing.

She tried to focus on it as they rode and found it satisfying. Riding this far away from the dwellings of man, whether during daylight or darkness, was something she hadn't done in a while. As she placed her hand upon her belly, she surmised that this kind of experience would be something she would not be doing for a long time again.

"We might need to seek shelter if this gets any worse," Akasati said as she brushed the snow away from her steed's neck.

"We rode through worse than this before," Schoenbach argued. "Remember the storm when the rukyul attacked us. That was much farther north than here. And the snow was up to the horses' shoulders in places."

"You exaggerate." Emily laughed. "I don't remember it being that deep anywhere. I remember that tempest as we crossed the plain on our approach to Whitekeep."

"Only, it wasn't Whitekeep then," Karlena put in. She turned to Alice, who was listening intently. She tried to make her words sound terrifying. "It was the White Witch's Lair."

Alice smiled, enjoying the entertaining conversation.

"We lost two good men there," Emily recalled.

"Ivo and Captain Tarkin," Alice recalled from the stories that she had been told before.

"Aye." Schoenbach nodded sadly. "I admit I didn't know Ivo all that well. He was very young. Very young. Too young.

"But Captain Tarkin," he continued. A glint of respect swept over the man's face as he reminisced. "Now, there was a man of quality. First one into danger. Last to leave. I think you would have liked him, Ruttger."

"From what I have heard," the other said, "I think you may be right."

"The only other man I found that surpassed Captain Tarkin's feature of valour would be your father, Alice." She looked over at Schoenbach, who seemed to peer fondly into the distance. "I remember seeing the two of them side by side. Fighting together. Now, that was something."

Alice saw a fleeting image of her father flash through her head. It was a moment near his end when he charged across a bridge on horseback during the height of battle, directly towards the White Mistress.

She wiped her eyes and looked over to the pine trees, focussing her senses to pick up the sweet aroma emitting from the trees again.

"Kayl'sro?" Nola'ee enquired, recognising the change in her leader's demeanour.

"I'm fine," the girl replied.

Twenty

A thin glow of deep purple sat upon the horizon. Even from this distance, through the haze of sleet and foam being kicked about by the heavy winds, Alice could see the waters were rough out upon the sea.

But it wasn't the sea that had her attention.

It was the six horses tethered by a small cottage near the side of the road leading into the ruins of Oakbeach far below them. The poor beasts, still with their saddles in place, were covered in freezing snow and were too cold, and too tired to move. Instead, they huddled together for warmth.

"How do you want to do this?" Emily asked.

The troop had paused on the top of a hill that overlooked the township. A small peninsula stretched away to their right, following the vein of a mountain's outstretched limb, of which the hill was a part. The village hugged the coastline along the peninsula before turning to the north.

The contours of where the land met the sea formed a small bay of sorts. Alice could see why some chose it as a point of anchor for ships. With another landform jutting out to the ocean, just a little farther north, it provided natural protection from any storm for any ship sheltered here.

Alice saw rotting pillars sticking from the water. They stood in straight lines reaching out from the shore, tilted this way and that like crooked soldiers standing in rows. A walkway had once stretched out from the land to form a pier. She imagined the *Adelandria* moored here many years before, or the black ship that had carried her aunt away to the north.

"We can't rush in," Alice replied. "It would be nice if we could take her alive."

"Do you think that's possible?" Ruttger asked. But before he could get an answer, there was movement near the cottage.

It was her.

Joanne moved from the hut towards the awaiting horses. A soldier had her arm and assisted her onto a steed.

The troop watched on, dumbfounded, as the Black Queen settled into her saddle and moved her horse away from the others. Six soldiers collected their chargers and prepared to mount.

Alice stared, as if transfixed, keeping her aunt in her line of sight. Almost everything else around her seemed to disappear. All she could see was the woman in black.

Their eyes met.

Joanne was peering directly at her.

Alice felt her heart standstill, and the world seemed to stop.

"Kayl'sro?" Yuri hissed, snapping Alice out of a trance.

Joanne had set her horse to the gallop, racing towards the north as fast as it could. The six soldiers frantically mounted their horses and started after her.

Alice kicked her steed hard, urging it down the embankment at great speed. Nola'ee was right behind her, followed closely by the remaining Agrodien warriors.

The girl didn't look back to see if the others had pursued. She assumed they had. She focused her vision upon the steed that carried her aunt.

The soldiers' horses kicked up slush and mud in all directions. Alice manoeuvred her charger wide to avoid the onslaught of muck as she overtook them.

One rider in black saw her catching up and moved to intercept. He lifted his sword out of his sheath and readied himself to swing it at the girl.

A bolt suddenly stuck into the back of his skull.

He dropped the sword and fell to the ground, leaving the horse to gallop on its own.

Alice followed his body with her eyes as it rolled across the ground. Another steed trampled over the soldier, causing him to roll some more. Upon the steed sat Akasati, who was stringing another arrow into her bow, allowing her horse to gallop free without the reins.

Another soldier charged for Alice. His sword came down in a long arc as he drew nearer.

She pulled one of her swords free of its sheath with her right hand and blocked his blow. With a quick glance to the whereabouts of her aunt, who was starting up another embankment, Alice let her reins go with her left hand and pulled her other sword free. She then jabbed it deep into the soldier's ribs and twisted it before retracting the blade.

Yuri caught up to one of the other men in black. He leapt from his horse and onto the enemy rider, tackling him to the ground in a flurry of mud and snow. Nakrah pulled his steed to a halt to help the older Agrodien, sliding off his horse with a curved dagger in his hand.

Alice continued urging her steed to gallop faster.

Joanne had vanished from sight behind a coppice of trees.

The last soldier waited on his horse at the top of the hill. He held his sword high as he faced the girl and the approaching troop.

As Alice climbed the embankment, she saw her aunt's steed lying on its side, writhing in agony. Its front right leg was twisted awkwardly, and it shrieked in agony as it desperately tried to get back to its feet.

The last soldier charged.

Alice thrust her hand forward, and using her power, knocked him from his horse.

He toppled over, striking stone and mud before smacking into a tree.

Alice dropped from her charger and pulled her blades free.

"You don't need to die for her," the girl shouted over the wind.

"I am Commander Leonard Funteyn," he called back as he rose to his feet. "I was appointed to serve the Black Queen. And I will serve her until my last breath."

Alice moved to the fallen beast's side as the other spoke. She looked down at it and saw pain in its eyes.

"I'm sorry," she whispered to it before plunging one of her blades into its skull.

The horse went limp and breathed a long exhale.

Funteyn raised his sword and ran at Alice.

"Stupid little girl," he hollered.

Alice blocked his blow with one hand and jabbed into his belly with the other.

A look of surprise flashed upon the commander's face as he pulled away from her, feeling the blade slide through his flesh. He glanced down to see his own blood trickle from the hole in his armour and shook his head.

The rest of Alice's troop arrived upon the hilltop.

"Where is she?" Catherine asked her mother, riding beside her.

"I don't know," Emily answered, peering into the forest to their left. She then looked towards the rocky peninsula past the coppice of trees and saw movement. "That way."

The commander attacked again, swinging his blade wide.

Alice ducked beneath it and plunged both swords under Funteyn's chest plate. The swords crossed somewhere inside the commander and popped out through his upper back.

She stood and placed a boot against his chest, heaving the blades free of him as he dropped his own sword to the ground. Funteyn stood for a moment, looking at the girl with disbelief.

"I was told about you," he muttered. Blood spilled over his chin. "But I didn't believe any of it. Until now."

With that, he fell upon his face.

Alice sprinted through the thicket towards the rocky point beyond without hesitation. Emily and Nola'ee were struggling to keep up. Catherine followed, moving as fast as she could manage.

Breaking through the treeline, Alice came to an abrupt stop. Emily almost ran into her as she burst through.

Standing before them, on the precipice of the jagged point, high above the waves crashing against the rock, stood Joanne.

She wasn't casting any spells.

She wasn't wielding any instrument of death.

She was crying.

"Stay back there," she yelled. The wind howled as white foam erupted about her. "I know what I need to do."

"Joanne," Emily called, stepping forward.

"Stay back," the Black Queen warned, pointing a finger at her sister. "I should have done this long ago. I should have done this before he made me…"

She bawled. Her legs shook, and she appeared as if she was going to fall to her knees.

Alice saw she was right on the edge of the high cliff.

"Come back this way a little," the girl pleaded.

"I still hear his voice," Joanne told them. "He still calls me *Mama*. After what I did to him, he still calls me *Mama*."

"Joanne," Emily cried, dropping to her knees. "You're not yourself. Come back with us."

"Please, Aunt Joanne!" Catherine reached her hands out.

"This isn't you, Mama," the Black Queen sobbed. "That's what he tells me. This isn't you, Mama." She looked to Alice. "Who am I?"

"You're Aunt Joanne." Alice wept. "That's who you are."

"I don't know," she wailed, looking to the sky. "I don't know anymore."

"Come home." Alice stepped forward and reached out her hand.

"The tree has been burned, Alice," the woman in black said, locking eyes with the girl. "But the roots grow deep."

She stepped backwards and looked at Emily, tears streaming over her face.

"Goodbye, sister."

Then she was gone.

Alice rushed to the edge of the rock and peered over. Her aunt Joanne lay dashed across the rocks below. Whitewash and large waves swept over her remains and claimed her for the sea.

The girl dropped to her knees, feeling helpless.

Catherine stared at the precipice blankly, as if she was trying to comprehend what she had witnessed.

Emily cried uncontrollably. Silent screams filled her lungs. Her mouth hung open as the wind howled about her. Then, without warning, she found her voice as her cries filled the air.

Twenty-One

Takmel almost fell, stumbling, so he had to grab the wall to steady himself.

He had been hit hard. He could feel it.

Joanne had fallen.

The prime of the Seven was taken from him.

She was a key, if not *the* key, to hold the others together. Without her, a large weakness existed. A great uncertainty festered in his mind.

Could any of them turn from him?

Would they band together and overthrow him?

Now that she was gone, he had no way of telling.

There was no time for mourning.

He needed to consider his options.

He needed replacements.

He needed new wives.

"Guard," he called as he sat on the edge of his bed. Isabel was gone again. He surmised she had spent another night with the twins.

"My lord," a uniformed man said, pushing the chamber door open. "You summoned me?"

"Yes," Takmel replied, wiping his brow. "Has Lieutenant Saruun Versel left the city yet?"

"I don't believe so, my lord," the other replied.

"Find her and bring her to me as soon as you do," Takmel commanded.

"Yes, my lord." The guard bowed, went out and closed the door behind him, leaving the Maji alone.

Takmel got to his feet again and dressed.

He felt weak and tired, as if he had just completed a day of laborious work. Yet, he had only just awoken from a good night's rest.

Walls were crumbling from within, weakening his defences. As he slipped his boots on, Takmel hoped his remaining queens remained loyal. But he had some misgivings.

He was afraid.

***

"I am sorry, Commander," Wake said from his chair by the fireplace. The two sat across from one another in the main room of the Petty Beggar. Brondt had brought a detachment of cavalry soldiers to escort him, most of which had stayed outside on their steeds. Two stood guard by the tavern door. The Sub-Commander continued, "I failed you. I did not know what I was doing and now look what has happened."

"What occurred here was not your fault," Brondt assured him. "This terrible thing would have transpired had I been here, too. They hit us by surprise.

"From what I hear," the commander continued, "you may have saved us with those beacon lights of yours. You could see into the woods and give the archers and catapults something to aim for."

"What good did it do in the end?" Wake asked, peering distantly into the hearth. "Those dark creatures just kept coming. And the Black Queen's men followed right behind them."

"And now they're gone." Brondt smiled, trying to change the other's mood.

"Thanks to you."

"No," the commander said. "Thanks to the resolve that you and the other officers displayed when you were captured. You sparked the resistance into a flame."

Wake thought back to the takeover.

"They just burnt the admiralty," he said. "The first thing they did. Took the superiors of the navy and lit them up. Then they did the same to the generals. They left me alive. They beat me, but they always brought me out to the square and made to watch."

"To break you," Brondt told him. "To crush your spirits. To make you less than what you are and to do so publicly. If they were to succeed in that, then they might just have broken the spirit of this city. But they didn't, Sub-Commander Wake. The city is ours again.

"I didn't come here to reprimand you or point the finger at you. My city is in ruins. Part of it still burns. There are dead in the streets and pools of blood leading up to the palace. But the people are united. And, for that, I thank you."

Brondt got to his feet and extended his hand. Wake attempted to rise from his seat, but winced as a sharp pain shot through his ribs and back.

"Stay in your chair," the commander ordered, taking the other's hand in his. "Take as much time as you need to mend. When you are ready, report back to the palace, Sub-Commander."

"Thank you, sir," Wake said.

Monteacute entered the room through the kitchen door.

"Not staying, Commander?" he asked. "The girls have got eggs and bacon on the skillet. The bread is a little stale, but I can make some toast for you."

"No, thank you." Brondt smiled as he walked to the front door. "I must continue on. I've a lot of surveying to do. My guess is there are many out there in need of help."

"Fair enough," the sheriff assented. "Be safe."

Brondt offered a mock salute and exited the Petty Beggar with his guards in tow.

Monteacute strode over to the fireplace and held his hands out to the heat.

"Nice man, that Commander Brondt," he said, looking to Wake seated beside him. "That woman of his. Fine lass, if I do say so."

"That's the queen you're talking about," Wake said.

The sheriff grinned. "I know. So, what? I'm a man. I'm not dead. I can recognise beauty when I see it. And she's a fine-looking woman. And Brondt is a bastard."

Wake chuckled.

"Ooh, that hurt," he said, and winced, fighting the urge to laugh.

"Toast?" Monteacute asked.

Wake looked at him curiously, then suddenly remembered the bacon and eggs.

"Please," he replied. He moved to stand. "I'll come and help."

"You'll stay right there," the other ordered.

"I feel I'm being treated like a cripple," Wake replied.

"That's not how Davine described you after last night," Monteacute teased as he opened the kitchen door.

"What?" the other called, turning to face the sheriff. "What did she tell you?"

But Monteacute had gone.

***

Alice kept her face as hard as stone, hiding her emotions deep inside. She kept to the front of the troop, riding with her hood over her head and her body rigid. Nola'ee stayed beside her, sensing the recent incident had hit that her leader hard. She didn't speak. She didn't peer over to her Kayl'sro. She simply rode beside her in silence as the wind from the north pushed them on.

Catherine continued to shake her head as she revisited the scene in her mind over and over. She saw Joanne simply step off the edge of the cliff and drop away out of view. Afraid to look over at what had transpired for her aunt afterwards, she had stood in place, unable to move. She wished with part of her she had simply run forward and grabbed the Black Queen's wrist. Or perhaps she and Alice could have used their powers to stop her from throwing herself to the rocks below.

She blamed herself for what had happened. Many *what if* questions raced through her head as she stared at the nag's mane before her.

What if I ran to her faster? Maybe I could have spoken to her and persuaded her to come back with us.

What if I had left Takmel and forced her to come with me when Alice moved to the glade? Then, we wouldn't be here right now.

What if I never loved Takmel? None of this would be happening.

Emily, however, was broken. She wept profusely, leaning this way and that as if she was about to fall from her horse. Karlena and Akasati rode at either side of her, consoling her as much as they could. But the auburn-haired woman was grief-stricken and unresponsive.

The snow beat down upon them and the waves crashed upon the rocks by the sea, roaring like thunder to their left. The riders pressed on to the south, leaving Oakbeach far behind them as they made their way back to Newholt. All travelled quietly for a long part of the return journey, keeping their eyes and thoughts upon the two.

"I don't think she'll be joining us from here on," Ruttger said to Schoenbach, riding at the rear of the pack and nodding towards Emily.

"Don't speak too soon," the other replied. "She's a tough one. Give her time to grieve and she'll be ready to fight again."

"I don't know," said the former soldier. "I mean, that was her sister. Seeing something like that does things to a person's mind."

"Between you and me…" Schoenbach looked to Ruttger. "I think this encounter had a result that is easier to deal with. Imagine how she would be if she had to cut her sister down. Or how she might be if her daughter had to do it. I think Joanne did the right thing. She was babbling like someone who had lost her mind. It may have even been a moment of clarity that gave her the idea to jump."

Ruttger nodded, agreeing silently. "What about her?" He jutted his chin towards Alice.

"I'm worried about her," he admitted.

***

It was dusk by the time they could see the palace tower in the distance. Many glowing lights dotted the land to the south. The expanse between them and the palace was devoid of anything living, as far as they could tell.

"They've moved everyone into one region," Ruttger said, pointing to the flickering orange sparks.

"Seems that they were hit harder than I thought," Schoenbach replied. "If those are the fires of everyone left in Newholt, then there aren't many left."

Alice peered at the ships anchored by the shore. She counted thirteen. Three were missing.

Yuri pulled alongside her. He lifted his heavy hood away from his face and stared at her for a long time. He was struggling with whether he should speak to her or not.

"What is it, Yuri?" she asked, relieving him of breaking the silence.

"Kayl'sro," he started. He kept his voice low and spoke to her in his tongue. "Are you feeling well? You haven't spoken, and we are all concerned." As he spoke, he turned to look at Catherine, who was still wearing a distressed expression. His eyes moved to Emily, who still cried but who had run out of tears to shed. Yuri then turned his attention back to the girl beside him. Nola'ee, riding on Alice's other flank, looked to him cautiously, offering a silent warning. "Your mother and sister don't appear fit. They could use your care."

"My attention?" She looked at him sidelong. "I saw Aunt Joanne dashed to pieces on the rocks. She was my enemy, but I loved her deeply. So, to answer your first question, no, I don't feel well. I don't feel well at all. My mother and sister are having difficulty dealing with the loss that they suffered today. I assure you, Yuri, that I would be the first to care for them both. However, I am having difficulty dealing with the loss that I suffered today as well. As soon as I am able, I will care for them. Right now, I just want to be left alone."

Alice moved her gaze to the tower and returned to riding in silence.

Yuri looked to Nola'ee, who replied with a silent, *I told you so.* He dropped back to the other Agrodien riders and lifted his hood over his head again.

***

The troop made their way into the warmth of the palace where they were greeted by Queen Amicia and Brondt. Only Alice remained outside, taking time to visit Liana who was resting by the wall of the courtyard, surrounded by four palace guards and two Agrodien warriors.

Incessant chirping and excited head bobbing met the girl. She rubbed the dragon's nose and scratched at the looser skin beneath the chin and jowls. Liana responded by half closing her eyes and purring.

"Has she been fed?" Alice asked in Agrodien.

"Yes, Kayl'sro," one warrior replied. "Two whole goats."

Alice seemed to consider this as she rubbed Liana under the neck with her hand.

"Harness her," she commanded the reptilians. "Ready her to fly."

"Yes, Kayl'sro," the two warriors replied.

Alice moved determinedly towards the palace. The dragon watched her intently as she disappeared through the doors and out of sight.

She entered the drawing-room, where everyone had gathered together. Amicia crouched beside Emily, who settled on a sofa by the fireplace. The queen had one hand on the auburn woman's shoulder and another on her knee. Emily held onto Catherine, nestled against her mother's side. The girl had finally broken down and sobbed profusely.

The others gathered about, looked away, or talked quietly amongst themselves. Ruttger and Schoenbach spoke with Brondt a little distance away from the others. Alice believed they were debriefing the commander on the day's events. The Agrodien stood together, warming themselves by the fireplace.

"I need some food for my journey," Alice said loudly.

All faces turned to her, surprised by the sudden interruption. They hadn't heard her enter but were more startled by the words she had spoken.

"Food?" Brondt asked.

"*Your* journey?" Emily furrowed her brow.

"Kayl'sro?" Nola'ee stepped forward. "We go?"

"Not we," Alice replied. "I."

"We just got here," Akasati reminded her. Nola'ee spoke to the other reptilians in a low voice as the Erilian woman continued. "Your mother and sister aren't up to moving on just yet. And you could use some time to grieve. That was no light thing you witnessed out there. You need to rest and recuperate before you move on."

Alice shook her head. "I don't. I need you to rest and recuperate before moving on to Dweagan in the morning. We need to see what we can salvage there, if anything. After that, you will return to the glade where I will meet up with you."

"And where will you go?" Amicia asked.

"I'm leaving tonight for Blackrock Haven," she replied.

The queen got up.

"Do you think this is wise, Alice?" Brondt enquired. "Taking on a witch without support? She will have soldiers and who knows what else at her beck and call."

"I'm stronger than Tricia," the girl answered. She stroked her braid. "I was before this happened. I'm stronger now." Alice saw the concerned faces peering at her. Even Catherine had stopped crying to stare at her younger sister. "I also have a dragon."

Akasati shook her head in disbelief. "Your overconfidence in your abilities could be your weakness, Alice," she said. "You should wait until we can all go with you."

"The Maji has lost three of his wives," Alice informed her. "It's only a matter of time before he finds substitutes. He may already be looking. If we can cut the tethers that bind them to him before he gathers replacements, we have a better chance of defeating him. They are a source of power. I know that losing Aunt Joanne has weakened him. She was the prime of the Seven."

"So," Karlena put in, "their ties are broken. Without their leader, they will fall apart."

"No," said Alice. "Aunt Joanne said something before she…" The girl stopped, pursed her lips and swallowed as she fought back her tears. "She said that the tree has been burned, but the roots grow deep."

"What is that supposed to mean?" Karlena questioned.

"I thought that the tree in Woodmyst was a source of power for the Seven," Alice explained. "So, I had Liana set it on fire. It's now a pile of ash. But the life source of the tree is beneath the ground, and it lives on. The remaining women of the Seven are still united. And if they are united, then they provide strength to the Maji.

"We can't dig up the roots of the tree," she continued. "They grow deep and wide. But, we can destroy the others of the Seven.

"If the captains of those vessels out there are up for it, they could navigate the coast and destroy any of Takmel's ships along the way." She turned to Brondt. "Three are missing."

"They are patrolling the waters down to Freymoor," he replied. "They should return in two days."

"I see. When I meet you back at the glade, we'll leave again to follow the coast," she explained. "If the ships join us, they can go ahead and meet us at each port town. They can prevent other vessels from leaving by sea while we attack by land."

The room was silent. All eyes were on Alice, absorbing her words and repeating them over in their heads.

"It's the best plan that I have at the moment," she said. "I admit, I am tired. I will sleep when I leave."

"On the dragon's back?" Brondt asked.

"I've done it before," she replied. "If any of you come up with a better plan in the meantime, let me know when we gather together again.

"Until that time, I need some food for my journey."

Twenty-Two

The dragon climbed higher into the night sky, trying to pass over the strong winds sweeping towards her from the north. The effort was in vain as the winds increased the higher she flew. She dived back towards the ground in search of an easier path through the barrage. Sleet spattered against her face and wings relentlessly as she pressed on.

The girl slept through it all. She wore layers of clothing, from her gloves, leggings and tunic, her regular hooded cloak, the bearskin of the Kayl'sro and finally, the thick earthen coloured leather robe, a gift given to her by the Agrodien females, covering it all. She had her scarf covering her mouth and nose; the hoods pulled over her head and her body resting against the dragon's neck.

Sheltered from the weather, warm beneath the clothing and soothed by the fluid motion of the flying beast, she had dozed off and let Liana fly. The dragon, fully aware of her passenger, did her best to ease up when the need to alter her course presented itself. Alice, however, had strapped herself in tightly. The only way she could fall from Liana's back was if the harness came loose.

It was dawn when her eyes opened again.

The dragon had stopped moving, and the wind had subsided somewhat.

Alice sat upright, removed the hoods from her head, and peered about. Liana had landed to drink from a thin, bubbling stream. The water wound its way through a wood nestled at the foot of a great mountain. Its peak was so high that it scraped the clouds above with a pointed spine.

Her gaze followed the stream towards the sea. There she saw the remains of a tiny hamlet with the buildings torn asunder There wasn't much left to recognise, but she knew where she was.

This was Whitekeep.

She had not been here before and had never planned to come.

This was Ursula's home before the dark creatures sent by Takmel overran it. It was also a small port village that marked the halfway point between Newholt and Blackrock Haven.

To Alice, though, it was the place where the Maji had been conceived. A place where darkness had almost destroyed her family before she was even born.

She still felt a coldness deep within that emanated from somewhere nearby. It could have easily been mistaken for the severe weather, and in fact, she even shivered as it touched her.

She knew better.

It was this place.

Something dark still lingered here.

She could see the stonework of a broken tower peeking through the snow-covered pines near a cleft at the base of the mountain.

It called to her.

Beckoned her to come.

Only, it used another's name.

Ivo.

Ivo.

It enticed her with a sweet sound that lured and almost seduced her.

Ivo.

The dragon lifted its head and gave a mighty shake before snorting abruptly.

Alice snapped back to reality, leaving the ghosts of the past where they were.

"Ready to keep going, girl?" she asked the beast. The dragon responded with a friendly chirp.

Liana took to the air again, taking off out over the shoreline, passing the small seaside on her left before circling around to her right, back towards the south. She used the wind at her back to climb higher as she swung back over the shoreline and passed above the forest.

Alice peered down at the base of the mountain to look at the ruins of the fortress. It was a crumbled mess with broken walls and toppled structures; barely anything recognisable as a complete structure still stood in place.

She could feel a presence there.

Something tangible.

Something old.

A memory that lingered and had found a home.

And it still called for him.

Ivo.

Ivo.

Alice lifted her water skin from her belt and took a swig. After setting it back in place, she pulled both hoods over her head and lifted her scarf over her nose. She turned away from the ruins and put her attention to the air before her as the dragon straightened its body out, continuing its course to the north.

***

Landon Wake leant upon a staff roughly fashioned from a pine branch by a man under his command. Beside him, with her arm around his waist, stood Captain Davine Staiger. Others from the Petty Beggar had gathered with them to see the mass of soldiers begin their march to the south.

They were standing on a hill to the south of the city. The sun was climbing above the sea and breaking through thick cloud cover with golden shafts of light. It was a welcome gift from above, considering that the stiff wind continued to sweep down from the north. But it was fleeting, as the clouds fought back and choked the sunbeams away.

"I'll return as soon as I can, Sub-Commander," Brondt assured the other. He sat upon his steed. The queen waited for him a short distance away. Wake couldn't stop staring at the reptilian warriors sitting high in their saddles. They were a very impressive sight to behold, with their weapons strapped to their bodies and long tails swaying over the sides of their chargers.

Amicia watched Ursula bid her friends farewell. The young woman was embracing the three girls that had come to be known as the Whores of Whitekeep. All were in tears, weeping as if they would never see one another again.

"Take care of my girls, Monty," Ursula told him. The sheriff wrapped his enormous arms around the four of them in one go.

"I won't take my eyes off them," he replied. "You just be sure and get back here quick."

The queen smiled, admiring the love shared between them. Although unrelated, they were bonded as tightly as any family could be. She then turned to see Emily and Catherine riding side by side. They were talking, but Amicia couldn't tell what about.

Yuri and the Agrodien warriors encircled them, offering protection as they moved. Ruttger, Schoenbach and the Erilian women followed closely behind.

"We need to go," the queen announced.

Ursula quickly kissed each of the others on the cheek before mounting her steed, being held for her by a palace guard. She then bade them farewell again with tears and a wave before turning her horse to begin the journey south with the others.

"Get your vessel ready," Brondt said to the captain of the *Gypsy*. "Restock her with everything you need."

"If you can find anything to restock her with," Wake added.

"We'll be here when you return," she replied. "No matter how long it takes, we'll be waiting."

Brondt mounted his charger and looked back at the palace.

"We only just got here," he muttered to himself.

"We'll be back," Amicia said, reaching her hand over to his. "But we won't be able to stay."

He looked over at her with sadness in his eyes.

"I know."

***

Arthur gripped the chestnut stallion's flanks with his knees as tightly as he could. The charger simply wanted to run, but the boy wasn't ready for such excitement yet. Every time the steed lunged forward, he pulled the reins to restrict the horse from bolting away. The stallion was compliant and adjusted its speed to suit the rider, if only for a short time. Then, it would try to run again.

"You're doing fine, son," David called from the bank of the stream.

"No, he's not," Lor muttered under his breath.

"Shut it," the other growled as Arthur wheeled the stallion about as best as he could with one arm. "That's it," David shouted. "You have him now."

"The boy's going to hurt himself," said Lor, watching on with a deep sense of fear. "We have readied the horse for battle, not simple back and forth riding like this."

"The horse is going to have to learn its place," David replied. "Alice gave it to Arthur. Arthur won't be riding into battle anytime soon. Therefore, neither will the horse."

The stallion trotted a short distance before leaping from its hind legs into a gallop.

"Try telling that to the horse," Lor said.

As quickly as it ran, Arthur brought the animal back into control and turned it about, slowing its speed to a gentle trot again. He pulled the stallion to a complete stop before turning it in a complete circle on the spot to the left. Then he turned it to the right. With a quick jab of his heels to the sides, the horse started forwards again.

"I think I have it," Arthur yelled.

And, indeed, it seemed that he did.

David watched proudly as his son turned the steed through some sheep that were grazing. The horse then made its way to the stream where Arthur navigated it towards his father. The stallion blew a loud snort as it approached the two men.

"Well done," Lor said. He clapped his hands to applaud the boy's efforts.

The horse bucked and bolted across the glade.

Arthur let out a cry as he tried to keep himself from falling off the saddle.

"Bugger," David gasped.

The boy leant forward, allowing the stallion some slack on the reins. He felt the rhythm of the steed's hooves hitting the ground. The wind-swept over his face and pushed through his hair. Before he knew it, he was laughing.

The treeline was coming up fast. He leant to the right, keeping his body forward. The stallion responded by turning to the right.

Arthur thought he might try to test the steed, as his confidence instantly grew. Simply by leaning to the right, he piloted the horse back onto the open ground. When he was far enough away from the trees, he leant to the left.

The stallion turned left.

Arthur leant to the right.

The stallion turned right.

The men by the stream were awestruck as the boy and his horse rushed past them like the wind. The thunder of hoof-falls and laughter had come and gone in a moment.

Finally, after rushing back and forth across the open ground several times, Arthur lifted himself upright.

The stallion slowed to a canter, then to a walk.

The horse made its way back to the men by the stream, where it pulled to a stop.

"That was amazing," Arthur huffed. His face was beaming with excitement.

"It certainly was," Lor said, surprised.

"I'm going to ride him back to the cabin," the boy said. "I'll meet you there."

Before David could answer, the horse leapt across the stream and galloped up the embankment.

David silently glared at Lor.

"What?"

"Well done," David said, repeating the other's words. He then clapped his hands.

Lor looked apologetic. "I was simply encouraging your son."

"Well done," the other said again, clapping his hands slowly.

"He's all right." Lor gestured towards Arthur. "He's not hurt."

"Well done." David clapped his hands again.

"I'm sorry," Lor said finally. "I really am."

David turned and made his way to the small bridge to cross the stream. He shook his head as Lor followed closely.

"Well done," the big man grumbled. As he walked over the bridge, he sniggered.

Lor said, "Bastard."

***

Takmel drummed his fingers on the armrest of the throne. With Isabel by his side, he watched the two girls playing with their puppies on the floor.

One dog simply wanted to be held and stroked by its new owner. Its personality appeared to be placid and submissive; not to Takmel's liking at all.

The other was attempting to bite at the other girl's hand playfully as she tried to pet its belly. It rolled and growled spiritedly, kicking its paws and slobbering profusely. For whatever the reason, it impressed him.

The twins' faces were alive with adoration and love for their pets. There was also a great deal of reverence and gratitude towards Takmel as they kept looking over at him with beaming smiles on their faces.

He smiled back dotingly as he continued to observe the exchange between the girls and their dogs.

In the back of his mind, he was wrestling with strategy. He could feel a breaking away between the Seven and himself. He sensed a vulnerability, a weakening from within.

The woman seated next to him appeared to be devoted. She had come to him in the night. She had stayed by him through to the morning. And she sat with him as he watched the girls play.

He wondered, though, just how true to him she was.

Would she be like these pups to the girls before him? Would she be loyal?

I am the Maji;; he kept telling himself. *I am far more powerful than all the Seven combined.*

But why did he need to remind himself of such trivialities? A part of him didn't trust her. It didn't trust any of them.

They could be plotting against him even now. They were connected before he had seduced them. Their connection might still hold together even now.

His fingers tapped against the armrest in a nervous reaction to the struggle within.

Could he trust her to stand by him, no matter what?

She placed her hand upon his, preventing his fingers from moving.

"You have done a wonderful thing here, Takmel," Isabel said. She looked at him in a way that only a devoted woman could. "Thank you."

"They needed something good," he replied, hiding his deepest thoughts away. He looked at the two girls on the floor. Although they were silent, he could tell they were laughing. "After what they have been through, they deserve this."

Twenty-Three

Soldiers draped in scarlet tunics watched from the top of the hill overlooking Blackrock Haven. Their small hearths, a series of fire pits, lined the edge of the yard in front of the mansion occupied by their queen. She was safely locked away behind thick stone walls, out of the harsh gale-force winds and sleet that swept across the view before them.

Giant waves pounded against the rocks by the docks, sending an explosion of whitewash and salt into the air. The ships moored nearby rocked and swayed violently, smacking against the piers with each upsurge.

But this wasn't what held their focus.

High-pitched screams, loud enough to be heard over the shrill of the zephyr, reached their ears. They were so far from the township, yet they could hear the creatures clearly. Every once in a while, they could see the dark forms scurrying along the wide paths between structures. The shouts of men would often rise upon the breeze.

"They've been at it for hours," one soldier remarked. He rubbed his hands over his arms.

"I think I'd rather be inside right now," another put in, stomping upon the ground to keep warm.

"Too cold for you?"

"Nah," the other replied. "It's all sunshine and toasty, isn't it? What do you think?"

"There's rum in the flask," another said, and pointed to a canteen lying by the fire pit.

"Probably frozen solid," the first commented.

"I'm more worried about those things down there than I am about the cold." The second gestured towards the town with his chin. "What are they going to go after when they're done with those fellers down there?"

"The queen said we'll be fine if we stay up here," the first reminded him.

"And you believe that?"

They looked at each other silently.

"Tell you what," the third began. "If we need to..."

A streak of fire burst from the sky and swept across the waterfront. The ships suddenly burst alight and the wharves burst into flame.

All the soldiers turned their faces to the sky but saw nothing. The wind and sleet provided too much of a haze for their eyes to see what was up there.

Another barrage of fire sprayed over the vessels. Moments later, they heard something tear through the sky above their heads. Its immense form drew the wind away briefly, drawing the snow in a different direction. A few men even fell to the ground.

"What was that?" one of them called.

"There!" Another pointed to the north, following something swinging back towards the coast.

"Where?" a man shouted.

They were all looking in different places.

Flames engulfed several structures in the town below them. The screams of the dark creatures being burnt alive crowded their ears.

A few soldiers watched as a mass of dark forms scurried across the open ground to the north of Blackrock Haven to escape the horror from above.

To their amazement, a great wall of fire erupted along the ridge bordering the town in that direction. Many of the creatures were swallowed by the inferno or driven back towards the town.

Another spurt of fiery light brushed over the town, moving from the shore towards the hill where the soldiers stood.

The men could not move, dumbstruck by the terrifying sight. The fountain of flame moved closer and closer. More than half of the town below was alight.

Closer and closer it came, until they could see the mouth of the dragon through the sleet and mist above.

Some screamed.

Some turned to run.

Others stayed in place as if frozen.

The flying beast swooped low, passing just above their heads.

As it swooped back to the sky, something dropped from its back.

The men were speechless when they saw a tiny figure, cloaked in thick coverings, standing before them.

The figure flung her covers to the ground and lifted two swords from her hips.

"It's just a girl," one man hollered to the others still fleeing. He pulled his own blade and charged.

She blocked his blow, ducked beneath his arm, and spun on her heels. As quick as a flash, his middle split open and he was lying on the ground.

Other men suddenly found their courage and turned to attack the newcomer.

The girl didn't wait for one of them to strike first. Instead, she leapt.

In one swoop, she landed feet first on the chest of one soldier while plunging her blades into the necks of two others. Quickly, she recoiled her blades and dug one into the forehead of the man beneath her boots.

She saw four more running to her from the left and another two approaching from the direction of the mansion in front of her.

The town behind her lit up as the dragon swooped by to send another bombardment of fire onto the ground.

Block.

Parry.

Stab.

The sound of clashing swords rang out as Alice cut her way through the Scarlet Queen's men.

One of them struck her across the face with his gauntlet. She tasted blood in her mouth and spat it onto the frozen earth. Her response was to place her blade through his chin and into his skull.

Another attempted to kick at her, but she ducked beneath his thigh and planted her weapon deep into his crotch.

More men approached from her sides as she defeated another and another.

Liana sent more flames over the township. Several dark creatures screamed in agony as the men on the hill kept falling at the hands of a little girl.

Blood drenched the snow-covered ground by the time Alice had beaten the last of her opponents. She saw a few men continue to flee into the storm. There was no use in giving chase. They would either die in the blizzard or return to seek shelter.

In either case, she wasn't here for them.

Her quarry was inside the stone manor before her.

She placed one of her blades back into the sheath on her left hip. With determination, she approached the door of the building, spitting out another mouthful of blood.

The façade of the mansion lit up in an orange glow as Liana spewed an onslaught of fire over the town, passing by from south to north.

Alice pushed the doors open. The wind caught the great wooden panels and slammed them against the walls of the foyer with a loud THUNK.

Almost immediately, it hit her; the sweet scent of blood and the foul odour of decay.

There was death here.

"Alice," a woman's voice called. She was almost singing, a gentle sound that shouldn't have reached her ears over the din of the blizzard behind her. "Alice."

The interior of the manor was dimly lit by small candles and a fireplace against a far wall in a sitting room to her right. She peered inside to see empty seats.

"Alice," the woman hissed. It was loud and felt as if lips had brushed against the girl's ear. She turned her gaze to a long corridor stretching away into the belly of the building.

There were many doors and openings lining the passageway on either side. Some were open, some not, and others partly so. Tiny cracks of darkness led into spaces that Alice couldn't see into.

A flickering orange glow emitted from the far end of the hallway. It beckoned to her.

Her fingers tightened around the hilt of her sword as she stepped forwards slowly, preparing herself for anything that might lie in wait behind one of the doors, or linger in the darkness of each room.

The hairs on the back of her neck stood on end as she passed by an open doorway to her right. She couldn't help feeling as if something watched her from within the darkened room.

Placing her feet carefully and quietly on the floor, she kept her ear cocked. A soft giggle reverberated along the walls of the narrow corridor.

"Alice," the woman hissed again.

A long staircase extended to the right and up to the next level. The girl placed her foot on the first step intending to climb.

"Alice," the voice bellowed. The room seemed to shake.

She turned her face to the far end of the hallway, where the orange light flickered.

"Tricia?" she called.

Playful, disturbing laughter echoed along the passageway.

Alice pressed on, leaving the stairwell behind her and passing by more entryways leading to dark empty rooms.

The stench of dead flesh filled her nostrils.

It was almost unbearable, growing stronger with each cautious step.

She entered a dining room with a long table. Silverware and white ceramic dishes adorned its surface.

Three young women sat to the side closest to a roaring fireplace, the only light emanating from the room. Their clothing removed and their heads taken from their necks and placed neatly onto plates before them.

Their matted, blood-soaked hair draped onto the table. Their lifeless eyes peered into nothingness.

Alice felt her stomach turn. A tear fell from her eye.

"What have you done, Tricia?" she whispered.

A vile snigger crept into the room.

Alice peered up at the wall above the hearth and saw a framed face staring back at her. She moved her gaze across the surface and saw more faces. All of them were women. One of them the likeness of Amicia.

Finally, her gaze stopped at two portraits above the head of the table. One was of a woman in green. The other was a woman in white.

The Mirikin.

Alice looked back at the three women seated nearby.

While she could smell their bodies, a stronger scent of death stemmed from a little farther away. There were other odours accompanying it. Something familiar, but not quite right.

Something was cooking.

She crept past the table towards another passageway, clutching her sword in her hands. The corridor was short, with two closed doors on either side. One had a thin strip of bright light spilling out from underneath.

Alice pushed the door open.

Light flooded her sight and the heat of an active stove along with the aroma of boiling meat attacked her senses.

"Alice," the woman said.

The girl focussed her attention on her adversary.

Across the room, behind a bench covered with freshly stripped bones and long shreds of flesh on a chopping board, stood Tricia dressed in scarlet. A large pot bubbled away on top of a stove to the left. A wood fire beneath it flamed away as the woman lifted a cleaver and sliced through the slivers of meat.

To the side of the table, Alice could see the partially skinned ribs and torso of a recent kill. A lump formed in her throat and a nauseating feeling filled her as she noticed the nipple and partial shoulder of the carcass.

It was too small to have been a man, leaving Alice to surmise that it had once been a young boy. A boy that was near her age.

Tricia used the cleaver to slide the strips of flesh to one side of the chopping board. She reached to another portion of the body that was resting at the other end of the table.

An arm.

The boy's left arm.

The little left hand slapped onto the chopping board loudly, splaying its little left fingers out wide.

Alice felt both sick and infuriated at the same time.

Her mind raced with images of a little boy suffering at the hands of the Scarlet Queen. She pictured Tricia slashing and cutting a terrified, defenceless child. She saw the woman laughing witlessly as she chopped and hacked, tore and rent bone, sinew, and flesh. The vision changed to that of Arthur being tormented by Takmel. She imagined her husband being beaten and bruised before having his arm removed.

His left arm.

"So nice to see you, Alice," Tricia said politely. "I'm just preparing supper."

Alice stepped on into the room.

"You need to stop now," the girl breathed. She glowered at the Scarlet Queen, who moved to the pot with the cleaver still in her hand. She lifted a wooden spoon resting on the edge of the stove and stirred the pot.

"Smells delightful," she said, pleased with herself. "You must try some."

"Tricia," Alice said more sternly. "You need to stop."

"Stop what?" the other woman asked. Her face was bright and smiling. "I had the captains and a skipper for dinner. My girls enjoyed him. Did you see them at the table? They must be getting hungry out there."

"Tricia?"

"This one is Samuel." She jabbed the spoon at the stew bubbling on the stove. "He is such a good boy. Not quite the same as Thedric." She looked away, as if in deep thought. "Nothing could replace my Thedric."

"Tricia, please," Alice urged, stepping closer.

"Alice, I must insist that you stop interrupting," the woman warned. She dropped the spoon and held the cleaver defensively in her right hand as she faced the girl.

"You need to stop," Alice yelled.

Tricia flicked her left wrist and held her palm up to Alice.

Alice slid backwards across the floor. She felt she was being pushed towards the door.

Planting her feet solidly onto the ground, Alice waved her hand from left to right.

"Enough," she retorted. Tricia suddenly lifted from the ground and thrown through the air. She smacked against a sideboard on the other side of the kitchen. The cupboard's doors flung open and its contents spilt across the floor.

Tricia's head hit the hardest. A large cut had formed on her forehead above her right eye, spilling blood over her face and down her neck.

Slowly, she lifted herself to her feet, cleaver still gripped in her hand.

She lifted her other hand to the wound and brought it back to see her fingers smeared in red. A furious scream followed as Tricia glared at the girl by the door.

Alice prepared herself for what was to come.

The Scarlet Queen sprinted over the floor, cleaver held high above her head. As she drew closer, she brought the blade down in an arc towards Alice.

Alice crouched as she swung her sword at an upright angle.

Tricia overshot her approach. Alice's blade sank into her torso as she plunged the cleaver into the doorframe behind her target.

Taking a few steps backwards, the Scarlet Queen removed herself from the sword in Alice's hands. She pressed her back against the bench top and touched the seeping hole in her belly.

A strange noise emitted from Tricia's throat that seemed to Alice to be a cross between a cry of pain and call of surprise.

"Look what you did," the Scarlet Queen finally said. "I thought we were friends."

"Friends?" Alice furrowed her brow as she lifted herself to full height.

Tricia reached behind her, slapping her hand onto portions of flesh, bone, table and finally a long carving knife.

She lunged for Alice again.

The girl saw the flames dancing in the fire.

In the blink of an eye, she waved her hand as if summoning the flames towards her. She twisted her hand, and the fire coiled together like a thick, glowing thread. It struck the Scarlet Queen in the back and spread across her shoulders.

Tricia dropped the knife and screamed in fright.

Alice stretched her hand to the woman as the flames engulfed the scarlet dress.

She clenched her fingers together tightly, making a fist. The fire grew with intensity and devoured Tricia's flesh.

A shrill, ear-shattering shriek streamed from the burning woman's mouth as her skin bubbled and cracked.

Suddenly, the screaming ceased, and Tricia fell to the kitchen floor in a fiery heap.

Alice watched for a while, telling herself that she was simply making sure the Scarlet Queen was dead. But a part of her, after seeing the remains of a young boy on the kitchen bench, wanted to watch the woman burn away to ash.

When she felt satisfied, she walked out through the door and back into the dining room.

The three women, murdered by Tricia, still sat by the hearth.

Alice didn't feel right leaving them like that for wild animals to find. She stretched her hand towards the fire as she moved through the room.

Streams of flames flowed from the fireplace and touched the hems of curtains, tapestries, and the canvas of the paintings on the walls.

As she walked through the corridor, back to the main doors of the mansion, fire moved through the building behind her. It rolled up the stairwell, surged along the walls, and set everything alight.

Alice moved back onto the open ground, and into the blizzard to recover her cloaks. She quickly put them on as the manor burst into flames.

Placing two fingers in her mouth, she gave a whistle.

Liana turned from her next attack upon the inferno that once was Blackrock Haven and glided towards the girl awaiting her on the ground.

Alice strapped herself to the saddle as she watched the mansion burn.

"Let's go," she commanded the beast. Liana leapt into the air and, within a few beats of her massive wings, she was soaring high above the ground.

With a quick glance about, Alice surveyed the damage. Every building in the township was aflame. Great pillars of smoke poured from the windows of the stone manor on the hill, forming a thick blanket of dark cloud before the gale spread it thinly into the air. Bodies of soldiers littered the ground near the mansion. Charred remains of men and dark creatures lay lifelessly in the streets below.

The girl lifted her scarf over her nose again before pulling the leather cowl of her outer layer over her head.

"Home, girl," she called over the howl of the wind.

Liana levelled herself and spread her wings wide. She glided at a tremendous speed as the wind blowing from the north pushed her from behind.

Alice took another look over her shoulder, watching the light of fire gradually disappear in the haze and fog of the blizzard.

Blackrock Haven was no more.

The Scarlet Queen was dead.

Twenty-Four

Takmel gripped the railing of the stable pen. His knees felt weak and his chest tightened. A few steeds, munching on stubble, twisted their ears as they watched him curiously. He was breathing slowly, gripping a bar that separated two chargers.

The scent of smoke filled his nostrils, and the taste of ash-covered his tongue. His skin felt hot and the backs of his eyes burned. He saw flames streaking across his mother's face. The canvas upon which she was painted peeled and bubbled as fire took hold. Hundreds of his dark creatures lay scorched and crumbling to ash in the snow.

The imagery vanished, and the feeling quickly subsided, and suddenly, he was back in the stable. The aroma of straw, horsehair, and manure sent his stomach into a spin. He could usually handle such odours. This sensation was strange to him.

"Maji?" A stable worker, gathering discarded straw into a pile near the rear of the barn, dropped his rake and rushed to Takmel's side. "Are you all right? Perhaps you should sit for a while."

"I'm fine," he replied, swallowing hard and regaining his composure. "It's nothing."

He turned and placed a hand on a grey mare standing in the pen with him.

"I can brush her, if you like," the worker offered. "You should get inside out of this weather."

The man, a young sapling not much older than Takmel, gestured to the snow gently falling outside the stable doors.

"I'll determine what I should and shouldn't do," Takmel replied.

"My apologies, Maji." The young man lowered his stare and bowed slightly. His voice quivered with fear as he suddenly remembered to whom he was speaking. "I didn't mean to disrespect you."

Takmel glared at him for a long time, contemplating ways to punish the stable worker. His demeanour relaxed as his stomach eased.

"Brush her and continue with your duties," the Maji instructed before walking to the doors.

"Yes, Maji," the young man answered.

Takmel trudged through the ankle-deep snow. He followed a lane, covered by the white blanket of powdered frost, that led around the side of his castle to a servants' access to the rear. By the time he reached the door, she was there waiting for him. Her eyes welled with tears.

"Tricia," she said. "They've taken Tricia, now."

He stepped inside the door and into a warm, spacious kitchen. His arms moved around her shoulders as she fell into him.

"I need to send patrols out," he told her. "I need to find more wives."

She pulled away from him a little. Her face wore the expressions of disbelief, confusion and a bit of disgust.

"How can you think in such a way?" she questioned. "Tricia was just murdered, and you want to replace her already?"

He sighed. "Isabel," he whispered. "I love all of you. I love Tricia, Joanne, Gilda and Lucy still. I even love Catherine. But this was inevitable. Alice and the others were going to try to attack, eventually. I just didn't believe it would be so soon.

"We now number five," he continued. "Catherine is no longer one of us. We are linked, but she sides with them. So, we need to replenish our numbers."

"Replenish?" She shook her head slightly. "Like provisions in the storehouse?"

"Of course not," he replied. His attention quickly moved to two figures standing in the space behind her. The girls were watching him intently, holding their puppies in their arms. They shared a worried expression.

"You mean more to me than the entire world. I will protect you and these girls until my dying breath. No one could replace you." Takmel pulled her into him and kissed her forehead. "I promise."

He looked at the twins again, quickly glanced at their dogs, and moved his gaze back to the girls' faces. They continued to look at him with concern.

He smiled sympathetically. "It'll be all right."

***

By late afternoon, the ground forces had marched to Belburn. Thornton and Yuri took a scouting party of eight additional Agrodien warriors and seven men into the empty township. They spread out into a line of sorts, moving from building to building and keeping within earshot and eyesight of each other.

A pack of hounds, turned feral over time, had found shelter in barns and damaged huts near the southern end of the large village. Yuri urged them out of the shelters, where he discovered them by clapping his hands and hissing at them angrily.

Others who had seen his success with this tried the same tactic. It worked mostly, but occasionally saw a pack turn on a soldier or reptilian. The result was always a call for help and retaliation with bows or blades.

"We eat them?" Yuri pointed to the recently killed dogs on the floor of a hut he had entered. "Cook on fire."

Thornton peered over at him with a disgusted face.

"You can eat them all you want," he replied. "I'll stick to the dried beef and fresh bread in my saddlebag, thank you."

"Good!" Yuri smiled. "Dog, good meal. Very good."

"I'll take your word for it." Thornton sheathed his sword and moved outside.

A gentle breeze blew from the northeast, bringing light snow that flittered in all directions. Some floated down and almost touched the white blanket draped over the rolling hills, only to be blown back into the air by the wind.

Thornton turned his head this way and that, stretching his neck and shoulders as Hugh Brook stomped over the frost, crunching it loudly beneath his boots.

"We've checked the last of the farmhouses on the hills down there," he said, pointing to a river that passed by Belburn, stretching from the mountains to the north and into the distance to the south-east. It flowed steadily and was hemmed by long stalks of browning grass and reeds. Some waterfowl lingered near the banks, playing and splashing in the shallows. "Everything is clear. Couple of cows got into a hut and got stuck trying to get back out. The lads helped them a bit by carving them up for supper. I don't think anyone will mind."

"Don't think so," Thornton agreed. He turned to the house and shouted into the door. "Yuri. You still going to eat those dogs?"

"Dog, good meal," the Agrodien called back.

"Just making sure," the other said. "My boys got themselves a couple of fresh cows, if you're interested. Probably not as good as dog, I suppose."

"Dog, good meal," Yuri repeated, walking through the door and into the open with a broad smile on his face. "Cow much better."

***

Yuri and Thornton took to finding huts close together, intact and clean enough for the queen, Ursula and Catherine to shelter in. Emily remained with her daughter and Nola'ee kept vigil over them both. The three were inseparable, and no one dared to make it otherwise. Brondt placed them together in one shelter and set two guards outside their door.

Ursula and Thornton set up camp inside a hut next to the mother, daughter, and reptilian bodyguard. The men under his command received two cabins a short distance away.

Amicia and Brondt settled for a small hut across the lane from the others. It was nothing more than one room with an iron stove to the side. The door had fallen off and rested on the floor. This was taken outside by soldiers and used as kindling for a campfire set in the middle of the street.

They hung two thick blankets over the doorway to act as a temporary flap, blocking out the elements and keeping the warmth emitting from the stove inside. As Brondt organised the night patrols, set the shifts and checked on the progress of his men who were setting up camp, Amicia fixed the cabin up. She set bedding down and arranged it as best as she could for both herself and her husband.

She looked about her and didn't know whether to laugh or cry.

The blanket covering the door moved aside.

"Am I interrupting?" Ursula asked, popping her head in through the door. She saw the sad look on Amicia's face. "What is it?"

"Just a silly thing," she admitted.

Ursula stepped into the room, letting the flap close behind her.

"Tell me."

"I was just thinking about my home," the queen said. "I was comparing it to this room. How my home has many large rooms with fancy decorations. And how this is a small box by comparison. But then, I thought of how people, possibly a whole family, had lived here once. And now I feel very guilty for comparing my comfortable lifestyle to the one that would have been experienced by the previous occupants of this room. This house."

She was a bawling mess by the end of this account. Ursula had some trouble understanding her completely.

"You'll be back in the palace again," the younger woman soothed, putting her arms around the queen.

"No," Amicia snapped. She shook her head and looked Ursula in the eyes with sincerity. "That's not the point. Part of me, deep, deep inside, believed myself to be better than these people. And, I'm not."

Ursula stepped back to allow the queen some room.

"I wasn't always a queen," she continued. "I took Newholt by force. I called myself Queen Elynbrigge and forced everyone to do the same. The people only made me their queen by choice after I rebelled against the Sovereign.

"I'm not a real queen. I think it might be time to cease being Queen Elynbrigge and truly become Amicia Brondt."

"What about Newholt?" Ursula asked. "They will need someone to guide them now, after what has happened."

"Maybe it's time for them to find a new leader," she said.

Ursula let out a long breath. "Have you talked to your husband?"

"About this?" Amicia asked. The other woman inclined her head. "No. But I will."

"Good," said her friend, placing her hand reassuringly on the queen's arm. "What I actually came for was to tell you they are roasting beef over the fire out here. Care to join us?"

Amicia wiped her eyes. She linked her arm with the Ursula's and together, they went outside.

***

Versel bit into a rabbit leg that had been cooking over the fire. She and her ten men had pulled their horses to a small oak grove on the edge of a field, where they sheltered for the time being. The trees had lost their leaves, exposing bare twisted branches that reached out in wide circles. It wasn't much cover, but it was better than being in the open.

The snow fell more rapidly, and two soldiers had requested to stop so they could relieve themselves and put another layer of clothing on. She obliged, but not because she wanted to comply with their demands or because it was getting dark. She was simply hungry.

Using a bow strapped to her steed, she took out the rabbit with one shot. Not all her men were so fortunate. Out of the ten travelling with her, one was left to pick at the scraps left by the others who could catch their own meals.

"Here you go, Willis," one man said, throwing a tiny front leg over to the unlucky man seated by the fire.

The tiny limb plopped onto the snow at Willis' feet. He grudgingly picked it up between his forefinger and thumb and scrutinised it, scrunching up his face as if the tiny leg were something that should not exist.

"Fuck you, Radcliffe," Willis snapped, throwing the little limb into the fire. "I wouldn't even be able to pick my teeth with that."

"If you had something in your teeth worth picking," another man jeered. The rest of the band chuckled, except for Versel. She looked towards Willis with a sideways glance and broke her roasted bunny in half at the waist.

"Fuck you all," Willis moaned, lowering his head and pulling his cloak about him tightly.

This amused the men even more.

"After everything I did for you," Radcliffe said, laughing and spitting pieces of meat in the process. "That could have fed some poor peasant and his family for a year out here."

Willis looked as if he might even cry as the men roared with hilarity.

"Here," Versel said, offering the fore-section of her rabbit to the soldier. Willis looked at her in question. "Take it before I eat it."

He didn't hesitate, snatching it from her hand and taking it to his mouth. He paused, holding the portion of rabbit an inch from his lips.

"Thank you, General," Willis muttered.

"Shut up and eat," she told him. "I can't have a weak man under my command."

Willis bit into the chest and tore away a flake of meat with his teeth.

"General," Radcliffe murmured with a shake of his head. "I think that might take me some time to get used to. I mean, how does that work?" He held a rabbit's leg in his hand and pointed it across to her casually. "One minute, you're a lieutenant. Then you're suddenly a general."

"Ease off," a man seated beside him advised quietly.

"I'm just asking a question," Radcliffe replied.

Versel ignored him and continued eating. The joviality shared between the men quickly vanished, and a heavy silence fell upon each of them.

"You're new to this company," the other man told him. "You would be better off eating your bunny and doing what you're told."

"Nah." Radcliffe raised his chin defiantly. "I want to know. How does a woman become a lieutenant in an army, anyway? There aren't any other women in the army that I know of." He turned his attention back to Versel. "So, how did you do it? Did you bed the boy back in Wintermarsh? Are you one of the Maji's favourite fucks? Is that it? I mean, you're a fine woman with your blonde hair and big tits. Anyone would want to have a go of you. Why not him? Did he make you general because you can spread your legs so very wide? Did you put your lips on his—"

Radcliffe gagged.

He wasn't able to breathe.

A gurgling sound emitted from his mouth as blood spilled over his chin and onto his chest plate.

His hand went to his neck, where he found the hilt of the dagger that Versel had thrown from across the fire.

When his mind stopped racing and the confusion subsided, all he could think about was how quick she had been. He didn't even see her move.

She got up and calmly walked around the fire to crouch in front of him. Slowly, she withdrew her blade from his throat and wiped it clean upon his tunic before placing it back into her belt.

"That's how I became general," she whispered. She took the rabbit from his hands and threw it to Willis.

"Thank you, General," he said gratefully.

"I told you to shut up and eat," she growled as she moved back around the fire to her place. "All of you shut up and eat."

Radcliffe wasn't gagging or spilling blood anymore. Instead, he tipped onto his side in the snow and stared lifelessly at the horses tethered to the trees nearby.

Twenty-Five

Alice passed over the Forest of Khun as the light dimmed upon the western horizon. Snow-covered mountain peaks drew nearer as Liana descended. The dragon slowly banked to the left, then right as she used the sweeping winds flowing through the gorges to glide in a south-westerly direction. The wind had carried them more quickly than Alice had expected. She increasingly noticed familiar sights such as the shape of mountains' peaks and landforms. At one point, for a fleeting moment, she saw the Rakmha Trench pass beneath her.

They were almost home.

Gradually, the land levelled more and more until Alice saw the glade before her. The dragon flapped her wings and angled her feet to the earth. She bounded once before stopping at the mouth of the cave.

Alice cocked her head, sensing something wasn't quite right.

Liana chirped and looked excitedly towards the cavern. She turned slightly, as if she was about to enter.

"Whoa," the girl called. "Wait until I get off."

The dragon froze in place and chirped again. Her voice echoed through the dark confines of the cave.

A chirp replied. Alice stared into the mouth of the cavern as she released her legs from the straps. She kept her gaze fixed upon the darkness as she dropped her pack and other supplies onto the ground by her dragon's side.

Liana chirped again, bobbing her head up and down eagerly.

The girl slid off the side of the beast and quickly unfastened the bridle and saddle. These she tried to remove in haste as Liana was becoming more and more impatient.

"Settle down," Alice said, rubbing the dragon's snout as she strode past to attend to more fastenings.

Finally, with all the equipment removed, Liana crawled into the cavern with no acknowledgment to her rider.

"And goodnight to you, too," Alice said with a smile as she watched the tail of the beast disappear into the darkness.

Several other chirps emitted from the cave. A chorus of excited beasts gathered deep inside.

Alice picked up the saddle and bridle together and moved them to a place just inside the cave's mouth, against the wall. She then picked up her other belongings, hanging her canvas bags over her shoulders before trudging towards the cabin.

She listened to the chirps reverberating from the shadows as she spied fires lit in the treeline to the northern edge of the clearing, where huts had been built for the Agrodien. The northerners also had a roaring hearth near their shelters to the western edge. Light streamed from beneath the door of her own house, but not a living thing could be seen, save for a few dogs running about and the livestock on the open field to the east.

She stepped upon the porch and stomped her feet to remove any snow from her boots.

"Who's that?" she heard a familiar voice call.

"It's me, David," she replied.

"Alice?" Arthur was on his feet and running to her. His arm was around her shoulders and his body pressed against hers before she had time to react.

She felt tired and heavily laden with all her equipment still attached to her. Her legs ached, and she almost fell back off the veranda when he embraced her enthusiastically.

A great beaming smile spread over her face, and she wrapped her arms around him and squeezed him tightly.

"I missed you," she whispered into his ear.

David moved to the door.

"We didn't even hear you arrive," he said, looking past her and towards the open ground. "Where's your mother?"

"On her way to Dweagan, I expect," she answered as Arthur pulled away.

"Dweagan?"

"I sent them to salvage what they can," Alice told him as she moved by him and into the cabin. Seated at the table were three Haigok, Gruloch amongst them. "It's good to see you again, my friend."

The Haigok rose to their feet politely.

"And you, Kayl'sro." Gruloch bowed slightly.

"When did you arrive?" she asked, plopping her supplies onto the sitting room floor.

"Around the middle of the day," he answered. She gestured for the guests to sit as she slid out of her cloaks. "We weren't sure whether we should stay when we were informed that you weren't here."

"I'm glad you did," she said as she sat down at the head of the table. "Have quarters been arranged for you and your companions yet?"

"Yes, thank you," the other answered as Arthur sat by Alice, and David by his son. "Your husband was kind enough to set up cots in your backroom here."

"In the storeroom?" Alice looked at her husband. She then peered at the door leading to the rear of the cave into which she had built her cabin.

"It's quite warm if we keep the stove hot and the door open," Arthur told her. "Besides, all the other huts are occupied, and the weather hasn't been the best for sleeping in tents."

"Where are Aunt Linet and Uncle Lor?"

"They've taken a hut from the northerners," David answered. "It's all right," he assured her. "Glaun, Kygra and their wives are sharing for the time being so your aunt and uncle can tend to Sevrina."

"The baby?" Alice looked at Arthur with concern.

"Not yet," he said and placed his hand on hers. "Soon though."

She turned her attention back to Gruloch.

"Sorry," she said.

"I understand," he said. "You are thinking of your people, just as a genuine leader should."

"And what brings you to my home again so soon?"

"I have instructed my riders to send word to all the Haigok clans about the need for an alliance," he replied. "They have all returned with a response. The leaders of my kind are willing to talk. I have invited them here to meet you.

"I apologise for being so presumptuous in this," he continued. "I didn't know you had gone and thought you would have remained either here or in Woodmyst."

"No need to apologise," she told him. "We had to act. The sooner we can defeat the Maji's queens, the less chance he has of reaching his full potential."

"So, he's not as powerful as he could be?" Gruloch asked.

"He is very powerful; more powerful than I believe even he is aware of. But, no, he isn't as powerful as he could be," Alice replied. "How soon before the clan leaders arrive?"

Gruloch took a moment to think.

"If my riders reach them and don't come across any trouble," he answered, looking at her with his bulbous yellow orbs, "it will be three days. Perhaps four."

"How many leaders?" David asked.

"There are five," answered Gruloch. "And they will each have an entourage of lieutenants and a handful of warriors."

"And a lot of dragons, I expect," David put in.

"This is accurate," the other said. "Each will ride a dragon of their own as well as others carrying supplies."

"Do you know how many dragons for certain?" Arthur asked.

"No," said Gruloch. "It all depends upon how much they bring with them."

"We'll need to move the livestock to somewhere safe," the big man muttered.

"We'll need to arrange lodging," Arthur fretted. "We don't have the room."

"You don't need to concern yourself with shelter," Gruloch informed the young man. "We bring our own when a gathering is called. But the livestock will need to be moved," he said to David. "For two reasons. The first is obvious and is, as you suspect. The dragons are not all trained as ours. Some keep a level of ferocity and will need to be kept away from by everyone. There is one clan of Haigok to the west who have a wild streak. Their dragons are as mad as they. We don't talk with them very often.

"They use their dragons to steal livestock from farmers on the plains between the inland sea and Spine Mountains. Or, at least they did before the Mirikin wiped out most of mankind in that region. How they have never been sighted by any of your kind is beyond me."

"The inland sea and Spine Mountains?" David quizzed.

"I think we refer to them as the Sea of Solace and the Ranges of Kailibard," Arthur explained.

"Kailibard." Gruloch pointed to the boy. "Yes."

"And what is the other reason?" Alice asked.

"Hmm?" Gruloch looked at her, a little perplexed.

"Why we will need to move the livestock."

"Oh! We will need a large area to establish a camp for at least two days."

"And you will stay with us during the gathering as our guests," Alice insisted, looking at the three Haigok. "All of you."

"We will," replied Gruloch, before gesturing to the Haigok to his left. "Except for Bhurukh here. He will leave for Mohaa in the morning to inform my people. The rest of my entourage will arrive a day or so afterwards."

"An army of dragons," Arthur murmured.

"Don't get too hopeful," the Haigok leader told him. "We have not involved our kind in open war for thousands of years. We have kept well-hidden from the eyes of man for all of that time. Some of the clan leaders may wish to continue to do so. Until now, they have had no dealings with your kind and might prefer it if they never do.

"If this is how the meetings end," Gruloch continued, "with none of the other clans agreeing to support you, I swear my dragons will fly by your side and see this through to the end."

"Thank you," Alice replied. "That means a great deal to me. To all of us." She looked at her husband and David, who both showed agreement.

David got to his feet. "We should eat and talk some more. Not about fighting or battle. Let's talk about things of goodness. As friends."

"Agreed," the lord of the Haigok said cordially.

"So?" David began. "Where's your mother and sister?"

"Possibly on their way to battle," she replied sheepishly.

Twenty-Six

The troop packed camp early in the morning, before the sun breached the horizon, and set out for Dweagan.

Brondt kept his word to Andris, allowing the former commander of the black forces to take his leave. The younger man packed his gear and opted to stay with the company instead.

They rode for most of the day, enduring a light snowfall and the occasional gust of wind at their backs.

During the crossing of the great plain, they drove their horses through a wide river. It wasn't deep, but the foot soldiers were forced to bear with the cold water that covered them to their knees. Still, none complained even when the chill wind attacked their damp legs, bringing a frosty sting upon their skin.

Some sang cheerfully to take their mind off the conditions.

I met a girl from Byview,
Who gave herself to me.
She had no teeth and had no hair,
And her eyes could barely see.
I gave her bronze for bedding,
She wrapped her legs 'round me.

"That's enough!" Thornton barked. He looked at the women travelling in the group remorsefully. His stare met with Amicia momentarily and he was about to apologise when he was forestalled.

"There's no other girl like the Byview girl," Ursula sang at the top of her lungs, "who made my balls itch-ee. I met a girl from Freymoor…"

"Ursula!" Thornton gasped.

"What?" She turned to look around her. "Why has everyone stopped?"

Laughter erupted in the ranks. Thornton eyed the men angrily. For a moment, he forgot who Ursula was, or at least who she had been.

She was the madam of three whores. She had spent most of her adult life in a tavern, exposed to the most vulgar talk and sailor songs in the world. Still, he didn't like the idea of her listening to such a degrading ditty. He was taken aback, even more, when he heard her singing along with it.

"Ease off, George," said Amicia. "The men need some release."

Brondt gave his wife an astounded stare. He then looked to Thornton, who stared questioningly to his superior.

"Don't look at me," Brondt instructed. "I take orders from her."

Ursula looked about at Catherine and Emily, who were both attempting to stifle their laughter.

"Excellent," she called out merrily. "Everybody. I met a girl from Freymoor, who gave herself to me."

The men marching behind the horse riders joined in enthusiastically.

She had a beard and a giant rump,

And was big as big could be…

***

Alice had gone to visit Liana twice in the morning. The dragon slept deeply through both visits, even with the noise of two more winged beasts chirping and coughing about her.

On returning to the cabin, she found Arthur pouring tea for two of their Haigok guests. They were all seated around the table again. Alice looked towards the bedrooms as she removed her cloak before hanging it on a hook by the door.

"Where's David?" she asked.

"He's gone to check on Sevrina," Arthur answered. "Have you seen them yet?"

"No." Alice reached for her cloak. "I should see them. Aunt Linet must be worried."

"You'll sit down, is what you'll do," the boy instructed. "You've not been home a day yet, and you haven't stopped fretting. You need to rest."

She left the cloak where it hung and moved to the table under the watchful eye of Gruloch.

"You do look tired," the lord of the Haigok told her.

"I have so much to do," Alice said as she sat down. "I haven't seen Galonia. She must be worried about Yuri."

"I'm worried about you," Arthur told her as he poured her a cup of steaming brew.

"How is Liana?" Gruloch enquired.

"She is still sleeping," she answered. "I think the journey took it out of her."

"Then, you should learn a lesson from her," the other instructed. "Take time to sleep. Let your body heal. Those other things can wait. If these people you are so concerned with really care for you, they would tell you the same as I have."

"There," Arthur said, placing the teapot onto the stove. "If you won't listen to me, listen to him."

She grinned as she lifted her cup to her lips. Arthur sat down beside her and lifted his own mug. His eyes moved to her braid. Neat intertwined hair rested upon her shoulder and draped onto her chest. He noticed, just behind her ear, that dark roots had formed near her temples.

She noted his stare and turned to look him in the eye. She smiled as she touched his thigh with her right hand, still nursing her mug in her left.

"What is it?" she asked.

He shook his head. "It's as if I have just seen the most beautiful girl in the world," he said.

Her cheeks turned red as she shot a quick glance towards the guests. They said some quick words in their own tongue and chuckled.

"Arthur," she chided, slightly embarrassed.

He put his cup on the table and reached his hand to hers, which rested upon his lap.

"I love you, Alice Gyfford," he announced. "And I don't care how many Haigok know it."

She giggled.

"Well done!" Gruloch thumped the table gently with his fist. "Honest words from a prince of hearts."

"My prince," Alice said with a playful grin as she leant in to kiss her husband on the cheek.

"My queen," he replied, lifting her hand to his lips.

Gruloch clapped his hands joyfully.

**

The township was busy with people bustling about in the market-place as horse-drawn carts paraded through the streets carrying supplies for digging, or the spoils of hard labour. Most of the men wore dirty coveralls and were caked in mud and silt from the work they did. Others wore the outfits of soldiers, merchants, and bookkeepers. There were women too. Some purchased stores while others sold themselves.

General Saruun Versel kept a hand squeezed around the hilt of her sword that was slung upon her hip. Her helmet's visor was closed as she scanned the scene about her.

"Stay focused," she said to Willis, riding by her side. "This is Iron-fields after all."

"Do you think Risha is here?" he enquired.

"Doubtful," she answered, eyeing a group of five warriors strolling along a boardwalk on the side of the muddy road. She gestured for her men to watch the approaching soldiers. "We're not here for him right now."

"Girls," Willis stated, remembering their orders.

"Not just girls, lad," one of the other soldiers put in. "The Maji has a particular taste. If it were just girls that he wanted, we could find enough of them in Wintermarsh for him to have his fill of."

"Ones with powers," the younger man clarified.

"Witches," Versel said bluntly as the soldiers on the walkway stepped in front of the riders. She pulled her steed to a halt. Her soldiers followed suit. "You're blocking our passage."

"It *is* a woman in there," one man sniggered.

"Shut up," an older one barked before turning his attention to Versel. "What business have you here?"

"We are here on orders of the Maji," she replied. "We intend to find lodging and use this village as a base during our assignme—"

"We don't recognise the Maji here," the other sneered. "We take our instruction from General Risha."

Versel glared at the older warrior for a moment. Her eyes flitted to the boardwalks on either side of the streets, the narrow alleys between buildings and the roads intersecting the path near to where she and her men were. She noticed more uniformed men with blades in their hands, ready to pounce.

"Is Risha here?" Versel queried.

"General Risha," the older soldier corrected her.

"We don't recognise his title as our master did not grant it to him," she told him. "So, I'll ask again. Is Risha here?"

The riders noticed their cue and pulled their blades halfway out of their sheaths, flashing a portion of their steel to those around them. Merchants, bookkeepers, workers and cart drivers froze in place. Some bystanders vanished into doorways or dashed away from the impending threat of violence.

"You're a smug bitch," the older man spat. "I'll give you that."

"Move aside," the general commanded. She pulled her blade free for all of Ironfields to see. "Or I'll give you this."

"You're a woman," one of the other soldiers jeered. "Show us what a woman can do to us?"

Versel pointed to the man.

An arrow suddenly appeared in his face, flung from a rider's bow.

"How's that, for starters?" she answered as the warrior fell face-first onto the ground. The arrow pierced the back of his skull as the ground pushed it through upon impact.

The rest of her band raced forwards and charged over the four remaining men, knocking them to the ground.

Versel dropped from her steed and strode over to the older soldier, who was on his back, scrambling to get to his feet. She plunged her sword deep into his chest and gave a twist.

He coughed, spitting blood over his chin as he stared at her with disbelief. His eyes flickered shut as she retrieved her blade.

She turned to see the other three men rising to their feet, drawing their swords and glaring at her wildly. Her hands gripped the hilt of her blade, and she prepared herself for an attack.

The riders leapt from their horses as more soldiers filtered through the alleyways and into the street. Swords clashed, and blood spilt as women screamed and working men fled in fear.

Versel cut down the first of the three with ease, lopping his head off in one sweep. She then lunged for the next, who blocked her blow with his own weapon. The third man attacked, trying to hit her in the back with a wide stroke.

The general jumped to the side.

The blade missed her by less than an inch.

She quickly leant towards him and jabbed her elbow into his forehead. The pointed steel guard covering her joint broke through his skull at the nose and teeth. He dropped his sword and fell to his knees as chunks of bone, mucus, and blood spilled over his torso.

He made a sickening sound of gurgles and screams as the general turned back to the other soldier.

She saw his sword coming for her head. In a flash, she brought her blade up and repelled the attack. The impact vibrated along her arm as she stepped back a few paces, knocked off balance by the blow. She almost tripped over the injured foe kneeling on the ground.

The screaming man continued to cry out as he tried to force a long trail of blood-soaked flesh back into his mashed face. Versel lifted her boot and kicked him hard with her heel. It sank into the same wound she had made with her elbow, only widening it, crunching more bone and flesh deeper into his head.

He fell lifeless to the ground as the last soldier lunged at her again. She stepped to the side, allowing the other to rush past her as he overshot his attack.

He stumbled and tripped over his fallen comrade before tumbling to the ground.

General Saruun Versel saw her opportunity.

She stepped after him as he landed spread-eagled on the road. His sword slid away, landing in a pile of horse dung.

"Shit," he spat.

She dug her sword into the back of his neck and pushed it through until it hit the dirt.

The soldier's body went limp.

Versel placed her boot on his shoulder blades and pulled her blade free of him. She peered over at her men, who were cleaning up the last of their foes.

"Do we clean this mess up?" one of her men asked.

"Leave it for the good people of Ironfields to take care of," she replied as she placed her sword back in its sheath. "With luck, Risha will get wind of this and come looking for us."

"Won't that take us away from our mission?" Willis questioned.

She lifted her helmet off her head. Her golden hair fell over her back.

"An added bonus," she replied as she peered along the street to see people reappearing from their hiding places. Walking confidently to the centre of the nearest intersection, a few yards away, she called with authority to all within earshot, "I am General Saruun Versel, first Garrison Commander of the Maji. This township is now under my command. Spread the word. You now all belong to me."

Twenty-Seven

"Spread out," Brondt shouted. "Keep formation. I want them to see how many we are."

"So many!" Ursula gasped as she scanned the opposing force that had gathered on the next ridge.

"It would seem that dragon fire wasn't enough to dissuade them," Schoenbach remarked as he peered at the still smoking city of Dweagan in the distance.

"I would say it probably infuriated them," Karlena opined. "Look at them."

Countless men on horse and foot were in formation. Their jade banners proclaimed their allegiance to their dead queen, and ultimately their loyalty to the Maji. Their numbers were immense and their discipline impressive as they stood rigid in neat rows and columns, waiting patiently as the snow fell upon their helmets and shoulders.

The surviving forces from Newholt and Woodmyst, made up of soldiers and resistance fighters, combined and formed up as best as they could along the crest of a smooth hill overlooking a wide vale. Archers made a line at the front with foot soldiers in rows behind them. Stretching in each direction behind them were two rows of cavalrymen.

"They outnumber us," Thornton grunted to his commander.

"We've both survived more dismal odds than this," Brondt replied.

"We were both a lot younger when we did," the other responded.

"I want you to remain here with Ursula and Catherine," the commander said, turning to his wife.

She peered at the army facing them, then looked along the line to the north of their own men still forming up.

"We can help," she told Brondt.

"Then you help from here," he insisted. "There are only three of you. Alice isn't with you. Her dragon can't assist us. That battlefield is going to get messy and people are going to die. I do not want you to be one of them."

She agreed, understanding his concern.

"I'll stand watch over them," said Akasati.

"As will I," Ruttger put in. "If any of them make it up here, they'll have the two of us to deal with, at least."

"Don't be daft." Emily shook her head and turned to face Catherine. "I'm not leaving my daughter alone. Never again."

"I'm staying," Karlena said. "And so are you," she said to Schoenbach.

"Whatever you command, my love," he said.

"I guess we're family," Andris said to Emily. "I should probably stay with you and Catherine. Lor would kill me if I didn't."

"Indeed," Emily said.

"I stay," Nola'ee said. She looked at Emily and Catherine. "Kayl'sro tell me to protect you. I stay."

Yuri gave a thoughtful nod.

"Agrodien fight," he growled. "This good fight, me think."

Thornton chuckled as he scanned the opposing force. He guessed there were at least three thousand jade soldiers on the ridge facing them. He looked along the line of men beside him in each direction and speculated that they were a little over one thousand in total.

"Good fight?" he queried. "I want you fighting by my side, my insane friend."

The reptilian smiled, taking the compliment to heart.

**

Alice slept soundly in her bed. Arthur had checked on her a few times to assure himself that she was all right. Not once did she stir, not even when he accidentally thumped the door against the wall as he opened it.

She sank into a deep dream where she saw arrows filling the air so thick it reminded her of storm clouds. She saw men smashing into one another as if they were waves crashing upon rocks by the sea.

Severed limbs fell to blood-soaked snow as a great and terrible din of blades clashing and people screaming in pain filled her head. Bloodied, lifeless faces stared at the sky silently as boot heels and tumbling bodies mashed them into the ground.

Then she saw them.

Amicia, Ursula, and Catherine were standing on a hill overlooking the battle. Surrounding them was a small group of others she recognised. Her mother, Karlena, Akasati and Nola'ee were among them. They were bracing for a fight. A large throng of men, smeared in blood and mud and carrying jade banners, ran up the rise towards them.

Alice sat upright and gasped noisily.

Her heart raced in her chest and pounded in her ears.

"No," she huffed as she flung the covers from her body. She slid her feet into her boots and wrapped her cloak about her before leaving the room.

Arthur was in the sitting room reading a book. He looked up at her. "You've been asleep for a long..." His demeanour changed when he saw the worried look on her face. "What is it?"

Gruloch, half dozing in a chair across from the boy, opened his bulbous orbs wide and peered at her in question.

"They're about to die," she said, still breathing hurriedly.

"Who?" Arthur asked, getting up and moving to her. "Who's about to die?"

"My mother. My sister. All of them."

David, stirring a pot of stew in the kitchen, turned. "What's that about your mother?"

"I think I sent them to their doom," she said as tears welled in her eyes. "I need to go to them."

"Go where?" Gruloch asked, wiping his face.

"Dweagan," she answered. "They need me. They need Liana."

"No," the Haigok responded. "She isn't rested. She needs more time."

Alice looked around the room, trying to find something to help her; an answer to her problem. A tight knot formed in her gut as she wept.

"This is happening now?" Arthur enquired. "It's not something that has happened or is about to happen?"

"I don't know... I should be there."

Gruloch turned to the other Haigok sitting at the table. He said something in his tongue. The other responded by getting to his feet and rushing out of the door.

"Jhakarh and I will go," the lord of the Haigok said. "We will fly like the wind to get there."

With that, he strode to the door and closed it behind him.

"Thank you," David called after him. He wasn't sure if the other had heard him and felt a small amount of regret for not announcing his gratitude before Gruloch had vanished from sight. He looked over to his son and daughter-in-law. She was crying on Arthur's shoulder and he was trying to console her as well as a one-armed man could by holding her tightly.

David flopped onto a chair by the table and stared numbly at the other two. His mind raced with anxious thoughts pertaining to Emily. He wanted to be by her side now more than ever. The dull ache in his thigh from the arrow wound reminded him of why he was here, in the cabin, and not upon the battlefield with the woman he loved.

A frustrating feeling swept over him as he suddenly felt useless. He had once been the one to race into a battle headlong, without consideration. He remembered how he and Tomas had often charged into a fight, side by side, bravely. Stupidly.

And now, here he was, cooking a stew that bubbled away on the stove behind him while Emily possibly fought for her life in Dweagan.

What a strange, long path we have travelled, he thought.

***

Versel leant back in a chair with her feet upon a table. She had discarded her armour and placed it in a neat pile by the wall, but her sword was still slung upon her waist.

A roaring fire blazed away in the fireplace near to her as she drank rum from a tall mug. Her men sat about her, nursing their own vessels of grog. The crowd in the tavern commended them for what happened in the street and, as a result, bought them drinks as a means of gratitude.

She sipped her rum slowly, maintaining a set level of sobriety as she watched the others in the room about her. They seemed to be a jovial and friendly group of men and women.

A little too friendly to her liking.

Several women offered themselves to her men, unbuttoning their blouses and flashing their breasts to entice them away for an adventure upstairs. Willis, at one point, found his face buried in the cleavage of a young, buxom lady who plonked herself upon his lap.

"I'll take this one," she cackled as she pulled his head into her chest.

"How much?" Willis gasped when he came up for air.

"You think I'm some slut?" she asked, seemingly repelled by the question.

"Well..." He glanced around the table at the faces of his comrades. They were all stifling their quiet chuckles as he looked to them for help. Finally, a small smile spread over his face. "Yeah. How much?"

The table erupted with laughter.

"You little git," the woman spat as she got up. "I would have been the best thing that ever happened to you in your whole life."

"What?" Willis looked dumbfounded. "You're not a slut?"

She moved away.

"She weren't no slut," one of the other men chortled. "Stupid boy."

Willis was on his feet within a flash and chasing after her. "Wait," he called. "I'm sorry. I'll do anything."

As he vanished into the crowd, one of the other men leant forward. He rested his elbow on the table and looked at his commander.

"What's the next move, General?" he asked. His voice slurred, and he swayed a little.

"First thing, Reilly," she replied, keeping her eyes on the crowd. "You sleep the drink off. Second thing, we wait until our garrison arrives. After that, we begin our search."

"And how long before the garrison arrives?" another asked, watching a couple of young ladies standing by the bar. They were eyeballing him and smiling bashfully. He raised his cup and acknowledged them both, at which they covered their mouths with their hands and giggled.

"Tomorrow," Versel answered. "The day after, perhaps. What are you looking at over there, Norris?"

"I have to go," he replied, pushing his chair back and leaving the table. The others watched him as he approached the maidens by the bar. They couldn't hear what he said to either of them over the din, but they were all envious when the girls both put their arms around his waist before he escorted them up the stairs.

"Lucky bastard," Reilly snorted.

Versel noted Willis standing by the stairs, attempting to talk the young woman who he had assumed was a tavern slut into taking him back. The woman was doing everything possible to play hard to get. The general could see the man was pleading with her, almost appearing as if he was about to drop to his knees. She got to her feet, about to go over to him.

"Where are you going, General?" another man at the table asked. "Need some company?"

"Willis is making a fool of himself," she replied. "You stay here. I'll be right ba—"

The door of the tavern thrust open violently and slammed against the wall.

"Who the fuck made that mess outside?" a voice hollered.

The room fell deathly silent as a large hulk of a man accompanied by four soldiers stepped into the room. The man was garbed in dress uniform and looked to be more of a desk sitter than a warrior, with his oversized belly oozing over his belt buckle.

Versel lifted her sword from its sheath.

The crowd parted, forming a space between the door and the general.

"Those were my men that you killed, bitch," the man announced, stepping into the room. His men lined up behind him, pulling their blades free.

"Funny," Versel replied. "You don't look like Dakoth Risha."

"I ain't no bloody Dakoth Risha," he answered. "If he were here, you would be dead already. I'm the man who runs things when he isn't around, aren't I?"

"I wouldn't know, you fat pile of shit," she said. "Would I?"

"Insolent slag," he hissed as he pulled a dagger from his belt. "I'm Farouk Rhamahn. First Officer to General Risha. You are my priso—"

She leapt in quickly, slicing his belly open with a quick swing of her blade.

The large man fell to his knees as his intestines slapped loudly on the floor.

Versel's men leapt from the table with their own swords in their hands. They rushed to support their commander.

The four soldiers gauged their situation immediately and dropped their weapons to the floor. They raised their hands above their heads and fell to their knees.

"We surrender," one of them called.

"I am General Saruun Versel," she announced. "First Garrison Command…"

"We know who you are, General," another said. "We are not loyal to this man or General Risha. He said, if we didn't follow his orders, he would slaughter our wives and children."

"My garrison will arrive soon," Versel told the soldiers. "No harm will come to your families. Join our ranks. Fight for us. Fight for the Maji."

"Anything," another said. "We'll do anything you command."

"Good," she said as she placed her sword back into its sheath. She then pointed to the large body on the floor by her feet. "You can start by cleaning up this filth."

"Yes, General," they chorused as she turned to face the bar. She reached into her pocket and pulled a gold coin free before tossing it to the barkeep.

"Keep my armour safe," she called. The barkeep agreed and held the coin up thankfully.

"Where are you off to then?" Reilly asked as Versel made her way to the stairs.

"I've got an itch," she replied as she strode past Willis and took the young woman he was talking to by the arm. She started up the stairs with the girl, who complied without a second thought. Versel turned her face to the bemused young man. "You coming or not, Willis?"

He raced up the stairs, following his general and the young lady to the upper level and out of view.

Reilly shook his head as the remaining men of the troop watched on in astonishment.

"That's a real lucky bastard," he slurred.

Twenty-Eight

"Here they come," called Brondt.

He galloped behind the line of archers who stood at the front of his forces.

"Hold the line," Thornton roared to the infantry. "Don't be hasty. Make them come to us."

Throngs of Dweagan's men tore down the embankment and into the valley. Their cries rolled through the air, sounding like heavy, tumultuous rain falling upon the ground. Their boots thundered over the snow, tearing up the soil and turning the land to mud in their wake.

"Ready your bows," Brondt called as he pulled his steed to Thornton's side. He shot a quick glance at the hilltop behind his position. Three women on horseback, surrounded by a small gathering of protectors, watched on nervously.

"Ready your bows," another repeated along the line.

The commander took a deep breath as he returned his gaze to the approaching horde. Even from this distance, he could tell they were eager to tear him and his men apart. They were angry and wanted blood. Brondt understood their position very well. He had felt a similar sensation when he had spied his own city in ruin.

Now, Dweagan burned, and he was here to finish the work of the one who had set it aflame.

But first, he needed to overcome the obstacle before him; a moving wall of angry men.

Their cries grew louder, and their armour clinked with each stride they made.

"Nock!" the commander yelled.

The infantry of Dweagan reached the valley floor and started across the open ground. Their weapons, ranging from swords to axes and farming implements, clasped steadily in their hands as they ran.

"They're coming in waves," Thornton growled, nodding towards the rise across the way.

Sure enough, another pack of men started towards the floor of the vale.

"We can spare a few extra arrows," Brondt replied.

The first wave bolted over the ground, kicking up snow and grit. Their war cry was impressive, as was their stamina. Brondt secretly hoped that they would tire out before reaching the base of his hill.

He turned to peer back to Amicia. She and the other two had dropped to the ground.

"What is she doing?" he gasped.

"Ursula," Thornton huffed before turning his horse towards her.

"Hold position," Brondt commanded. He gestured towards Emily and the small band of people surrounding the women. "The others will protect them."

"They'd better," Thornton replied.

Brondt watched as Catherine reached her hands out to Ursula and Amicia. They each took hold; the queen on the left and the woman of Whitekeep on the right.

Ursula reached her hand to the sky as Amicia crouched and touched the ground. Catherine stood facing the valley. Her eyes were closed, and her face composed.

"Unite," she whispered, but her voice rang out like thunder through the air. A wave of energy expanded over Brondt and his army, into the valley and up the embankment across the way.

For a fleeting moment, the ground shook, and the air seemed to tremble.

The clouds above the vale darkened and appeared to bubble slowly as more and more snow fell through the sky.

The approaching infantrymen ignored the strange occurrence and pushed on.

"Draw," Brondt hollered.

The archers pulled back on their bowstrings. The sound of cords being tightened resounded along the line.

The men of Dweagan continued to call as they ran bravely towards the combined forces of Newholt and Woodmyst. They were nearly at the base of the rise.

The ground shook wildly beneath them as a shaft of crooked light shot down from the clouds.

White-hot light hit several men as the rest fell to the snow.

"Loose." Brondt pointed to the men in the vale.

A thick cloud of arrows flung into the sky. They arced high, clearing the embankment before plummeting towards the toppled men below.

Screams and cries of pain filled the air as shafts pierced the multitude of men.

"Again," Brondt called as he eyed the next wave vastly approaching.

"Draw," another called from down the line. "Loose."

More arrows streaked through the sky.

Some screams fell suddenly silent as others intensified.

Another shaft of light fell from the clouds and snaked its way along the fallen men.

A great clap of thunder erupted, causing the approaching throng to stop in their tracks.

They had barely made it halfway across the narrow valley when their bravery fell short.

"Now, they're having second thoughts," Thornton growled.

"Won't last long," Lieutenant Hugh Brook put in as he eyed the cavalry on the opposing hill.

As if to answer his intuition, someone blew a horn amongst the enemy.

"You had to open your fucking mouth," Thornton snarled.

Brook shrugged apologetically.

Countless steeds charged down the embankment at an immense speed. Their riders held swords high above their heads and flaunted the jade colours for all to see.

"We can't fight them up here," Brondt surmised. "It would bring them too close to the women."

"The Agrodien have already decided where the battle should take place," Symond Jendryng, the youngest of Thornton's men, announced. He pointed a little farther along the line to the south.

Yuri led a charge of reptilian riders down the hill at breakneck speed. The bulk of Brondt's cavalrymen followed keenly behind the Agrodien warriors.

Infantry and riders in the immediate vicinity of the commander looked to him for instruction.

"What are we waiting for?" he bellowed. "A formal invitation?"

With that, he kicked the sides of his steed and raced down the hill.

A great roaring cry discharged around him as his men raced after him towards the valley.

The men, already upon the open ground, braced themselves as horses hurried towards them from both directions.

"You need to stop," Emily instructed the three women. "They're going to fight."

Catherine opened her eyes and let the other women's hands-free.

"What?" Amicia got up and peered towards the valley. She saw mud and snow flying in all directions as the ground forces charged down the embankment.

"We could have taken them all from here," Catherine said coldly. "We still could."

Ursula shook her head.

"We can't risk it," she replied. "My George is down there."

"And my Jonathon," added the queen.

Catherine looked away and nodded. Tears welled as she turned away. Emily noticed and put her arms around her daughter.

"You did your best," she assured. "You did all that you could."

The girl nodded again and buried her head against her mother's shoulder.

"Perhaps we should reconsider," Ursula said, peering across the narrow valley to the ridge beyond. "There are more men over there. Waiting."

Amicia moved to her side, pulling her cloak tightly about her shoulders as the snow fell more steadily. She gave a small nod.

"We need you, Catherine," the queen said.

Yuri roared with fury as he urged his steed into the throng of Dweagan's men. They pummeled a few of the soldiers to the cold ground where they met the hooves of the horses following the Agrodien into battle.

One infantryman ducked below Yuri's outstretched blade and swung his own into the front leg of the horse. The steed let out an ear-shattering squeal as its limb came away at the joint. It toppled headfirst to the earth as Yuri leapt from its back.

The Agrodien angled his blade to the men below him as he arced through the air. The soldiers below turned their weapons in their hands to prepare for defending themselves.

But they were too slow.

Yuri landed on one man, crushing him to the floor as he swung his sword with ferocity. Another four were on the ground bleeding out before the others realised what was happening.

One attacked from behind, only to be cut down by Nakrah, who charged into the fight upon his horse. He crouched, perched upon his saddle as he stabbed and hacked into the enemy. The horse continued to charge through the horde, knocking men to the ground as it galloped.

Nakrah quickly considered whether he should continue with his horse, moving away from Yuri and the others who had joined him in the fight. He grabbed the reins with one hand and turned the steed to the left as he slashed and chopped down man after man.

The horse turned in a wide circle, galloping hard all the way, knocking many men of Dweagan to the ground. Some gathered themselves and rose to their feet, while others found a fatal end from the touch of the steed's hoof.

Eventually, one of the Dweagan soldiers attacked the approaching horse with an axe. The blade sank deep into the charger's muzzle, sending a spray of thick blood over Nakrah.

The steed fell, landing heavily upon the axeman. Nakrah rolled over the ground, caking himself in mud. He leapt to his feet and started cutting men down remorselessly.

He could see the other Agrodien warriors and men a short distance away. Only, there were countless men with jade tunics between him and his friends.

With a set determination, he started fighting his way through, cursing quietly for allowing himself to get so far away from his comrades.

A great rumble filled the air for all to hear. A woman's voice was carried upon it, speaking one solitary word.

"Unite."

Thornton crashed his steed into the foot soldiers as a blinding flash lit up the hill from where the enemy had advanced. He peered up to see several horses on the ridge set aflame from a shaft of light.

Ursula was hard at work, it appeared.

Several of the Dweagan soldiers stopped to gawk at the sight, giving Thornton and his men an advantage.

Without hesitation, he started cutting into the soldiers. He turned his horse to the left and urged it to walk sideways, to its right. The steed's body pushed the men on the ground, forcing them to back away. Thornton quickly plunged his sword into the three jade tunics next to him, dropping the men to the ground. His men followed suit, turning their horses similarly to form a line before hacking into the enemy relentlessly.

Another flash of light blared from the enemy's ridge. A low rumble emanated from high above. Thornton thought it was nothing more than thunder from the clouds.

That was until he heard Dweagan soldiers swearing and pointing back to the hill from where their comrades were descending.

He took a quick look and saw dust clouds bursting along the ridge. Large chunks of ground, rock, and soil spewed towards the sky like a water geyser, pushing man and horse into the air like tiny children's toys.

Part of the hill gave way and slid towards the valley floor, chasing after a second wave of charging horsemen.

Thornton lowered his gaze to the valley and saw the first wave of riders still approaching.

Brondt moved into the throng of infantry with his men, a little farther south. He charged towards the cavalry, knocking foot soldiers to the floor as if they were mere flies being swatted away.

"Oh shit," Edmond Cobham cried as a man of Dweagan reached up and dragged him from his horse and down to the ground.

Daniel Bacon moved in to assist his friend, slashing his sword at all who stood in his way. He could not see Cobham, who had vanished from sight. He knew the other to be there as he heard his voice calling over and over.

"Oh, shit. Oh, shit."

"Bloody heck," Bacon spat as twenty men pressed against his steed's flanks. The horse gave a squeal and lifted itself onto its hind legs, kicking wildly with its forelimbs.

One of the enemy soldiers plunged a pitchfork into the horse's ribs. Bacon slid off the right side of the beast and chopped into soldier after soldier as his horse crumpled to the ground behind him.

From his new vantage point, he could see Cobham stabbing his weapon into the enemy surrounding him. He was on his back and trapped beneath the crowd. Each time the man seemed to make room to get to his feet, another pack of soldiers filled the gap.

Bacon hacked and slashed his way through the mass, copping a few blows from bare knuckles, sword hilts and gauntlets along the way. Blood filled his mouth and a numbing sensation spread over his gums and lips. He spat, losing a few teeth in the process.

"Oh, shit," Cobham called as one of the Dweagan infantrymen fell over his belly, jamming his weapon arm against his legs so he couldn't move it. The soldier had merely tripped as the crowd surged in one direction. His eyes were full of fear as he stared at Cobham's face. He was a young man, Cobham thought as he pulled his dagger free from his belt with his free hand.

"I'm coming," Bacon called, slashing through two men that blocked his way. When they fell to the ground, his gaze fell upon his comrade.

Cobham's throat had been cut from ear to ear. His stare met Bacon's as he tried to breathe, reaching his hand out to his friend. Blood gurgled and spat against his chin and neck.

Sitting on top of Cobham's belly, plunging a dagger into the fallen man's chest over and over, was a young man of Dweagan.

Bacon swung his blade downward, taking the soldier's head from his shoulders. The body slumped to the side and fell onto the muddy ground as his head rolled away into the throng.

A sharp pain struck Bacon from behind. He felt a strange sensation as a shaft of steel pushed through his ribs and out of his chest.

The unmistakable form of a sword tip stuck from his body.

"Bloody heck," he gasped before the blade retracted.

His legs felt wobbly and his head spun.

He fell to his knees hard and dropped his weapon to the ground.

A deep darkness enveloped him as he fell forward, landing at his friend's side.

Yuri leapt upon a man of Dweagan, sinking his teeth into the soldier's face. He tore a large sliver of flesh away from the man's skull with one horrendous tug. A gurgling scream ensued as the man flailed wildly upon the ground.

Many bearing the jade tunics stopped and looked on in horror as the reptilian lifted himself to his feet, strips of bloodied skin dangling from his jaws. The rest of the Agrodien warriors pummeled most of the gawkers to the earth. The remaining onlookers were treated to the blades of the men that had followed Yuri into battle.

"Bastards!" one of the jade soldiers hollered. He was running full pace towards Yuri, his sword held high.

Yuri crouched, ducking under the other's blow, and whipped his tail around to smack the attacker hard in the back.

The soldier fell flat into the mud.

He pushed himself back to his feet as the Agrodien stepped towards him.

As Yuri lifted his blade, intending to pierce the soldier where he lay, the man looked up at him with sad eyes.

Yuri hesitated. He had never seen a foe so depressed and angry at the same time.

Suddenly, a team of horses charged by, pressing the soldier into the sludge.

Something made him stare at what remained of the soldier.

As the din of battle filled the air about him, his stare remained upon the crushed and battered remains of the man. He couldn't figure out why he felt so remorseful.

"Yuri," he heard a voice call, sounding like a distant echo.

He looked over to his left to see Bein pointing into the fray with his sword. Following the gesture with his eyes, he saw Nakrah surrounded by jade soldiers.

Yuri tightened his grip on his weapon and charged into the fight with seven other Agrodien warriors immediately behind him.

With a great leap, they tackled the men in jade to the ground. Blades flashed, and blood flowed as Nakrah focused his attention on two enemy soldiers attacking him from either side.

Yuri barely had time to pounce back upon his feet when five more jade soldiers charged at him from the right. With his tail and sword, he blocked their assaults and knocked them back a few paces.

It wasn't enough to stop them, but it allowed him a chance to examine the situation a little.

"Mralner," he called to a young warrior to his left.

The other was retrieving his sword from the chest of a fallen body. He peered over to the older Agrodien and saw the five soldiers lunging with their weapons.

With haste, Mralner sprinted into the bout, swinging his sword from behind his back and upward as he brought it before him. The scream shook the reptilian's ears as the blade cut deep into the groin of a jade soldier.

Mralner pulled the weapon free. A little more than blood slapped to the earth between the soldier's feet as the reptilian turned to strike another man down.

Yuri hacked into another man of Dweagan with his weapon. As he did so, he saw the same sadness in the soldier's eyes as he had with the one who had just been crushed into the ground by horses.

Something about their expression made Yuri feel uneasy.

Something didn't feel right.

At the same time, he was following the instructions of his Kayl'sro and needed to see this through to the end.

So, he fought on.

Brondt burst through the throng of foot soldiers, his cavalry riding by his side. They charged out of the fray and towards the oncoming riders from Dweagan.

Two walls of man and horse closed upon each other at high speed.

Hooves chewed up the ground.

Snow, slush, mud and flint sprayed about them.

Rushing wind filled Brondt's ears as another flash of light filled the sky above the ridgeline.

His vision fixed upon the approaching wave of chargers, but he could see the hilltop behind them being torn apart in clouds of dust and swirling rock.

The jade riders' eyes filled with rage.

Their spears and swords held at the ready.

They drew closer together.

Closer.

Closer.

The lines smashed into one another.

Several horses collided violently, breaking limbs and opening flesh.

Riders vaulted into the air, their arms and legs trailing like rag dolls.

Weapons flew in all directions. Some cavalrymen on both sides were unlucky enough to receive a sword or spear as a parting gift to the head or chest.

Then there were those who were fortunate enough to evade any damage, such as Brondt.

He cut down two men as he passed them by. He swung his steed around sharply. The horse squealed.

Brondt looked down to his right and noticed blood on his shin. A thick red ribbon stained the flank of his horse.

A quick observation informed the commander that someone had hit the steed with a blade across his right shoulder. A deep gash stretched across the edge of the animal's breast, almost to Brondt's leg.

It was enough to cripple a horse, but this one wasn't ready to give up yet.

The beast snorted and nodded its head as it stomped its hoof into the mud. It wanted to go again.

The commander looked at the scene before him. He was now facing back towards the hill where Amicia and the other three women were located. Between him and them was a hellish scene of death and pain.

His cavalry had engaged with the enemy. Horseman battled horseman with clashing swords.

"Come on," Brondt called as he gave a kick to the steed's ribs.

The horse lunged. It wasn't long before it was charging at full pace back into the fray.

William Vawdrey found himself on the ground and surrounded by foot soldiers. He spied Thornton and Brook a few yards away, still seated atop their steeds and swinging their swords into the jade soldiers below them.

Vawdrey's horse kicked frantically in an effort to get back up on its feet. Its intestines oozed from a gaping wound in its belly and its left hind leg swung at an awkward angle below the thigh. The poor creature would never stand again.

Getting to his feet, Vawdrey saw a quick glint of steel to his right. He lifted his weapon high and blocked the attack. The sound of iron rang in his ears as the vibrations of the swords clashing ran along both of his arms.

He kicked out with his boot and snapped the knee of his opponent. The jade soldier fell to the mud, screaming in agony. He dropped his sword, which disappeared under the feet of others nearby.

Another man charged, bringing his long blade around like a wood-cutter lopping a tree with an axe. Vawdrey saw it coming and stepped aside. The soldier overbalanced and stumbled. He almost toppled, taking three gigantic steps.

Vawdrey used the opportunity to plunge his blade into the fallen man with the broken leg. He jabbed his sword into the soldier's neck hard and fast, rapidly recoiling to attack the other man who had just moved by.

The other turned about, spinning on his heels as he brought his sword over his head and back towards Vawdrey.

Again, he stepped to the side. The jade soldier's oversized blade sank into the ground.

Vawdrey swept his weapon upwards, slicing through the enemy's neck with ease.

Before the jade soldier's head had hit the ground, Vawdrey was already engaged in battle with another.

This opponent had him matched blow for blow. He blocked every attack. He parried every thrust.

Just when he thought he was at an advantage, chopping and hacking with his sword, hitting steel and pushing the soldier back, the other would see an opening and return with similar action.

On and on it went. Chopping, swinging, slashing and neither hitting flesh all the while.

Others around them fell to the floor, never to rise again. A few times, both fighters almost stumbled over the dead as they fought.

At one point, Vawdrey found himself on the defensive. He stepped back carefully, hindering the heavy strikes from the jade soldier with his own blade. He strove to keep his footing as the muddy ground caused him to slip.

Something uneven beneath his boots caused him to fall. He landed on his back, right on a pile of dead men.

With one arm, he held his blade out to block the insistent blows from his challenger. The other arm was frantically feeling about for something sturdy enough to help lift him back to his feet. His fingers touched the wet bodies of the fallen. The bodies slid and slipped over one another as Vawdrey attempted to clamber over them backwards. Dead arms slapped him, and others rolled upon him as he continued blocking blow after blow.

The jade soldier roared with rage as he desperately hacked his blade towards the other. Several dead men received extra wounds as they got between the sword and Vawdrey.

"Why don't you just die?" the jade soldier hollered.

"I'm beginning to wonder that myself," he replied as sword met sword again.

Vawdrey believed that he and his challenger were going to be stuck in this predicament for eternity; he, with the unsuccessful attempts to get to his feet; the soldier, with the failed attack.

Again, and again, the clang of steel rang out like temple bells. Vawdrey's arm was turning numb. He could feel his grip loosening with each strike.

This is it, he thought as he felt the hilt of his sword slip slightly.

Suddenly, the attack stopped.

The jade soldier fell to his knees and dribbled thick, dark blood over his chin.

He made a strange groan before falling face-first into the mud.

Vawdrey peered up to see Thornton seated upon his steed. His blood-stained sword pointed towards the ground.

"Don't ever say I don't do anything for you," the older man growled.

"Thanks, Captain," the other replied, rising to his feet.

Thornton was peering over the battle to something behind Vawdrey; something that couldn't be seen from ground level.

"Bastards got by us," the captain snarled.

Brook rode to Thornton's side and stared in the same direction.

"We could go after them," the lieutenant suggested.

"What's going on?" Vawdrey asked, jumping on the spot to see. They were looking back to the hill where the three witches and their guardians were located.

"Some of the enemy have broken through and are making their way up the hill," Brook answered.

"We won't get to them in time," Thornton said, judging the distance between their people on top of the rise and the soldiers clambering up the embankment. The other two men heard the concern in his voice.

"She'll be all right, Captain," Brook assured the other. "She has protection."

Thornton nodded.

"We keep fighting here, gentlemen," he said. "We keep the rest of these bastards down here with us and try not to let any more get by."

Twenty-Nine

Ursula, holding Catherine with her right hand, reached her left hand towards the ridge across the way. She spread her fingers wide as a bolt of lightning shot from the sky and struck her in the back between the shoulder blades. Four thin, twisted and jagged streaks of light were instantly flung from her fingers. They flashed across the expanse and hit several jade horsemen on the ridge top.

Armour and swords sparked wildly as branches of light spread into other men surrounding the struck riders. As the lightning dissipated, men and steeds fell to the ground lifelessly. Thin plumes of smoke poured from the joins of their armour as their bodies continued to cook inside the metal shells.

"We have visitors," Catherine announced.

She looked down the embankment to fifty soldiers climbing towards them. Their tunics soiled with mud and blood, making it difficult to determine the jade colour beneath the muck.

Amicia, holding Catherine's hand, crouched and reached her free hand to the ground.

"Wait," Emily called. "What are you doing?"

The queen gave the other a quizzical look.

"I'm going to make the earth swallow them," she informed the auburn woman.

"You might cause the land to slide." Emily pointed to the valley with her sword. "Our own men would be in peril."

Amicia got up and considered the situation. Emily was right. "You will need to protect us," she said to their guards.

"That's why we stayed, my lady," Andris said as he moved to the edge of the crest.

Akasati lifted her bow from her shoulders and placed an arrow on the string as she moved to the older man's side. With a quick aim, she flung the arrow down the hill. It skimmed the surface and struck the lead soldier on the bridge of his nose, piercing through to the nape of his neck.

He fell face-first onto the slope. His leg twitched slightly as the life drained from his body.

It wasn't enough to deter the others from approaching.

Onward they climbed, peering up now and then to gauge the distance they needed to tread.

The Erilian woman strung another shaft into her bow and took aim again.

Another jade soldier fell.

"I don't think you have enough arrows for all of them," Schoenbach remarked as he looked at the quiver on Akasati's back. There were about ten darts left by his count.

"Then you had better pray I don't miss," she told him as she loaded another shot. The arrow sped through the air and passed through an iron breastplate sticking deep into the chest of a soldier. "Otherwise, we'll have more of them to deal with than I would like."

Brondt noticed the band of jade soldiers climbing near the top of the hill. He was too far away to get to them before they reached his wife and the others on the ridge. There was also the immediate threat of the enemy soldiers and cavalry surrounding him and his men.

He made a quiet prayer under his breath as he continued to fight.

"You may not be real," he said, clashing swords with a jade rider. "Maybe the girl was right when she said there are no gods." He plunged his sword into the shoulder of the opponent's steed. The horse fell with a loud squeal, sending the jade cavalryman onto the ground. "But, you have done something to all four of them." He watched as some of his infantry dug their blades into the fallen rider. "So, if you have any power at all, keep my wife safe and give us victory."

With twelve of their comrades lying face first in the grime upon the hillside, all with arrows sticking from their bodies, the jade soldiers seemed more compelled to reach the top.

"I'm out," Akasati called after reaching for another shaft and finding nothing in her quiver. She dropped her bow to the ground and lifted her sword from its sheath.

Nola'ee's tail coiled as she bared her teeth and tightened her grip on the hilt of her blade. Ruttger and Schoenbach moved to either side of her and prepared themselves for the impending attack.

Emily stood near the three witches, who were still focusing their attention on the hilltop across the way. Plumes of dust erupted violently, and jagged fingers of light continued to tear the ridge open. The screams of the men amongst the carnage couldn't be heard over the din of battle coming from the valley below. Still, Emily imagined it would feel like hell was being unleashed on any jade soldier still breathing over there.

Karlena stood by Emily's side. She looked over to the backs of the reptilian female, the Erilian warrior and two men positioned between her and the approaching soldiers.

"I don't think I like this one, Emily," she said.

The auburn woman peered over her shoulder at Catherine.

The girl's eyes were black as night. Tendrils, like black veins beneath the skin, stretched across her face as she gripped the hands of the other two women beside her. Ursula stretched her fingers out, sending another barrage of lightning from her fingers over the valley and onto the hilltop across the valley. Amicia, crouching by Catherine's side, touched the ground and spoke to the earth. Another eruption of stone and soil exploded into the sky, carrying men and horses with it.

"Me either," she replied to Karlena. "Not one bit."

Yuri and the Agrodien warriors raced along the base of the hill. He kept peering up to the top now and then to see how far the enemy soldiers had climbed.

There was no way they could reach the jade soldiers in time to prevent them from reaching the small team on the ridge. His aim was to form a blockade of sorts to prevent more enemy foot soldiers from following their comrades.

Running swiftly, on all fours at times, the reptilians swiped with their claws, hacked with their blades and bit with their teeth, cutting down horses and men that were in their way.

"The enemy thins," Mralner shouted in their tongue.

Yuri shot a quick glance around and noticed bodies piling up throughout the valley. The young warrior was correct. Their allies were winning, but it was at a significant cost. Many jade soldiers had fallen, as had many of their own.

"We don't have time to congratulate ourselves yet," Yuri called back. "They are losing, but that will simply make them more desperate and angry. A trapped animal facing death is always the most aggressive."

A deep horn resounded from somewhere on the battlefield.

He knew it wasn't from a man of Woodmyst or Newholt, as none of them carried one. With a scan of the valley, he saw the jade riders turn their horses to the south, where a large group of enemy cavalrymen had gathered.

"Will they charge us?" Bein asked, noting the horsemen's position was almost parallel to where the foot soldiers had climbed the hill.

"If they do," Yuri answered, "they will have to run right over the top of us."

"We're not going up to help the mother and sister of the Kayl'sro?" Nakrah enquired.

"No," the older Agrodien replied. "We stop as many of these men as we can."

"Fight until we fight no longer," Bein said.

The warriors faced the enemy and formed a line. They gripped their weapons and prepared to battle the growing ranks of jade riders.

"Fight until we fight no longer," Yuri agreed.

Brondt and Thornton met up on the battlefield. Their enemies were spent, bleeding out or lying dead around their feet.

"Where are they going?" Sparrow asked, pointing to the jade cavalry racing towards the south.

"They're mustering together and forming ranks," Brondt replied from atop his steed.

Thornton peered to the hill behind them and back to the riders of Dweagan.

"They're going to take the hill," he growled.

Brondt frowned. "We don't have many of our men down there."

"The Agrodien have gathered together in their way," a horseman called, peering into the distance.

Thornton looked concerned. "There's not enough of them to hold that lot back."

"Then we help them," Brondt replied. He pointed his sword at the base of the hill where nine reptilian warriors stood, and shouted, "To the Agrodien!"

The surrounding men, on steeds and on foot, gave a great shout as they ran towards Yuri and his warriors.

Ruttger blocked the blows of a young jade soldier as best as he could. He watched for an opening so he could attack rather than defend. His adversary was faster and more agile than he.

Emily, after cutting another man down, swung her sword around and slashed Ruttger's opponent across the back of the knees. The soldier stumbled, giving the older soldier time to plunge his sword into the other's chest.

There was no time to thank the auburn woman. She was already engaged in another scuffle. Within moments, Ruttger was also under attack by another jade infantryman.

Nola'ee swung her sword about her with grace, speed, and precision. She instantly cut those who dared to do battle with her down. None could get close enough to harm her.

She moved herself closer to the three sorceresses, who were still assaulting the hilltop across the valley with violent spells. As each man who made it past the other protectors attempted to attack the witches, Nola'ee would simply put them down.

"Last one," Andris announced as he pulled his sword out of a dying man of Dweagan.

"Not quite," Schoenbach replied as he pointed to the valley with his sword.

At least one thousand horses tore across the ground towards the base of their hill.

Amicia got up and let go of Catherine's hand. Catherine's eyes returned to their piercing blue as she seemed to come out of a trance. Ursula shifted her focus to those around her.

"What's happening?" the woman from Whitekeep asked.

Amicia peered to the valley floor and saw the mass of chargers racing towards the nine Agrodien warriors. Some distance to the north, she noticed the remaining forces of Woodmyst and Newholt moving to intercept.

The attempt would be futile.

The horsemen would reach the hillside well before Brondt and his men ever did.

"I don't think Yuri will stop all of them," Ruttger put in.

"If they make it past Yuri," said the queen, "then we attack them on the slope."

Ruttger looked at her strangely.

"We can't stop that many," he told her.

"Not you," Amicia informed him as she linked hands with Catherine again. "We."

"It's too late," Thornton huffed, slowing his pace. He watched Brondt lead the remaining cavalrymen towards the jade horsemen. But he knew, no matter how fast the commander and his men rode, there was no way that they would reach the Agrodien in time to help.

The men of Woodmyst and Newholt running on foot slowed their approach. Thornton bent over, still holding his sword, and placed his hands on his knees to catch his breath.

"Fuck, I'm getting old," he managed between gasps of air.

"What do we do?" Jendryng asked, watching on helplessly as the enemy riders rapidly closed upon the Agrodien.

Thornton straightened a little and pointed into the valley.

"Kill as many of them as you can," he growled.

The men turned their attention on a few hundred jade soldiers regrouping near the middle of the battlefield. There were more making their way to the centre from a variety of places throughout the valley.

Brook turned about and quickly calculated their numbers.

"We have about two hundred strong here," he informed Thornton.

"Then the odds are in our favour." Thornton smiled as he stood upright.

The jade riders drew spears and swords.

Mud, slush, and blood sprayed up from the ground as hooves tore through dirt and fallen bodies as they raced towards the hill.

Yuri tightened his grip on his sword and tensed the muscles in his legs.

Closer, the horses drew.

Closer and closer.

Yuri crouched slightly. His tail straightened out.

With a great roar, he leapt forward into the air. He tackled the lead rider to the ground and plunged his blade into the man's belly.

His warriors followed suit and took down another eight. That was nothing compared to the mighty force that continued to charge past them.

Yuri quickly jumped to his feet and slashed out at a passing horse. It crashed to the ground, sending its rider headfirst into the muck.

The Agrodien swung his sword at another horse and another, causing further casualties. A few men lifted themselves to their feet with their swords in their hands. Others tumbled and snapped bones upon impact or landed on the ground, only to have their own steed roll over them.

As Yuri engaged in battle with five men on the ground, he watched the last of the horsemen charge by and begin the climb up the hill. A quick glance told him the bulk of their cavalry was heading for their friends at the top. Nearly one thousand strong.

There was nothing else to hold them back.

Yuri thought about how he needed to survive just so he could make it home to his beloved Galonia and his three younglings. He hoped the three witches at the top of the hill could stop the riders in their tracks on the hillside.

He held little hope of gaining a victory.

Not now.

As he fought valiantly on the battleground, his fellow Agrodien warriors by his side, his mind turned to his Kayl'sro and how he intended to inform her he had failed her.

Brondt pulled his horse to a halt and watched helplessly. Tears welled in his eyes as he observed the jade riders galloping up the hillside. They were less than a quarter of the way, but too far to intercept.

It was too late.

"No," he gasped as he moved his gaze to the hilltop, to his dear Amicia.

His men looked on, understanding his sorrow and frustration.

Plumes of dust broke the surface around the jade horsemen, sending a few steeds and riders into the air.

"Look," one of Brondt's men called. "Our queen is fighting."

The men gave a cheer as Brondt's anxiety grew.

"Come on," he urged his wife under his breath.

Another eruption of dirt and rock burst into the sky, carrying more cavalry.

A quick shot of lightning streaked down the hillside and into the approaching force.

Brondt's men gave another cheer.

"Come on," the commander said again, gritting his teeth and leaning forward in his saddle.

The attack from the ridge wasn't enough to slow the assault. A large throng of horses burst from the dust cloud and continued racing up the hill.

"There are too many," Ursula announced.

"Just do what you did to that hill over there," Karlena suggested. "Rip it apart like that. Stop with the little blows you've given so far."

Catherine shook her head.

"We can't," she replied. "We have people down there. Neither of these two wants to put our own people at any more risk than they are at already."

"But you're all fine if we die instead?" said Karlena.

Amicia looked at her sternly. "Those men who fight for us have families of their own," she said. "Many of them won't be returning home. I would prefer it if I could get as many back to their loved ones as possible, rather than making widows and orphans of people back in Newholt and Woodmyst by the doing of something with my own hands."

"Besides," Ursula put in, "we need our men for the battles yet to come. If we attack with full strength, we could destroy our own forces."

"And how do you feel about this?" Ruttger asked Catherine, expecting her to reply with a similar argument.

"It makes sense if we're playing a numbers game," she answered. "Personally, I would like to tear the side of this hill off with them still riding upon it and throw it into the sea."

"You could do that?" Schoenbach inquired.

"Yes," Amicia acknowledged. "But we would come tumbling down and perish as a result."

"Then, let's not go with that idea," Ruttger said to Catherine.

She shrugged and turned to face the approaching riders.

They were almost halfway up the hillside.

"Then we die," she told them blankly.

Emily moved to her daughter and took her in her arms. She kissed the girl's forehead and pulled her in tight to her chest.

"So, that's it then?" Akasati asked, peering at the clouds swirling in the sky.

"Of course, it isn't," Schoenbach told her. "We keep fighting until we win, or the other one."

"Lose, you mean?" Andris asked.

"I don't like that word," the old sea-captain remarked with a wry grin.

The rumble of horse hooves grew louder as the ground beneath their feet trembled.

"Well," Emily said, letting her daughter go and pulling her sword from its sheath again. "I don't intend on letting them just simply take me."

"Me either," Karlena said, moving to the auburn woman's side.

Akasati and Nola'ee took up position beside the other two and peered over the hillside to the rapidly approaching jade riders.

"To the death it is," Ruttger said, moving to the end of the line.

"Aye," replied Schoenbach. "To the death."

The ground shook more vigorously. The sound of hoof-falls increased like a growing wave of thunder.

Closer, the enemy drew.

The calls and cries of men urging their beasts onwards reached the ears of those standing at the top.

Closer and closer.

The seven protectors prepared for the imminent attack, correcting their footing, gripping their weapons.

Closer.

The three women standing behind them grouped together and formed a triangle by holding hands. They lowered themselves to their knees, closed their eyes, and bowed their heads.

"Unite," they said in unison. The sound of their voices rang out like thunder throughout the valley.

Ursula tilted her head to the sky and opened her eyes.

They were pitch black.

A single bolt of lightning fell from the swirling clouds above them and into the midst of the jade riders.

Two men fell to the ground before being pummelled by galloping hooves as the others rode over the top of them.

Another jagged line of light hit another rider. Then another. And another.

Closer and closer, the horsemen came.

"May the gods help us," Ruttger murmured.

Emily gritted her teeth and glared at the enemy. "There are no gods."

A strange noise echoed from the sky towards the north. Emily turned her head to see two giant forms breaking through the clouds.

Dragons.

One of the great beasts dived towards the hill, tilting its colossal membranous wings slightly to skim over the sloping land. The air seemed to tear open with a loud ripping sound as the beast raced through the sky.

It opened its massive jaws and spewed a long, wide trail of flame over the lead riders climbing the hill.

The other beast hurled another barrage of fire over the tail end of the cavalry.

Horses and men screamed as they flailed in the fire before falling silently to the earth.

The men trapped in the centre of the two thick lines of flame stopped in their tracks.

Several horses bucked and kicked at the horrific sight, sending riders crashing to the ground.

Emily watched in awe as one of the flying beasts shot into the sky, where it turned quickly and dived back towards the trapped men on the ground.

Another attack of fire streaked through the centre of the remaining cavalrymen as the dragon and its rider shot back to the north.

Plumes of dark smoke rose into the air as anything and everything in the flames below burned away.

The second dragon moved over to the battlefield as it flew parallel to its comrade.

Men bolted across the valley to the western hill and started clambering up its side to get away from the monsters.

The beast quickly turned on them, engulfing a crowd of soldiers on the hillside as it flew by. Flesh melted from bone. Bone charred and turned to grey ash. Ash carried away in the wind.

"I hope none of those men were people we know," Schoenbach gasped.

Both beasts turned about again and returned to finish the remaining jade cavalrymen, flying side by side as they threw fire over the last riders.

Together, the dragons turned to their right and swept over the valley to the hill across the way. Within moments, they set the entire hillside alight, engulfing all upon it and preventing any jade soldiers still alive from escaping from the valley floor.

The beasts moved back into the air. One turned to the west and flew towards Dweagan. The other circled around at the north end of the valley and made its way to the hilltop, where the small band of ten gathered.

Amicia, Ursula, and Catherine were on their feet, surrounded by the other seven.

"Is it Alice?" Andris asked.

"No," Catherine replied. "Neither of the dragons is Liana."

The dragon landed a few yards away, sending an almost solid gust of air over the others standing nearby. The rider, hooded and robed in black, slid from the creature's back, over its side and onto the ground effortlessly. As the figure stepped forward, it raised its hands to remove the hood, revealing its grey skin and large, bulbous yellow orbs.

"Gruloch?" Emily gasped. She raced over to him, dropping her sword in the process to wrap her arms around his neck. "Thank you," she said.

He placed his arms around her.

"It is my pleasure to help the mother of the Kayl'sro," he replied. He turned and gave a sharp whistle.

The dragon spread its wings wide and bounded into the sky. It swept over the plain, past the hill opposite theirs and onwards, chasing after the other dragon flying to the west.

"Where is it going?" Ruttger asked, peering after it admiringly.

"To assist Jhakarh with the destruction of Dweagan," Gruloch answered.

Emily looked at him curiously. "They go to destroy it all?" she asked.

"Yes," he said with a hint of sorrow. "It is necessary."

"Why?" the auburn woman enquired. "There are people there."

"I know," he said, looking at the battleground. "They are loyal to the Maji. All of them."

"Alice hoped we may salvage something from that city," Amicia put in. "I interpreted that as meaning that we should explore a treaty with the people of Dweagan. Make them allies, if we can."

"They won't ally themselves with you," Gruloch told her.

"And how do you know this?" she pressed.

He gestured to the valley where the dead were piled in heaps and not a sign of snow could be seen because of the bodies lying in mud and blood.

"That is how I know," the Haigok answered.

Thirty

He took a deep breath as he rode his steed to the top of a knoll, where he could look down upon the township of Ironfields. The streets appeared empty, which was unusual for this time of day.

Usually, the hustle and bustle of merchants, couriers, workers, and soldiers would be energetic. The market would be alive and corner stall keepers called out what bargains were to be had to passers-by. The guards would be hard at work keeping an eye out for thieves and pocketing their take of the stall profits. Whores would stand on the tavern porches, waving their hands and flashing their tits hoping to empty the pockets of miners and goat herders.

But not today.

A lone dog rushing along the main street, barking, and several horses tethered to posts outside the taverns were the only signs of life that he could see.

His horse snorted as another rider pulled to his side.

"General Risha, the men await your orders."

"Make camp at the foot of the hill behind us," Risha replied. "We wait for the scouts' reports."

"Yes, sir." The rider turned his horse around to pass on the instruction to the other five hundred men waiting on the lower ground at his rear.

***

Saruun Versel woke up and stretched her arms and legs. She moved Willis' arm from her chest and pushed him away to her right onto his back. He remained asleep, murmuring slightly as he rolled over to his side.

The girl grumbled as Versel pushed her off to the left. She then pushed the covers away, revealing their naked flesh to the cold, before clambering over the young woman in order to get out of the bed. She felt clumsy and awkward as she carefully placed her knees and hands on either side of the girl's body.

Willis reached for the covers instinctively and pulled them over himself.

"Why are you leaving?" the girl groaned, putting her hand on Versel's bare waist.

"I need to see to a few things," the general replied, placing her feet onto the cold timber floor.

"Like what?"

"Like telling your innkeeper to purchase some fucking rugs for your floor," she replied. She lifted the covers back over the girl. "Go back to sleep."

Within moments, Versel walked down the stairs to the tavern. Raucous men celebrating the arrival of the new commander still filled it.

A loud cheer went up as several men saw her descending the stairs.

"There she is," the barkeep called. "Our protector."

Another cheer ensued.

One man by the bar, an old merchant judging by his clothing, approached her with a mug in his hand.

"For you, General," he slurred, holding the vessel in front of her face.

She looked at his drool-covered chin and stared at the cup for a long time.

"It's fresh," he assured her. "I ain't had a drop. I swear."

She peered to the barkeep, who nodded in reply.

With a smile, she took the mug and sculled the ale.

The room erupted with yet another cheer as she held the vessel upside-down to show that it was now empty.

"Come on." The old man put his hand on her back and guided her to the bar. "Let me buy you another."

She quickly scanned the room for her men. They were nowhere to be seen. Even her armour, which had been resting against the wall by the fireplace, had vanished.

The barkeep poured ale from a flagon into a line of mugs along the bar.

"Where are my men and armour?" she asked, trying not to sound grumpy.

"Your armour's safe," the other replied. "I put it back here, out of the way."

"And my men?" She lifted the mug from the bar.

"Upstairs with some ladies," he said, lifting his eyes to the ceiling.

She nodded, accepting his answer.

"Don't worry 'bout them, love," the old worker said with a beam. Half of his teeth were missing and the other half was yellow with rot. "Drink up and be merry." He held up his mug to hers. "To the new order."

"To the Maji," she replied.

"And him too," the other said.

As they drank, four men in cloaks sitting by the door got up and vanished into the street. No one noticed them leave.

But no one saw them arrive either.

***

Alice sat by Liana deep in the cavern. She stroked the beast's snout gently. Liana breathed deep and emitted a low purr that rumbled through the ground. The vibrations moved through the girl's body, almost tickling her and causing her to giggle.

The dragon had awakened from a long sleep, but still appeared sluggish. It was clear that the great creature wasn't ready to fly yet. She needed more rest.

Alice had killed a sheep and brought it into the den for Liana to eat. The dragon devoured it in one bite. Nothing remained of it except for a small sliver of blood trickling from the beast's jaw.

"Hold still," Alice whispered as she took the hem of her cloak and wiped the stain away.

Liana continued to purr.

"Sleep, girl," Alice urged her. "I need you strong."

The dragon closed her eyes and drifted away again.

"Alice," Arthur called softly. His voice reverberated through the cavern.

Liana stirred and turned her head towards the source of the sound. She let out a soft, friendly chirp when she saw the boy approaching.

Alice got up and rubbed the beast on the neck.

"Sleep," she repeated.

The dragon lowered her head back to the cave's floor and closed her eyes.

"I'm sorry," Arthur said in a low voice. "Did I wake her?"

"No," Alice replied as he moved to her side. "She's being stubborn. She wants to be with the other dragons."

Arthur placed his hand on Liana's snout and rubbed the rough skin near her nostril. The dragon started purring again.

"You won't be staying long," he said melancholically. "Will you?"

"No," she admitted, looking to the ground first, as if ashamed, before raising her gaze to his. "We'll leave after the gathering of the Haigok."

"I understand," he said. "You don't have long. Before your bond to whatever this power leaves you, I mean."

It surprised her he would know such a thing.

"How do you...?"

"Your hair," he said, moving his hand from Liana to touch his wife's braid. "It's changing back."

"I can feel it," said Alice. "I need to finish what Takmel started before it leaves me entirely, and before he becomes too strong."

"I wish I could go with you," he told her. She could tell he meant it.

"I don't," she replied. "I need you to be ready for when I return."

"We will be," Arthur said.

***

Ruttger and Andris watched the orange glow illuminating against the clouds in the distance. It was a sure sign that Dweagan burned.

"I need to return to Alice," Gruloch told the gathering. He peered to the west, where two dark silhouettes had formed in the clouds.

"Will your people fight with us?" Brondt asked.

"You have my people," the Haigok answered. "I cannot speak for the other clans."

Thornton watched the two dragons circle the valley.

"While I am truly grateful, Lord Gruloch," Amicia said, "I am unsure whether the destruction of Dweagan was necessary. There were families in that city who may or may not have been loyal to the enemy's cause."

Gruloch considered her words as the dragons came to rest behind him.

"Dweagan was a great vantage point for the Maji," he replied. "Its wharves were central to the trade routes of this land. Everyone knows this. Even the nomads I have traded with, in the Core Lands.

"In fact, most produce and supplies that have travelled across from the Eastern Sea to the west had passed through Dweagan at some point. Including weapons, iron, timber and black powder.

"How is it that the port towns and strongholds like Dellmoor, Blackshore and Erimoor have come back into realisation if it wasn't for the help of Dweagan? These were places once destroyed by the Mirikin. Now, according to my kin, they thrive.

"Ironfields sent its ore through the docks of Dweagan to Blackrock Haven. Were you aware of this?"

The queen shook her head.

"It was our understanding that Newholt controlled the routes of the Eastern Sea," Gruloch added. "It appears that a great deal was being done without your approval."

"That doesn't justify why the city burns," she told him, with a hint of emotion.

"It most certainly does," he said calmly. "They were loyal to him. If they regroup, they would cause you more grief than you would care for. This war would continue long after the Maji is defeated. Sometimes, a cause to fight for is more powerful than the origin of the cause.

"Dweagan sent every soldier," continued Gruloch, "every shop-keeper, every father and every son out here today to face you. I can see spades, picks and wood axes amongst the weapons of warfare.

"They didn't come because a jade witch queen commanded them. She's long dead. The Maji wasn't standing on that hill over there. He is far away in the west.

"They fought you today because they believed. They were commit-ted to *his* cause because they believed. And you can be sure that every woman, child or man remaining in that city believed as well."

Amicia stared after him silently as he withdrew towards the await-ing dragons. She wanted to say something as an angry, hot flush ran along her spine and over her face. Instead, she held her tongue. She knew he was right.

"We did you a favour today," Gruloch called from the back of his dragon. "We prevented the chance of any future enemies rising from Dweagan, which they surely would have.

"Mark my words," he continued. "You will need to do the same to every seaside port town, village, or farmhouse you come across be-tween here and the Maji. You have no way of knowing who is for us or against us.

"Alice would agree with me. You know this to be true."

He turned his dragon and prepared to take flight.

"Gruloch," Emily called after him. The Haigok turned to face her. "Thank you. And please tell my daughter that her sister and mother are all right."

He gestured he would.

Both dragons took off into the sky and made their way to the north.

"Do you think he's right about Dweagan?" Ursula asked Catherine quietly as they watched the massive creatures fly away.

"Yes," the other answered, turning her eyes to the valley floor filled with death. "He's right about everything."

Thirty-One

Four cloaked figures scrambled through the lowlands between the snow-covered hills and crags, keeping out of sight of the township as they ran. They passed through open farm ground, smeared with a thin blanket of snow, before navigating through seemingly endless fields of dried wheat stalks and corn.

Eventually, they came upon a throng of armed men, dressed in dark armour. A large camp with fires and tents had been established. They raised no banners nor wore colours.

"Halt," a soldier called.

One figure pulled off his hood.

"It's us, stupid," he remarked. "We have news for the general."

"He's busy taking a shit," the soldier replied snidely. "You'll have to wait."

"Well, we'll talk to him when he's done, then," the other said back in kind. "Won't we?"

"Can we just get to a fire?" another cloaked man enquired. "It's fucking cold."

The first man turned to the soldier and held his hands out as if to ask permission to pass by.

"Go on." The soldier gestured towards the camp.

It wasn't long before Risha found the four spies sitting by a fire near a group of tents. The men were digging into bowls of hot, steaming stew with wads of bread they broke from a shared loaf.

"What news have you?" the general asked.

The men stood up and lowered the bowls to their sides as best as they could without spilling the contents.

"General," they all responded.

"Sit and eat your stew, boys," the other ordered. "You can talk and eat, can't you?"

"Thank you, sir," the first man replied, returning to the stump of wood he was using as a seat.

"So?" Risha asked as he sat on the edge of a felled log positioned by the hearth. "What news?"

"There are men from Wintermarsh," the other informed him, muffling over the mouthful of bread he had just placed in his mouth. He swallowed hard and winced as the large portion of food slid down his throat slowly. "A woman leads them."

"A woman?"

"Fair-haired. Good looking. Big tits," the man answered. "They call her general."

"Saruun Versel," Risha sneered. "How many with her?"

"I saw nine," another man reported. "But the folks in the tavern kept saying that she was the First Garrison Commander of the Maji. I didn't see no other men. Not enough for a garrison."

Risha contemplated this for a moment.

"Nine?" he asked. "Are you sure?"

"Positive," the other replied.

"Easy enough," the first man remarked. "We could sneak in tonight and take them all."

"They said garrison?" the general pressed.

"Yes sir," the second said.

"There are only nine," the first assured him.

"That you could see," said Risha. "The rest of her troops may be on their way or hidden from sight. Saruun Versel is a formidable tactician, gentlemen. We will be best to play this with caution."

"Sir?" The first man gave the general a puzzled look, not understanding the meaning of Risha's words.

"We should double the guards tonight," he said, more to himself than for the benefit of the others. "And we should prepare to attack at first light. Before she is given the opportunity to draw first blood."

***

"What is she doing?" Becka asked, looking from the door of the cabin to the lone, hooded figure sitting cross-legged on the snow by the blazing fire on the ground a few yards away. The tents and wagons were now gone, leaving open ground where the camp had once rested.

"Talking," Arthur replied as he brought a mug of hot tea to the woman.

"Talking?" the other questioned, taking the mug and looking back at the girl curiously. "To whom? There isn't another soul in sight."

"To the others," Linet answered from the kitchen. She and Courtney were preparing a meal of baked venison, boiled potatoes, and bread. Linet carved the meat while Courtney sliced the bread.

"Can't she do that in here?" asked Becka. "It's cold out there."

"Cold in here too, with that door open," David commented.

"Leave it open," Arthur ordered, as he moved back to the kitchen to fetch his own cup. "I can see her from here. I need to see her."

David sighed. "Sorry, son," he said. "I didn't mean to upset you."

Arthur turned to his father and gave a small grin.

"It's all right, Papa. I just have seen little of her and she will be gone again soon. I don't want her to go."

"I know." David moved to Arthur's side and placed a hand on the boy's shoulder.

"You fret over her, Becka," Lor said from the sitting room. He slouched upon the couch, sharing a blanket over his legs with his sister. "I've never seen you act like this for anyone."

"Richard loved her like a daughter," she explained. "Or, a grand-daughter. I'm not sure. I just know he was very fond of her. I think she was his favourite child of Woodmyst. I guess a little of his affection for her rubbed off onto me. She's special." She looked to Arthur and David before turning her eyes to Sevrina's belly beneath the blanket. "I don't mean to cause offence, but she may be the most special child I have ever known or will ever know."

Becka turned back to Alice. The girl was facing away from the hut. Tall flames danced before her as she sat silent and still in the gently falling snow.

"Just look how far she has come," the woman by the door said. "The little girl who would once rather be exploring the woods and training with our warriors, and besting them before her twelfth birthday, is now a leader of people. No..." She shook her head, considering. "Not just people. That's the wrong word. A nation. None of us could have foreseen this. Not even Richard or Tomas would have dreamed of this.

"She has seen too much for someone as young as she," Becka continued. "Too much blood and death." She shot Arthur a quick glance. "Too much of you. And you, too much of her." Arthur almost blushed as her eyes returned to the girl. "I wish you and she had waited just another season or two before committing to one another as you did. But, nevertheless, I am proud of her. I just wish she'd come inside and get out of the cold."

"She's not the same," Sevrina said suddenly.

"What?" Lor asked, turning his face to his sister.

"Alice," she replied. "She's not the same girl that I knew before she came out here."

"What do you mean?" Arthur asked.

All focused on her. Becka stepped away from the door and moved inside the room a little.

Sevrina shook her head, sensing that she may have said something out of turn.

"Doesn't matter."

"Say your piece, girl," instructed David. "We're all family here."

"Well..." Courtney piped in.

"We're *all* family here," David repeated.

Sevrina murmured her acquiescence. "She was happy." Her hand moved over her round stomach as she felt the child inside kick. "Do you remember? She used to chase the ducks by the river and roll in the mud with the swine. She simply didn't care what anyone thought of her. Right until Tomas died.

"Then she trained with weapons," Sevrina went on. "I don't remember who started that. Perhaps it was Akasati or Emily. Maybe you." She looked at David. "It doesn't matter. It was around that time she changed. But she would steal away whenever the chance presented itself. We wouldn't be able to find her anywhere because she would be running or hunting in the forest or exploring the caves here. That was when she was truly happy. When she got to be a little girl. When she got to be herself.

"Now, she has responsibility. She's not a little girl anymore. She's grown up. She's not the Alice that I remember."

"That Alice is gone," said a voice at the door.

All turned their attention to the girl. She stepped inside the hut and closed the door behind her.

"Alice." Arthur brightened. "Tea?"

"Yes, please. And keep that stove stoked. It's freezing."

Becka sat down in a chair and looked at Alice curiously.

"What do you mean, that Alice is gone?"

"Aunt Sevrina is right," the girl explained. "I have changed. I have responsibility and I'll never be able to go back to what I once was." She placed her hand on her belly.

The others understood.

Arthur poured a cup of hot brew and placed it at the head of the table.

"Smells good," Alice said, looking over to Courtney and Linet.

"Won't be long," Linet told her as the girl sat down at the table.

"Any news?" Arthur asked as he returned to the stove to test the potatoes.

Alice took a sip of her tea.

"Mmm," she breathed. "That's good." She placed the mug back on the table. "Dragon fire has destroyed Dweagan. No one survived. Our people prepare to march to the west. I told them I'll meet them as soon as I can."

"Dweagan destroyed?" Courtney sighed. She shook her head before turning her attention suddenly back to Alice. "What of Ruttger?"

"He's fine," she assured her. "He returns with Andris. They have departed from the others and make way for the Twisted Road."

"Andris is alive?" Sevrina's face lit up.

"And well," Alice relayed, allowing herself to smile.

"Thank the gods," the other said, clasping her hands and peering to the ceiling.

The smile on Alice's face disappeared for a moment. She wanted to say her father's words, but knew the time was not appropriate. So, she held her silence and forced the cheer back to her face.

"Emily?" David enquired. "Catherine?"

"They're all right," she replied. "Many men were lost. Some we know. Most, we don't know so well. We still have a large force. We have Gruloch and his dragons. We may yet have even more allies to join us."

"She's not coming back though?" David pressed.

Alice shook her head. "She intends to stay with Catherine."

"I should go to her," the large man told her.

"You should stay here," she instructed him. "You should prepare for when we return. Arthur will need your help."

David plopped into a seat beside Alice.

"She's out there and I'm here without her," he said, tears welling in his eyes.

"I need you here, David," she said, and touched his hand. "Please."

He looked at her for a long time. She watched his beard quiver and thought he was about to argue against her wishes.

"All right," he said. "But you make sure that she comes home safely to me."

"I promise," Alice answered, squeezing his hand reassuringly.

***

The troop moved over the plain in loose formation. Brondt led the procession with Amicia by his side. Following closely were Catherine and Ursula. Surrounding them were Emily, the team from the glade, Yuri and his Agrodien warriors, as well as Thornton and his men.

The cavalry rode in groups as infantrymen walked in clusters, chatting and reflecting upon the day they'd had. Bringing up the rear were wagons and horses carting supplies for the combined forces of Woodmyst and Newholt.

"How do you feel?" Emily asked her daughter. She had noticed a blank look on Catherine's face as they had been riding.

"I feel better after talking with Alice," she answered. "She fretted for us."

"Of course she did," the auburn woman asserted. "She's Alice. But that wasn't what I meant. I saw you on the hill. Something wasn't right."

Catherine frowned and peered towards the sea far to the left of their position. The sun was getting low, its golden orb penetrating through the clouds that covered the sky not far above the horizon.

"Alice is the balance we need," she admitted to her mother. "She holds the power that brings healing and encourages life. I hold death in my hands. Without her, we three are dangerous weapons. There were moments where we lost focus today…" She stopped and corrected herself. "I lost focus. I let my feelings influence the connection. I didn't consider the lives of our allies. I just wanted to win."

"It's all right," Emily said. "It's over now."

Catherine turned to face her mother. Tears were streaming down her cheeks.

"I wanted to kill them all," she confessed. "I wanted to take everything."

"But you didn't," her mother reminded her. "You *did* control yourself. I'm very proud of you, Catherine. Very proud."

The girl sniffled. "Thank you, Mama."

Ahead of them, the men conversed. Thornton peered at the setting sun.

"How far do you intend to take us?" he asked his commander.

"I think we should try for the borders of the Lunkhul Forest," Brondt answered. "We can camp by the mountains overnight and try for Oldcastle in the morning."

"Ain't nothing in Oldcastle, sir," the youngest of Thornton's men commented.

"Shut it, Jendryng," Thornton growled.

"I'm fully aware of that, young man," the commander replied. "I have seen the ruins of the citadel with my own eyes. But Oldcastle has a freshwater river running through it and provides some shelter against the weather. I intend to locate our men there so we can recuperate before moving on. There isn't much to protect us between there and Dellmoor."

"Dellmoor, sir?" Jendryng asked.

"The first location on our trail of where one of the Maji's wives' lives," Catherine answered. "The Olive Queen."

Epilogue

Isabel entered the throne room, expecting to see Takmel in the marble seat. Apart from a few guards posted near the door and at their posts along the length of the walls to the side of the white room, the chamber was empty.

She retreated towards the foyer as heightened anxiety took over. She had not seen him for some time. Not only that, but the twin girls were missing as well.

She started up the wide stairs to the living quarters. Passing tapestries, fine trinkets on expensive tables and more guards, she continued her search. She stopped to speak to a soldier standing in the doorway to a large sitting room, which was also empty.

"Where is the Maji?" she asked.

"My queen." The guard bowed. He pointed along a wide, stone corridor lined with doors to the bed chambers. "I last saw him heading in that direction."

With a quick turn on her heels, Isabel started down the passageway. She tilted her head, directing her ear towards a soft murmur coming from the far end. The closer she drew, the clearer the sound became. His voice reverberated along the stone corridor. It came from an open door on the right. The last door in the hallway.

The twins' room.

She stopped in her tracks as she considered how to approach. She thought about walking in, as if it was a casual visit. She contemplated storming in and rousing on him for not telling her where he was, leaving her to look all over the palace grounds for him.

Instead, she trod carefully and approach the door in silence. She intended to watch in secret.

"How much do you love me?" she heard him say. She moved closer to the wall and nearer to the open door. A moment later, she heard him chuckle. "And what about you? How much do you love me?"

She pressed herself against the wall and poked an eye around the doorframe. The girls' beds sat side by side. Takmel rested upon the edge of the one closest to the door. The twins were on the floor, cross-legged, with their puppies resting in their laps.

One girl held her hands out as wide as she could stretch them.

"That much?" Takmel asked.

The girl nodded.

"Good," he said as he pulled a dagger from beneath his cloak. He turned the blade in his hand and held the handle out towards the twins. "Prove it."

The girls looked at the knife curiously. Takmel gave them a stern look and shot a glance at the dogs in their laps.

One twin understood immediately and sobbed. She reluctantly took the dagger from Takmel and held it over the puppy's ribs.

The second twin moved her eyes from her sister and pleaded silently with Takmel, shaking her head.

"Prove it," he said again. "Prove that you love me."

Isabel felt compelled to step from her hiding place and confront him. But she didn't. It was as if something held her back.

She understood what Takmel was doing to the girls. He needed their complete devotion. She remembered the sacrifice she had made for him. She remembered the sacrifices they had all made for him.

However, she could no longer remember her husband's face.

She knew his name. John.

She knew she had loved him dearly.

She also remembered how she had devoured him.

Part of her wondered how she could have done such a thing. How they all could have committed such a fiendish deed.

Takmel.

She felt a warmth flow over her body.

It was all for him.

The first twin plunged her dagger into the pup's side. It yelped as the blade popped through its skin. The other puppy woke from its sleep with a start.

She pulled the knife free and dropped it on the floor by her side. It seemed as if the reddest blood spilled onto the white rug beneath her legs. The girl got up and dropped the dead dog on the floor as she wept.

The other girl was already a blubbering mess. The pup in her lap was licking her hand. She continued to shake her head as she peered at Takmel.

"How much?" he asked her. His voice gentle and soothing. "Prove it."

She grudgingly picked the bloodied knife up and looked into the large eyes of the tiny dog. With a quick thrust, she stabbed the puppy through the chest. It thrashed a little before falling limp.

She too, got up and moved to her sister's side. Both girls cried profusely.

"Come," Takmel said gently, holding his arms out to them. "I know that was hard for you. But it needed to be done."

The girls shuffled over to him and pressed their faces against his shoulders.

"I love you both so much," he told them.

Isabel watched as he moved his hands to untie the lacing on the backs of their dresses.

The bitter taste of bile burnt the back of her throat.

She heard a voice screaming inside her head to stop him.

But she couldn't move.

She watched on helplessly.

He turned his head, glanced over to Isabel, offering a dark grin.

"So, so much," he whispered to the two little girls as he slowly waved his hand.

The door gently swung closed, giving Isabel enough time to see Takmel finish unlacing the girls' dresses.

With a soft click, the door shut.

She stared at the wooden panel, uncertain of what she was feeling. Was it the fear and anxiety that gripped her, as she considered what the two little girls were about to endure?

Was it disgust that she felt?

Perhaps contempt?

Isabel's stomach knotted and turned. A deep loathing for Takmel swept over her as she compared her childhood nightmarish experience on the black ship that carried her to Blackrock Haven, to what might occur behind that blasted door.

Her hands shook, and her heart thudded in her ears as she tried to listen to what was happening in that room.

Jealousy.

Jealousy overtook her as she believed she had a right to him more than they. She belonged to him. Surely that was enough.

She wept and dropped to her knees on the stone floor.

"Why, Takmel?" she whispered as tears streamed over her cheeks, dripping upon the floor.

Staring blankly at the door, she waited for an answer.

One came.

The sound of the locking mechanism snap into place.

The Maji shut the White Queen out of the room and left her in the long, stone corridor to weep alone.

All alone.

About the Author

Robert E Kreig was born in Newcastle, Australia and grew up in its outer suburbs.

He has always had a love for books, particularly well-told stories involving action, adventure and fear.

Some of Robert's favourite authors as a young reader included J. R. R. Tolkien, Stephen King, Orson Scott Card, Ray Bradbury and Frank Herbert. As he grew into adulthood, the list continued to lengthen, adding more influential writers such as George R. R. Martin, Matthew Reilly, Nathan M. Farrugia, Dan Brown, James Patterson, Michael Connelly and Lee Child just to name a few.

Inspired by movies like Star Wars, King Kong, Jaws, Jason and the Argonauts and other great adventure pieces, Robert listened to the voices in his head and entertained the strange visions dancing through his mind to assist him with writing his fantasy series The Woodmyst Chronicles.

Robert has penned ten books for the series which follow the lives of many characters, particularly focussing upon a family who must face many trials before the epic conclusion. Clashing swords, strange creatures, flying dragons and sorcery inhabit the world surrounding Woodmyst.

Robert has also written a standalone book, Long Valley.

Robert currently lives in Canberra, Australia where he hopes to one day become a full-time writer.

Other Books By This Author

THE WOODMYST CHRONICLES

From a faraway land...
...comes a new adventure.
The Woodmyst Chronicles is the story of a small community that faces the hardest of trials in a world filled with darkness, violence and magic.

Books In This Series...
THE WALLS OF WOODMYST
THE SONS OF WOODMYST
THE HEIR OF WOODMYST
THE WARLORDS OF WOODMYST
THE HUNTRESS OF WOODMYST
THE SHADOW OF WOODMYST
THE BRIDES OF WOODMYST
THE GODS OF WOODMYST
THE WEAPONS OF WOODMYST
A FAREWELL TO WOODMYST

LONG VALLEY

In the small community of Long Valley, nestled comfortably beneath snow-capped mountains, people quietly go about their business. Everybody knows everybody and there are no worries to give mind to.

But something has awakened.

A tragic accident near the valley's army base sparks a number of terrifying events, placing the local civilians in mortal danger.

A contagion is subsequently released into Long Valley, infecting pets, livestock, wildlife and people.

It's up to the local law enforcement and a small band of citizens to try to keep the town safe.

In the end, it becomes a struggle for survival as the people of Long Valley are overcome by the urge to feed.

www.robertekreig.com

www.whitekeepbooks.com

www.ingramcontent.com/pod-product-compliance
Lightning Source LLC
Chambersburg PA
CBHW020344120726
47904CB00002B/442